AME
RI
CAN
PET
RIC
HOR

Acknowledgments

Writing's a funny thing. There's no wrong answers. No right one's, either. Maybe that's why it's such a hoot. Either way, I owe you a debt for reading these words and an even bigger one for reading the ones to come. I would also like to say a sincere thank you to Charlotte, who edited this story, and my beautiful wife, Mary, for putting up with my endless hours of playing author. This story wouldn't exist without her. Furthermore, I would like to thank every one of you that took a chance on reading A Vantage of Darkness. It takes a leap of faith to pick up someone's first novel and those of you that did gave me the confidence to bring American Petrichor into being. And finally, I want to say thank you to my high school English teacher, Ms. McDermott. I've had many great educators over the years, but I'll never forget the day you told me that I "step to the beat of my own drum." A better compliment I've never received. I try to live up to it every day.

This is a work of fiction. All characters, events, and institutions are a result of the authors imagination and are not intended to represent any real persons, events, or organizations.

ShrakeWrites.com

Copyright © 2026 by Nathaniel Shrake and Menagerie Publishing House.

ISBN: 979-8-9989970-3-7

First Edition.

"The Tower" – Illustrated by Koltyn Barber.

Cover art designed by Nathaniel Shrake.

No portion of this book may be reproduced in any form without written permission from the publisher or author, except as permitted by U.S. copyright law. All rights reserved.

Menagerie
Publishing
House

For Mom, for teaching me how to dream

and

for Dad, for showing me that hard work is magic incarnate.

The hillside cascades like the dappled skin of God;
a slow pirouette of the Earth's laughing clay.
Above it roll the clouds, those jagged crowns of August
on the whims of nothing. And slowly
from its anvils rise a voice masquerading
to pull back the curtains; to deglove the skin,
to displace a sea upon the God dappled soil; its
past lives recalling a thousand sailors drowned, still
recalling the sand of the soft ocean's floor, still
recalling the call of thy God's love begotten.
The roots are devoured of the pale ancient tree,
while thy good lord abstains and the devil cuts the cards.

THE TOWER

One

Of all the holy places that he'd ever known, Shae Mackenzie thought the saloon of Bastion, Wyoming to be the finest.

He was biased, of course, being the establishment's proprietor, but he nonetheless revered its walls and everything within it. Dionysus would agree, he would muse on occasion—the Greek god of wine and theatre being the only parcel of ancient history that he could, for whatever reason, reliably recall.

The building's high, front facing windows flooded the space with light, bestowing the recently polished pine of its floors with a glistening shine. Behind the bar stood Shae, straightening the seven display bottles of bourbon that served as a menu for those inquiring. Each bottle long ago consumed and thereafter filled with Hess apple juice; likely, by now, fermenting anew.

He stepped back to admire their symmetry before pulling out a high-top stool to take a seat; something he hadn't done in hours. It was a fine thing to do so.

He retrieved a handkerchief from his pocket and wiped the sweat from his face, turning to gaze out the windows overlooking the dusty street. Within an hour, Sunday's service will conclude and the saloon will be once again filled. He'd be well suited to rest as much as he could before tomfoolery itself came trouncing back inside to accumulate sins anew.

Through the lens of the window, the fluttering of sage and rabbitbrush danced in the breeze across the way. At the sight, he realized that he hadn't stepped outside in days. Considering that he lived in the room upstairs and rarely had reasons to step off to places beyond the saloon, the warmth of sunshine upon his skin was a rarity.

Not to mention, replacing the oiled oxygen of his lungs with something cleaner would serve him better than sitting idle.

Shae collected his crowned Stetson and pushed open one of the two mahogany doors to greet the morning. A touch of petrichor lingered in the air, and his boots creaked the floorboards of the pine walkway separating his saloon—and its adjacent establishments—from the hard caked earth of College Avenue.

Shae detested the fact that the road was called such. Not only did the road not have a college on it, but neither did the entire town of Bastion.

It was Mayor Hess that had the grand idea of suggesting that the road be named College Avenue at a contentious town hall meeting only a few months prior. It was before a boisterous crowd that his excellence—as Shae sometimes called him—made a verbose case that it was unquestionably necessary to be ambitious in engagements, such as the naming of roads.

"Let us announce to the world," the mayor pontificated, "that in the year of our lord, 1898, the town of Bastion, Wyoming is a town populated by those ambitious of both mind *and* spirit. But to do this, to reflect virtues that we already know ourselves to possess, we must go forth and place upon our establishments names that reflect these axioms of truth. If we were to endow our roads with names like 'Dust Street', 'Empty Road', or even worse, leave it without a proper namesake, the implications of such indecisions will pull upon our community's future like a millstone." He sweated profusely as he spoke, pacing about the room. "You see, my dearest of friends, that by naming our proudest street in reference to a University of Bastion's future, we are asking, no, *imploring* providence to smile upon us and bless this community with prosperity, for manifestations of will are rarely, if ever, ignored by God." Mayor Thadeus Hess turned to Reverend John Gilroy as he continued, grabbing the man by the shoulders, "Reverand, did Jesus not say in the book of Matthew, *'Ask, and it will be given to you; seek, and you will find; knock, and it will be opened...?'*"

Things were changing quicker in Bastion than most within it cared to witness. In the past five years alone, the town had seen its population grow from a few dozen to nearly a hundred—primarily due to its location being at a convenient crossroads between the larger towns of Gillette, Miles City, and Casper. Thus, as the months inevitably rolled past—as they insist on doing—more and more buildings came to flank Bastion's widest road.

What, not too long before, had been but a dusty trail touching only the saloon, blacksmith, livery, and general store, had grown to accommodate a barber, gunsmith, bank, post office, and even a halfway decent restaurant—Sal's Eatery.

It was hard to ignore the advantages of the growth, of course. With the budding population came an influx of money and hands with which to labor. Sheriff Vale Kingsbury finally got himself a proper jail, Beatrice Valentine taught the dozen youth of Bastion in an actual schoolhouse, and Mayor Hess presided over all from within the walls of the brand-new courthouse that stood like a gilded bookend upon the western end of the avenue.

But change is hard for most, especially those accustomed to certain dispositions. Shae had—from his position as the town's tap handler—heard it all, and had come to understand that most within Bastion liked what they knew and feared what they didn't. And to have people come from yonder to change what few monoliths of stability they had... well... it was an obvious result, he supposed.

Shae stepped from the creaking floorboards and onto the dirt of College Avenue. He raised his sight down the long and dusty corridor of storefronts and businesses that led to the courthouse at its end. Mayor Hess's words at the town hall meeting echoed in his memory, threatening to undo the bliss that his manual labor had roused within him.

But before he could indulge the gluttony of his anger, an unkempt wind rose at his back, nearly sending him and his Stetson tumbling. He spun about to acknowledge the anvil face of a cumulonimbus rising high upon the eastern horizon.

"A man steps outside for sunshine and gets you," he muttered aloud.

As if in response, the wind rose once again, this time sending a volley of dust into his face. So much for getting fresh air.

Shae made to walk back inside, but before he could reach the door's handle, a voice called to him from the alleyway running between the saloon and "Ginny's Gunsmoke" next door. Shae had thought it a poor decision to place the gunsmith immediately next to a saloon, but when he brought his concerns to the powers that be, he was again educated on the fact that his opinion mattered very little in the eyes of city planners. Mayor Hess made that fact very plain, indeed.

"Master barkeeper!" called Quinn O'Callaghan, the town's most prolific drunkard, "S'pose since I'm first in line I'm due a free drink? It is the lord's day, after all, and the lord is nothing but merciful."

Quinn had a weathered old face, a fact all the more impressive after one witnessed the quantity of whiskey that his gullet could contain. Shae had—on more than one occasion—asked Quinn how old he was, but in response the Irishman would only cackle and meander into the telling of a story about a dog that had lived to the age of thirty.

"If he were merciful, he'd-a left me free of you for another hour, at least!" said the bartender, wrestling the door open against the rising wind.

Quinn's unbathed stench dovetailed with the scent of polish and bay oil as he strolled happily to the already pulled-out high-top, the same that Shae had been sitting upon before stepping outside.

"Ya got Rye?" he asked, plopping himself upon the seat's cushion. He knew the answer, of course.

The clock read ten-forty, and both men were plenty aware of the town's ordinance stating that no alcohol be served before two PM on Sundays; not that it would stop them from a neat sip. Sherriff Vale Kingsbury would be in church for another half hour and would be none the wiser if such a harmless transgression were to occur. After all, being the sheriff of a town like Bastion was only a step or two higher than being its bartender. As far as Shae saw it, Vale had his jurisdiction and he had his.

It was also a poorly concealed secret that Kingsbury was generally too lazy to arrest anyone on any charge that could otherwise be resolved with a simple talking-to. There was less work involved in talking, and Shae took advantage of the fact on more than one occasion.

"I'll give ya one drink, Quinn, but ya gotta promise me one thing. You'll make it past ten o'clock tonight. You understand?" There may or may not have been money riding on the matter.

Quinn shook his head in stoic agreement. "I wouldn't dream of goin about it any other way, master barkeeper. I'd be much obliged ta ye, too."

Shae popped the cork from his cheapest bottle of whiskey and poured a finger into a pair of simple glasses. He handed one to the stinking man sitting across from him, noticing, as he did, the increasing ferocity of the wind outside.

Rain was soon to follow.

"I spose we've been needing this," he said aloud.

"I've been needing this all-damn day, praise the lord," said Quinn. Shae looked back at Quinn to see him staring longingly into his glass. "Especially with what's heading our way, and all."

Shae furrowed his brow. "What do you mean?"

Quinn smiled. "Don't mind me, master barkeeper. We've all got our proclivities. For me, maybe it's just the moss of my age, but from time to time, an odd dread visits to whisper worries."

"Oh?" Shae asked, amused. "And what worry does today's dread speak of?"

"Ahhh! Now..." laughed Quinn, "wouldn't that be a convenient thing to know."

Although he was a notorious drunk, Quinn was known for being deliberate with it, an oddity for those so consumed by the bottle. Most, in such circumstances, pulled their liquor as soon as they had it, as if compelled to envelope the liquid before it could speak any truths to them. Shae knew many that drank in such an unconscious manner. But not Quinn. Even in his deepest of stupors, he was known to examine his glass, smell its accents, and even sip slowly from its brim. That's not to say—of course—that he would stop at any hint of overindulgence.

Raindrops soon dappled the tired beams of the outside walkway and the meager roof overhead.

"Quinn," Shae began, suddenly thinking of his own Irish mother. "Would you tell me a story about Ireland?"

Quinn concluded a slow sip from his glass, replacing it upon the countertop with care. His eyes remained closed for a long while.

"I'd be happy to, master barkeeper. I'd be quite happy to, indeed."

Two

Near the westward conclusion of College Avenue, just before the road met the gaudy steps of the courthouse, a rough dirt path led north and into the hills overlooking Bastion. The path concluded in cobblestone as it met the tall cherry doors of the First Methodist Church of Bastion. The building sat nestled in a grove of yellowed, quaking aspens surrounded by sheer cliffs on its northern and western sides. As such, the cliffs would reliably drown the church—and its old graveyard—in shadow long before dusk could properly arrive each evening.

The building's sharp ceiling crescendoed in a bell-less belfry encased in unpainted bricks—a sharp contrast from the otherwise plain white of the rest of the building.

Within the church's walls, six white pillars of plastered wood held the relatively crude ceiling aloft. Eight fully occupied rows of pews dissected the space, while a modest foot-tall rise supported a cross-engraved pulpit that Reverend Gilroy stood beside, gesturing emphatically to the congregation before him.

"...and it is these pulls of the earth, these weights of imagined importance that drag us down into the dirt and away from righteous benevolence. For it is the path of the..."

A crack of thunder rumbled the church's walls. Reverend Gilroy paused his soliloquy, allowing the bellow of the encroaching storm to fully pass before summoning a gentle laughter from his chest. It proved contagious amongst the audience.

"Well, as if John hadn't already proclaimed it to be true: '*Then I heard what seemed to be the voice of a great multitude, like the roar of many waters, and like the sound of mighty peals of thunder, crying out, 'Hallelujah! For the Lord, our God the Almighty reigns!'* My friends, we forget that God's voice still speaks true and clear to us, even to this day, even in voices cloaked in nature's humbling tenor. May each of you have a blessed day, and may each of you get home safe. God bless you all."

The pews emptied slowly beyond a few hasty exceptions. The contingent had grown sizable in the past year, and as the reverend moved toward the door to shake hands with the masses that awaited him, pride swelled unchecked in his heart.

When he bid farewell to the last that stood to leave, he looked back inside to find one still seated in the pews; still facing toward the pulpit and the stained-glass sunlight that drenched it. He knew it immediately to be the disheveled hair of young Jebediah Lovely.

The reverend sighed mightily. What a shame. What else could be said?

From what little scuttlebutt the reverend had heard, Jebediah's parents had come to a mysterious, grisly, and bloody end only a few weeks prior. Apparently, when the milkman, Kline Bennett, made his morning delivery to the Lovely home on the third day of July, he found the front door cast open. Neither Susan nor Thomas came to answer when he called inside. But when he stepped within, Kline discovered a scene that had subsequently driven him to become a church-going man for the first time in his life.

Silver linings, thought Gilroy. Silver linings.

Speaking of which, Jebediah had *somehow* escaped the massacre. Many had initially thought that he had been kidnapped as he was, at first, nowhere to be found. But on the following day, the boy was spotted descending a nearby hillside with a limp.

Due to the claw marks and bloody decoration of the home, the growing assumption was that a bear had somehow snuck in. But as to how Jebediah had escaped the same fate as his parents, that remained a question rife with speculation.

"Screams and grating sounds," was all Jebediah would ever say on the matter.

Gilroy approached the aisle in which the boy sat, his own uneven gait announcing his approach. The confederate Minié ball that had dug itself into his hip, decades back, continued to insist that such a limp would forever be his. He sat beside Jebediah with a grunt, joining him in gazing into the stained-glass window behind the pulpit.

"Is this where you tell me that God operates in mysterious ways, Reverend?"

The reverend didn't respond. He was just glad that the boy was still to be found amongst his pews on Sunday mornings. He had known men that had undergone less and subsequently used their circumstances as an excuse to abandon their faith; as if it were a fickle thing, something easily doffed.

He thought it telling of the boy's character that he remained.

That being said, he knew that all he could provide the boy in that moment was steady and quiet company. Words did little in the face of whatever it was that Jebediah Lovely was enduring.

"No," was all he eventually said.

Reverend Gilroy allowed his eyes to stray, soon catching sight of the rafters overhead. For the first time in what felt like months, he thought of the vacancy in the belfry above them.

From what he had been told by Mayor Hess regarding the history of Bastion, the first church constructed by the town's founders, John and Matthew Brightly, was a modest building erected near the town's center, many years prior. Mathew Brightly was the primary engine behind its construction, while his brother John—the more secular and pragmatic of the two—attended more commonly to matters of law enforcement, housing, and trade.

So devout was Matthew, that he initially wished to bestow the virgin settlement with the more godly name of 'Monastery,' but he was ultimately forced to compromise with his brother John, lending Bastion its namesake.

But Bastion's first church wasn't long for the world. In the year of 1891, a lightning storm's resulting fire left the church a smoldering heap. For years thereafter, other matters of reconstruction held precedence, and with both of the Brightly brothers having died the year before the storm, another church wasn't immediately constructed. It wasn't until a traveling missionary by the name of Father Samuel Rigley became stranded in the town—bucked from his horse on his way to San Francisco—did another seek to build a church in Bastion.

He chose the hills north of town.

As construction progressed, Rigley ordered a brass bell from the San Julio Bell Company of San Francisco to fill the church's belfry. It seemed that the Californian city, of which he had initially set out for, had never lost its romantic grip on the man. And although bells could have been made and delivered from places resoundingly more practical, he all but demanded that the bell be one constructed in the city by the bay.

The San Julio Bell Company requested, in its mailed invoice, that its hefty price of five-hundred dollars —nearly a quarter of the cost of the church itself—be paid up front, in person, and in gold.

"It's a tithing to God that shall, in its fine California crafted metal, last longer than you or even I," insisted Father Rigley while requesting the funds from the town's treasury committee. "It's an investment in our commitment to this town's salvation. For such, I dare say we pinch no penny."

Father Rigley's request was granted, and young Frederick Samson, Ginny Samson's boy, was given command of a cart, a mule, two month's rations, a pistol, five-hundred dollars in gold, and instructions to deliver the payment all the way to the San Julio Bell Company in San Francisco. He was to return with the bell when it was crafted to the *exact* specifications of Rigley's designs and nothing less.

"Consider it a pilgrimage," said Rigley to the boy on the bright spring day of his departure. Frederick had been a devout altar boy for Rigley, and as he came of age, the father saw growing promise in the boy. Frederick was soon to be eighteen, and Rigley thought bestowing him with increasing responsibilities, such as traveling to San Francisco in his stead, would further endow Frederick to the service of both himself and the church. Father Rigley might have gone himself—he repeatedly professed to the crowd as Frederic prepared to depart—if he hadn't only recently developed a cough in chest.

He died three days after Frederick's departure.

As such, in Reverend John Gilroy mind, at least, it was providence that had bought him through the streets of Bastion on the very same week of the Father's passing. He had only recently been run off by his previous congregation in Gillette—not that anyone in Bastion needed to know that. All the town of Bastion needed to know, as he rode through the dusty long street of College Avenue for the first time, was that a new man of faith had arrived—in just the nick of time—to lead their congregation.

And thus, in short order, The First Methodist Church of Bastion was christened on Easter morning, 1896. It wasn't as difficult to convert the Catholic idolators to a protestant faith as Reverend Gilroy had initially feared, for, as it turned out, the vast majority of Bastion's flock just wanted someone—anyone—of authority to take over the job of leading them on Sunday mornings.

To many, the minutia of the finer details of faith were just that: minutia.

The building's Catholic imagery was disposed of unceremoniously, although Reverend Gilroy quietly took a liking to the building's tabernacle, ensuring that it found its way to his personal quarters in the church's basement. Within its doors he stored his gin, a revolver, and a French post card of a bare breasted woman riding a bicycle.

But as the years went by, an aching, sad question began to settle itself upon the collective lips of the town: where was Frederick Samson? Three years passed without so much as a whisper as to what had happened to the boy, the gold that he carried, or the bell that he was tasked with delivering. The most prevalent theory was that he had gotten lost and perished somewhere along the winding and perilous route to and from California. Some even whispered that Frederick had grown wise and had taken the gold for himself to start somewhere anew, although the voices that championed this theory were often the same to proclaim that they too would have done the same if given such an opportunity.

But no theory—likely or otherwise—gave solace to Ginny Samson at losing her only son to the endless yonder. As such, it was ultimately decided it best to leave the belfry uninhabited, at least for the time being. Its hollow space an unofficial remembrance of the boy that disappeared into the unfurling west.

Reverend Gilroy turned to look at Jebediah Lovely, still seated patiently and unmoving beside him. He himself had never met Frederick, but at examining the untouched youth in Jebediah's cheeks, lamented the loss of innocence all the same.

The day had turned grey and the sound of rain began to tap upon the wooden roof overhead. The smell of rain drifted in through the still open doors behind them.

When the storm soon became accompanied by violence, Reverend Gilroy rose to close the cherry doors before turning his attention to his various obligations within.

Jebediah Lovely remained unmoving, still patiently seated in the pews.

Three

Sheriff Vale Kingsbury was amongst the first to exit the church upon the conclusion of Gilroy's service. The skin upon his right pointer finger had grown raw as he had spent the final minutes of the sermon subconsciously rubbing his thumb and forefinger forcefully together.

Before the Reverand could finish uttering the word "bless" in his final address to the crowd, the sheriff was already upon his feet, heading for the door.

Outside, he hooked a sharp left and hugged the side of the building to protect the match that he had already lit. He cradled the flame as it settled into the match's wood and raised its heat to ignite the tobacco leaves stuffed into the pipe clutched tightly within his lips. He inhaled sharply, simultaneously shaking the match's flame into extinguishment. He closed his eyes, relishing in the nicotine blanket that then enveloped him.

"Well ain't that inspirinn," bemoaned the approaching voice of his wife, Susy. He kept his eyes shuttered.

"Dontcha think this town deserves a sheriff that can last more than a few short hours without a smoke?!"

Vale intended to finish his pipe's tobacco without acknowledging her but was left without a pipe to do so when it was pulled from his mouth and thrown to the floor. He opened his eyes and imagined what his father might have done, his tombstone only a stone's throw away.

"There ain't nothin wrong with a smoke, Sally."

"Cept that you said you was gunna give it a break," she replied. "You promised me, Vale. You said that you was gunna cut back to suckin on yer pipe only after breakfast and after supper. And yet here ya are, hardly waiting to step outsida God's house to fill yer lungs with tar."

"Who said anything about tar, Sally?" he replied, avoiding the premise of his wife's frustrations.

Sally huffed in exasperation, shaking her head. "Vale, you've never failed to convince yerself of a truth you'd crafted all yer own. But as far as yer question is concerned, the blood that mingles in your coughs spittle, Vale. That's who."

Sally turned and, like a drop of rain finding a river, integrated herself into the slow-moving crowd meandering down the hill towards town.

Vale puffed again from the pipe, knowing she was right. He watched her integrate with the descending crowd before allowing his attention to drift to the wide, black cloud approaching the valley from the east.

Distant flashes of lightning descended from the cloud's flat underbelly. A moment after each, rolls of thunder cascaded along the hillside.

He sat quietly watching the scene for some time.

When the pipe's tobacco was at last exhausted, he emptied its remnants into a nearby sagebrush and followed the well-worn path down the hill.

He ought to see how Luke has been getting on without him. God only knew what the young deputy had gotten into while he was off making a favorable impression upon the lord—as Sally insisted he do.

Luke was a well-intentioned concrete thinker, to put it kindly. And that was fine and all, as Vale didn't consider himself all that bright either, but with Luke being not a day over seventeen and the nephew of Mayor Hess to boot, well... that made things complicated.

The question of what Luke had been up to without his supervision summoned an image of the boy in a Mexican stand-off with the coyotes that grew bold whenever Vale was away from the jailhouse.

The thought made him laugh, concurrently summoning a cough in his lungs, convulsing his chest and compelling him to bend over and cough a puddle of muddled mucous into the dirt below him. Vale knew it wasn't a good omen, but at least the doctor had ruled out consumption.

"Nooo, sir," Dr. Stevenson had bellowed, examining him the week before. "If you had the consumption, you'd be burning up and losing weight. And by the looks of you," he peered openly downward at the gut protruding from Vale's abdomen, "I'd say that you have not yet been consumed."

The storm proved to be quicker moving than Vale had initially thought. Before he could do anything about it, the sheriff found himself descending a muddy hillside in the midst of a full-blown thunderstorm. By the time he reached the door of the jailhouse, his boots were coated with mud and his Sunday's best were soaked rightly through.

A crack of thunder marked his arrival as his soggy boots squelched upon the wooden planks of the jailhouse floor. He slammed the door closed behind him.

Luke rose sharply from his chair, offering a polite hello as the sheriff entered the room. "Relax, boy," replied Vale, not looking up from his waterlogged pipe.

Vale sensed that the kid wanted to talk, but was still processing Luke's presence in the first place. He decided it would be best for everyone if he retained a grumpy silence over an outright airing of grievances. It wasn't the boy's fault, after all. No, Vale blamed the mayor for appointing his own nephew as the town's newest—and first *ever*—deputy.

"We don't need no deputy, Thadeus. Shit, we hardly need a sheriff!" argued Vale, barging into the mayor's office after first hearing the news.

"Watch your language, Vale. You'll respect this place even if you don't respect me," said Hess from his chair. He wasn't a fan of the sheriff's insistence at using his first name.

Vale bumbled and paced about the room but could think of no-good argument beyond the fact that he didn't need to be babysitting a child. In truth, he had grown enamored with his long hours of solitude in the jailhouse and couldn't fathom sharing the space with a child not yet eighteen.

"We've only got one Goddamn chair, Thadeus."

He was sternly encouraged to leave.

But as he hunched over the trash bin, refilling his pipe with dry leaves, Vale looked up to see a wide smile beaming across Luke's face.

"What is it?" he asked slowly, fearing the answer.

"I made my first arrests, Sheriff!"

"You did what?!"

Before waiting to hear Luke's response, Vale stepped briskly around the brick wall separating the building's office from its holding areas. He found two of its three cells occupied. One held the frustrated demeanor of Shae Mackenzie, while the other contained Quinn O'Callaghan, happily grasping the proximal bars.

"Sheriff!" exclaimed the latter in a joyful, Irish tenor, "So good of you to join us!"

Four

Vale's eyes shot to Luke in impatient suspense.

"What'd *they* do?"

"Well," began Luke with pride, "I was on patrol, just as you told me, and when I passed by the saloon's open windows, I saw these two drinking to their happy delight during the hours of prohibition."

"Are you kidding me?" shot Vale in open disdain. Luke's smile evaporated.

"Am I kidding? No... They broke the law so I apprehended them, as is my right as a representative of..."

"You ain't a representative of shit yet, kid!"

Shae laughed aloud.

"Shut your mouth, Shae," shouted Vale, turning to face the bartender in the proximal cell. "How many times have we been here now?"

"By my count, this is incident number six."

"Are you lame then?"

"No, sir."

"Insubordinate?"

"You know me well enough to know that the answer to that question is yes, but not towards you directly, Vale..."

"Sheriff."

"Right... Sheriff. Point being, I was only housing poor Quinn here from the approaching storm, and it felt silly for us to be sitting in such circumstances without having but a single drink to dull the dread of the storm's passing."

"Spoken like a weak man," said Vale sharply as a roll of thunder passed overhead.

"Yes," Shae admitted. "But either way, I'm only insubordinate to broad strokes. I consider the nuance of immediate circumstance to be more worthy of respect."

"Good. I hope you can then respect the nuance of your immediate circumstance." Vale turned to again address his deputy. "Outside!"

Vale again slammed the door behind him, this time re-entering the storm's cacophony. He and Luke stood beneath the doorway's awning that protected them from the direct sight of the rain. A flash of lighting briefly turned their surroundings to brightness before the storms midday darkness returned, accompanied by a roll of thunder.

"Listen, kid," he began, his throat raspy, "the law is the law, sure, but there's more than one way to enforce it. And I prefer not pissin off the very people most likely to be breaking grander laws tomorrow by enforcing lesser ones today."

"That's poppycock, Sheriff," barked Luke. He no longer cared what the sheriff thought of him. "You've talked with them plenty and there's signs posted all over that saloon. It sounds to me that you've tried being gentle before and it's not fixing the problem. It sounds to me like you're just being a coward."

"You really think I give a damn about that ordnance, Luke? Don't be simple, son. I couldn't care less if those miscreants decided to drink the town dry by Sunday supper. What I care about is them not murderin, shootin, and stealin. And if what they're doin ain't one of those three things, hell... You know what they say about your enemies?"

Luke just stared at him, off-put by the Sherrif's sudden verbosity.

"Keep em close."

Luke stared into the growing puddles at his feet, shaking his head softly.

"But more than that, son, I need you to not be taking initiative just yet, okay? Let me show you how things work round here. Cause, before you can go about enforcing the hard rules, I need you to understand the soft ones. You understand what I'm sayin?"

"You shouldn't have spoken to me like that. Not in front of the criminals," said Luke. The deputy turned, opened the door, and walked inside.

Vale thought to follow him and apologize, but decided it best to give the boy some time to cool off before doing so. He lowered himself onto the old wooden rocking chair beside the door, stuffed his pipe with fresh, dry tobacco, and watched the storm pass in leisure. He thought of his rangering days; days now long gone. Days spent on the plains under storms far mightier than this. Days when things were simpler albeit filled with more lead in the air and blood on the ground.

Within an hour's time, the storm proved transient and the clouds gave way to the August sun.

Vale stepped inside and walked close enough to Luke to whisper.

"I'm gunna make towards College. See how everyone fared from the storm. In twenty minutes, let em go."

Luke only stared passively into the distance. Seeing that such was all he would receive in that moment, Vale knocked on the desk with the bare of his knuckle, confident that the message was understood.

Vale enjoyed the short walk that separated the jailhouse from the avenue. He always did. It was an unnecessarily twisting jaunt through the trees, but it never failed to inspire him. Over the years he'd placed various boulders along the path, each chiseled with the words of various pillars of character that he wished to inspire in others and himself. From the jailhouse to the livery, the stones read as follows: Integrity, Honesty, Trust, Patience, Empathy, Dependability, and finally, a word that Vale was convinced his father had made up, Higherosity—the reverence for perfection. Vale might have simply used the word idealism, but his father's word for the concept conjured in him some of the few fond memories that he had of his dad, and chose to leave it be. Even if it meant baffling the remainder of the town.

Vale passed the boulder in question as a cough leaped at him from the lower chambers of his lungs.

He stepped from the tree-lined pathway onto College Avenue intending to go door-to-door inquiring about any damage from the storm. But as he strolled onto the road now glistening in a thousand muddy puddles, something else entirely caught his eye, capturing his attention. As he gazed east down the long narrow road, a lone rider could be seen approaching upon the distant horizon.

It wasn't every day that Bastion had visitors of a lonesome variety. Most were trading caravans or cowboys taking their respite from the trail. Rarely did visitors come in ones. Vale was glad he had his pistol on him, and was even more thankful that he just so happened to be walking past as the rider drew near. He preferred to lay eyes on newcomers that rode into town, and he liked it even more if he could be the one to introduce Bastion and its disposition. God forbid the opportunity instead fell to Mayor Hess or one of his slack-jawed lackeys.

Vale walked casually to the conclusion of the road and the approaching rider, still only a speck in the distance. But with every step he took in its direction, Vale gained a better view of the encroaching visitor and its steed.

Upon a black mare rode a bald, pale faced man brandishing what appeared to be a long unkempt beard speckled in grey and black. He wore tattered ebony robes that blended seamlessly into the mane of the mare. It was hard to tell for sure—based on the distance that still remained between them—but the horse didn't appear to be carrying saddlebags, or even a saddle for that matter.

That was curious.

Vale stood at the edge of the road with his hands confidently resting on his hips. When the rider drew within earshot, he let out a holler somewhat lower in tone than his larynx typically produced.

"Howdy, partner!" he shouted, a hand raised in greeting.

But the rider didn't respond. Not at all. Not a glance, a wave, or a word.

When the rider grew within a short distance, Vale saw that the man's left eye was milky white and he indeed rode without saddle or bags of any kind. His bald head was without cover and his gaze rested steadily forward, continuing to give no entertainment to Vale's obvious attempts at garnering his attention.

"Welcome to Bastion, traveler," spoke Vale in descending volume. "My name is Sheriff… Kingsbury…"

The rider rode past him.

Perplexed, and slightly annoyed, Vale turned to watch as the rider rode right along the center of College Avenue into Bastion. The crowds that had since amassed watched silently as the man languidly rode down the artery of the town.

Vale thought the rider might take his horse right up the steps of the courthouse at the western conclusion of the road, but before it could do so, the horse took a sharp right turn and began trotting up the winding pathway toward to church.

Five

Jebediah Lovely remained seated in the church pews when the sounds of an approaching horse rose from outside the sealed cherry doors behind him.

The sound roused him from passivity, prompting him to look slowly and deliberately about his surroundings as if it were his first time sitting within the confines of the church. He considered its walls. The metaphors of its architecture. The stained-glass windows promising hope and individual relevance to all that filled the pews.

Its intermittent inhabitants were but moss, worshipping the sun in forest chapels.

How he despised them.

The pillars within the space seemed like soft pitons against a sky resolutely demanded the felling of the churches ceiling. He wished it would get on with it already.

It was all so tiresome, these people, their aspirations, their imagined salvations...

If nothing else, it was at least easier to sit in the space alone with its visiting masses since departed. He enjoyed it even more with Gilroy in his quarters down below, attending to himself and his various vanities.

He wouldn't be required to wait much longer. The rider, at long last, approached. His brush would soon be in hand, and with it, his oils would meet the canvas.

He would soon dance once again.

When the horse's hooves ceased outside the doors, the resulting silence was replaced by the sound of soft footsteps approaching. Jebediah kept his gaze forward as the doors crept open, flooding the space with daylight. A tall shadow stood amongst its deluge, enveloping the center pews, the head of Jebediah Lovely, and the pulpit upon the wooden rise at which Jebediah still gazed. The soft sashaying of cloth accompanied the shadow's movement while a rasping breath escorted its presence.

Jebediah lazily raised his right arm to point toward the stairs descending to Gilroy's quarters below.

"In the basement you'll find God," he said. "Speak truth to him so that he may see."

The sashaying cloth and rasping breath of the visitor moved toward the descending stairwell without hesitation. Although Jebediah never turned to look at it directly, his right periphery acknowledged its figure traversing the room and descending the stairs with deliberate footing.

Creak.

Creak.

Creak.

Creak.

Creak.

... Then silence.

From the bottom of the stairs, three sharp knocks rapped against the door of Reverend Gilroy's quarters.

"I'll be out in just a minute, Jebediah. Why don't you go send for water, we'll..."

"John... it's Mary-Lou...." spoke a woman's voice from the stairwell's depths. "John...it's me..."

From Jebediah's unmoving perspective in the water-colored pews, Reverend Gilroy could be heard crudely stumbling to his feet as he scurried to the door of his quarters. From there, four distinct sounds emitted from the stairwell's landing in quick succession.

First, came the sound of Gilroy's door being flung open in a high-pitched squeak.

Second, the reverend could be heard stammering "wha, wha, wha, wha," in a pathetic and fruitless dread.

Third, the inhaled, guttural growl of a predatorial beast rumbled the buildings foundation.

And finally, a brittle crack, as if emitted by the decisive snapping of a twig, preceded a dull triplet thump.

The sound of firewood dropped carelessly to the floor.

Six

Watching the rider trot past him without so much as a glance was ammunition enough to roil Vale's suspicion, sending him promptly after the man with a quickened step. Although his gut had indeed grown large over the years, his instincts still served him well.

But when the rider turned north and began ascending the path to the church, his pace quickened further still. What business could he possibly have in the hills? That pathway concluded at only one building, after all.

Vale walked briskly to the livery opposite the church-bound trailhead, intending to pull Jacob, his speckled Gelding, from boarding. Vale had already summited the hill once that day and he was in no mood to do it again.

It was only a half hour before that he was forced to pour water from his boots.

"I need Jacob!" he hollered, entering the covered stables.

"Ya know, Sheriff," began Willie, pushing a wheelbarrow about, "there was a time when you'd say hello when you walked in here."

Vale huffed and then coughed, his lungs suddenly squeezing him in intervals, forcing him to once again bend forward and rest his hands upon his knees.

When he finally caught his breath, he rose to wipe a dribble of bloody spittle from his lip. Thankfully, Willie didn't stand by and watch. Vale didn't wish to offer condolences for himself on behalf of someone new.

The act was growing exhausting.

Willie put the wheelbarrow to rest near the gate of a wide stall containing a pair of young colts. He dug his pitchfork into the barrow's pile of hay, forking it into the stall.

"I need Jacob," Vale repeated, "and hello."

"Jacob's not feeling well. Hasn't eaten in two days. Plus, he's been doing nothing but stand in that corner since yesterday."

Indeed, as Vale then acknowledged, Jacob stared emptily into a corner while a tall pile of hay sat untouched near the stall's entrance.

"I'd be happy to saddle you up Valley Girl or Lucky, but you'll have to give me a few minutes. These horses have been waiting all morning to get their breakfast. I wasn't exactly feeling up to braving the weather earlier, although, I know I should have."

Vale again coughed and only barely fought off the tickle of another fit.

The rider was surely heading for the church, but Vale still couldn't think of any good reason as to why that might be. The appearance of the man on a saddle-less mare was odd enough in itself to warrant his suspicions, but the man's unblinking demeanor warranted more than that. He felt compelled to follow up with the man's intentions, and something inside of him suggested that he'd do well to do so quickly.

"I don't have the time, Willie," he said, turning from the livery to walk toward the trailhead across the avenue.

"YOU USED TO SAY GOODBYE TOO!" hollered Willie as he left.

With another huff in his chest, Vale began his trudge up the muddy path into the hills for a second time that day. But as he began his trek, he looked up to see a figure already upon the path ahead of him. The soot coated jeans and stodgy white T-shirt identified the man as Xavior Jenkins, the town's blacksmith.

"Ahhhh shit," Vale spoke under his breath, walking toward him.

Apparently hearing either Vale's grumbling or heavy breathing, Xavior turned about to see Sheriff Kingsbury approaching not far behind him.

"Ahhhh shit," he too muttered before turning to walk on, not waiting for Vale to join him.

"Xavior!" called Vale.

Xavior slowed to a reluctant stop without turning to face his pursuer.

"Where ya headed?" called Vale once more, drawing near.

"What's it matter, Sheriff? You gunna point yer gun at me if I say something ya don't much like?"

"Stop that," responded Vale, taking note of the bags below Xavior's sky-blue eyes. "I'm following after that rider. You know anything I don't?"

Xavior hesitated, just enough for Vale to notice.

"I know just as much as anyone else does, Vale. Just getting my exercise. Or am I not allowed that?"

Vale squinted in distrust. "What aren't you telling me?"

"Look, Vale. I'm just walking. Sure, that one eyed weirdo rode passed in an odd way, I'll give you that, but just cause I happen to be walking in the same direction don't mean I've got anything to do with it. Now, if you wanna follow behind me like some sort of creep, be my guest. It's a free country, as I'm sure you're plenty aware.

Freer for you than any of us, of course. Yer free to accuse us simple folk of stealing, hell, yer even free to steal our women if it pleases ya."

Xavior paused as if to see how Vale might react to his latter words but the sheriff gave him nothing. Xavior waited a while for Vale to say something, anything in his defense, but when neither said a word and only a slight breeze accompanied them, Xavior peeled away and continued up the trail.

"Come or don't, Sheriff," he called over his shoulder. "But I don't have to tell you that. You're the king of Bastion, after all."

Vale marinated in the man's words before eventually continuing behind him. He was all-too aware of the resentment that Xavior held for him despite the years that had passed since his rendezvous with Susy in the back of Shae's Saloon. If the incident hadn't resulted in his eventual marriage to the woman, he might have felt even more sorry for the act.

But ultimately, Xavior's notoriously capricious emotions were a fickle consideration at the moment. Vale's attention remained on the rider and his still yet to be known intentions.

"As far as I'm aware, Hess is king!" shouted Vale, hoping to encourage even a sliver of playfulness in the man. But

Xavior only continued onward, refusing to acknowledge the statement.

The sheriff maintained a respectful distance behind Xavior as they trod upward into the hills. Puddles of quickly congealing mud clung to level pockets of the trail.

When they reached the plateau holding the church against the sky—the encapsulating cliffs looming behind it—Vale paused to catch his breath and survey the scene. A dozen feet ahead, upon the cobblestone steps leading to the building's open cherry doors paced Xavior, biting at his oily nails. Every few steps the blacksmith altered his gaze between Vale, the rider's black-haired mare—grazing in the nearby grass—and the wide-open doors of the church.

It was clear that the rider was within the building and the analytical portion of Vale's brain encouraged him forward to approach and investigate its interior. But when he went to take a step forward and do just that, something stopped him where he stood. It was as if the more ancient folds of his cortex, the portions of his cerebrum dedicated to the interpretation of things beyond the spheres of conscious recognition, demanded he step not another foot closer to the building's open doors.

But then, something happened that stopped even the cyclic pacing of Xavior. An impossible and metallic vibration of the air.

The repeating sound of a church bell.

Vale looked up to the once vacant belfry to see that the space was indeed occupied by a cast iron bell swinging from side to side.

But... how?

As far as Vale could tell, no bell existed in the belfry's open chamber when he arrived for the service that morning. Plus, it was a well-known fact that the bell had never arrived after Frederick Samson's presumably ill-fated departure years before. If Frederick had indeed arrived, bell in tow, the news would have spread like a wildfire upon the buffalo grass. Not a single person in Bastion would have been unaware of the fact come the end of the arriving hour.

And yet, the bell undeniably rang out with wide arching swings, smacking its interior walls against whatever metallic clapper was hidden within its curved crevasse.

Xavior too stared steadily upward to the church's pinnacle chamber. Vale heard him mutter a single word against the bell's metallic clamor.

"Glory."

Vale's curiosity shifted to who was pulling the bell. He noticed a rope dangling out the belfry's left edge, alternating between tautness and slack with each swing. He stepped around the building's left face to find Reverend John Gilroy heaving upon the rope. A bumbling smile traversed his face as tears of joy fell from his cheeks.

Then, just as Vale came to observe him, the reverend ceased his pulling, allowing the rope to hang in silent slack. In his periphery, a figure emerged from the church's open doors. It was the rider; his shoulders now draped in ceremonial crimson stoles, his palms outstretched to the sky.

He spoke in a slow and pausing cadence.

"The mayor... I'd very much like to speak with him..."

Xavior stepped forward, startling Vale with his boldness. "Who are you, damnit!?" He trembled as he spoke. "WHO ARE YOU?!"

The man's outstretched arms rose higher into the sky. "A messenger. A catalyst. A harborer of joys."

As the words escaped his chalky mouth, Reverend Gilroy emerged from his position around the church's corner to stand beside the man, quivering with joy.

"Cut the rosary!" responded Xavior with a tremble. "I want you out of my head! Out of my dreams, now!"

Vale's astonishment shifted from one incredulity to the next. No wonder Xavior looked as if he hadn't slept in days.

The rider slowly dropped his hands to his sides where they disappeared into the enveloping sleeves of his cloak. A thin, wiry grin grew upon his face.

"I wanted you to see... He, wanted you to see..."

"I said drop the rosary!" exclaimed Xavior. With speed, Xavior reached under the curtain of his long white shirt to produce a poorly maintained peacemaker, aiming it at the man.

The rider didn't flinch.

But before Xavior could pull the trigger, Vale pulled his own 6-shooter from its holster and made a point of loudly cocking its hammer to announce its presence.

"Drop the gun, Xavior."

"You don't know what you're doing, Vale," cried Xavior, still training his gun upon the rider, his hand shaking.

"There's such a thing in this town as due process, Xavior. But it's something you won't get if you don't give this man his. Now put down yur gun."

"Vale!"

"I'm gunna count to three, okay? And on three..."

"He's the goddamn devil, Vale! Look at him! He's a vile thing and you'd know it if you just looked at him!"

"One…"

Vale's finely oiled sights rested evenly upon Xavior's head as Xavior's own extended arm shook with growing vibrance.

"Two…"

"Goddamnit, Vale, you don't know what you're doing!"

Vale began tightening the pull of his index finger when he became distracted by the sound of fast approaching footsteps, footsteps sprinting up the pathway behind him. They were accompanied by the voice of Ginny Samson calling brightly into the open air of the plateau.

"Frederick!!!" she hollered in a frantic bellow. "Freddy!! Where are you my sweet boy?!"

Comprehending the woeful scene approaching, both men lowered their arms to see Ginny Samson rising above the crest of the pathway; a rolling view of Bastion glistening behind her.

Joy christened her face.

Vale shifted his sight back to the rider and increasingly began to suspect—despite the bells call—that the plateau held no Frederick for poor Ginny to embrace.

Seven

Thadeus sat in the office, scribbling upon a legal pad with a feathered quill. It was an outdated writing utensil, he knew, but he nonetheless appreciated its delicacy.

A frustration was strewn across his face as he mouthed the words as he wrote them. In excerpt, the cursive upon the page read:

"*...If not for ourselves, we must act for the sake of the proud state of Wyoming, the God warranted union of The United States, and the providence of the entire world! We must create within ourselves—and our community—the very personification of idealism that we wish to see in others! My friends, such manifestations require actions not only bold in thought, but also in action...*"

He paused to stare at the paper before scoffing and flinging the quill across the room.

"Hollow... through and through," he bemoaned, ripping the page from the pad. He crumpled the paper into a loose wad, dropping it atop a pile of similarly fated words in the wastebin near his knee.

The townsfolk, he knew, weren't simple. Not all of them, anyway. If he were to suggest the legislation that he wished to, well, it would require fine acrobatics of word. He would be required to present his ideas subtly at first, in ways that led the masses that heard them to construct similar concepts of end in their own minds so that they might nurture such thoughts as their own. In that way, when he was to later reveal his plans in the plain light of day, the audience would sigh in relief and be allowed to forgive themselves for having harbored such ideas already.

Just as had been done to him.

Three weeks before, he had gone for an early morning stroll through the Hess apple orchard when he noticed a sparkle of sunlight reflecting upon something leaning against the trunk of a tree. He bent down to receive what had so reflected the sun's narrow rays, discovering it to be the golden clasp upon a book titled, '*The Taiping Rebellion in China*'.

The book enraptured Thadeus and his imagination at once.

Within the tome's pages, the author—a British adventurer by the name of Augustus F. Lindley—journaled his time spent among the Taiping Rebellion of 1860, chronicling his first-hand observations of the group's pursuit of utopia.

The Taiping Heavenly Kingdom, as the rebellion preferred to call themselves, was led by a man that claimed to be the younger brother of Christ. But whether or not that was indeed true was irrelevant, considered Thadeus. His followers believed it to be true, and *that* is what ultimately mattered.

Through the kingdom's theocracy, the group doffed the slogging bureaucracy of democracy, and in their streamlined manner of governance, declared alcohol, gambling, and prostitution illegal. But most importantly, Thadeus thought, was that they enforced the compulsory reading and memorization of scripture.

What a righteous pursuit!

Could such policies be implemented in Bastion? If they could, Thadeus mused for days, what rewards could be wrought from such legislation. Although the Taiping Heavenly Kingdom met an early end, he knew that if he could somehow implement such a concept, such an inspiration in Bastion, that he would see to it that it be done the right way, in the American way, the Hess way. A way distant from Washington and its sluggish bureaucracy and secular prejudices.

The founding fathers were enlightened theologists, after all, willfully blind to the revelations handed down by God every day. Their "separation of church and state" would be their undoing, eventually. Why should Bastion be fettered to such a corpse?

And yet, in a similar vein, the most troubling question that festered itself within Thadeus's mind thereafter wasn't if a Godly governance would be of merit. No. The real question was could he implement such a thing while evading the heavy thumb of Washington. If the south, with all its industry and armies couldn't succeed in implementing their convictions, how could the meager town of Bastion break free from the Godless—albeit powerful—American government?

The question lingered unanswered and heavy in his mind.

Thadeus rose from the cushion of his tall-backed throne to reclaim the quill resting upon the floor. It lay at the foot of an elegantly carved pedestal that rose to support his namesake's most prized possession: an engraved burgonet helmet that had been handed down to him through the fraternal Hess line for generations. Retrieving the quill, Thadeus rose to appreciate and examine the helmet. He removed it from its stand and carefully turned it about in his hands, studiously taking note of every angle of its finely preserved craftsmanship.

It was a golden and steel helm; its sides and back descending to protect the neck of its wearer. A narrow, vertical fin of steel accentuated its top. Engraved upon each of its sides was a well preserved double-headed eagle clutching a cross in one talon and a sword in the other. Beneath the eagle were the words: "*FIDES ET IMPERIUM*"; *Faith and Empire.*

According to the family lore, the helmet had been worn by his eighth great Grandfather, Albrecht von Hess, a man that'd fought amongst the ranks of Emperor Charles V's landsknecht forces at the siege of Münster in 1534. It would have been a prized piece in any museum celebrating the Holy Roman Empire and the fragmented histories of 16th century Germany. But its reverence was held to an even higher esteem in the Hess family, and to Thadeus in particular. To him, the helm symbolized the bravery of his lineage and a clear mandate of excellence and providence to come.

He walked to the door, slid the deadbolt into the housing of the doorframe, and returned to his desk where he sat. Carefully, he placed the helm upon his head before returning his attention to the legal pad resting on the desk before him.

But just as he moved to fill the unmarked page with fresh ambitions of literary inception, the distant sound of a church bell lifted his chin to give him pause.

As he listened intently to the muted sound, he squinted and stared into the corners of the room as if their shadows hid the answers to all of his questions.

Had the Samson boy returned?

The sound left his previous thoughts abandoned. He stood, returned the helmet to its place atop its pedestal, and walked briskly from the room.

Eight

When he emerged onto the landing of the courthouse, Thadeus looked out upon the length of College Avenue to see more than a few men and women gawking at the bell's toll in the hills.

Upon the twelfth strike of the bell, it fell silent at last.

In the resulting hush, a figure that had previously been standing alone in the street began a frantic sprint toward the church. It was Ginny Samson.

If he were her, he'd be running too, thought Thadeus. Of course, at the same time, he was without children and could only imagine what terrors haunted parenthood.

His curiosity soon turned to how the bell had arrived without his knowledge. All things new to Bastion required his awareness, and to have such a fundamental investment arrive without his knowledge... well... that pickled his pride.

At once, he descended the steps intending to make for the church himself. He wished to invite Frederick to the courthouse to hear of his travels.

As he walked, a half dozen hat brims dipped with corresponding—and restrained—murmurs of, "Mayor..." Thadeus only nodded in response to each. All were happy, he reasoned, to give their minimal acknowledgements to his position when it was paraded before them, but not one of them had reported the arrival of the bell to his office. There was no initiative in this town, it seemed. No appreciation for the hierarchy of its leadership. All everyone wanted was their handout before retreating to their grovels to drink and tend to their gluttonies. It was a pity to see such decadence and sloth making inroads among Bastion's population.

His mind flickered back to the Taiping Heavenly Kingdom and its example; its inspiration.

At the turn-off that led to the trail, a small crowd gathered, whispering in hushed tones. As Thadeus approached, the murmuring diminished as Dr. Stevenson—the town's lone physician—stepped forward to greet him. The doctor wore a shellacked top-hat to match the neatness of his mustache.

"Mayor," he said, pulling at the brim of his hat.

"Doctor," replied Thadeus in a tone more respectful than what he had given the faceless others. There had always been a shared respect between himself and the doctor, both acknowledging a need for each other in their respective fields of practice.

"Why didn't anyone tell me that the bell had arrived?"

The doctor shrugged. "Nobody knew. We all just heard it ourselves. I can't imagine Samson would have raised it over those hills without coming through town first, unless, that is, he intended to make a flamboyant entrance, which," the doctor threw up his hands, "he very well might have done! It doesn't seem much like the style of the boy, but who knows? Maybe he picked up an appreciation for the eccentricities of things in San Francisco. I hear they have excellent playwrights out that way."

"I doubt it," said Thadeus. "Has anyone gone up yet?"

He was eager to step up the trail himself.

"The sheriff and Xavior hiked up on the heels of the rider not too long before the bell began ringing, but nobody was carrying a bell. Frederick must have snuck it, and himself, past us all!" Dr. Stevenson chuckled. "And then, just a moment ago, Ginny went rambling..."

"A rider? What rider?" interrupted Thadeus.

But before the doctor could reply, a murmur rose from the surrounding crowd. Thadeus turned to see a black horse descending the trail from the church ridden by a man in black robes. His shoulders were draped in what appeared to be thin strips of crimson cloth.

"That rider," said Stevenson, pointing in its direction.

Thadeus couldn't take his eyes off the man. Even with the distance that separated them, he sensed a tremendous weight in his approach. It was as if something in his mind couldn't decide if he ought to run or grovel. Ultimately, though, his pride chose neither and the mayor instead strode forward to be the first among them that the rider would encounter. He preferred it when he could be the first to greet any newcomers to the town.

When the rider drew near, Thadeus saw that he was a bald man with a long black beard and a milky left eye. The man wore a black hoodless robe that engulfed his arms and legs while crimson red stoles draped his shoulders.

When the mare reached a stone's throw from the crowd, it slowed, then stopped.

The rider gazed wordlessly at the crowd before patiently dismounted to bring his bare feet to the moist earth beneath him.

The tattered ends of his robe lingered in the mud.

The man turned to the mare and whispered a word into its ear. Upon hearing whatever it was that was said, the horse ambled slowly forward and through the crowd that intuitively parted to let the animal through.

Thadeus turned to watched it stride into the livery's wide-open maw.

He returned his sight to the visitor who was now raising his arms from the swallowing shadows of his sleeves. Thadeus thought his arms to be outlandishly thin.

He spoke in a slow, vanilla rasp.

"Mayor Hess. Long have I traveled to make your acquaintance. May we speak in solitude?"

Thadeus felt the milky eye of the man piercing him.

"What is your name, traveler?" Thadeus inquired. "I wish to give respect to your father by knowing whose lineage I am so happy to converse with."

The man brought his right hand to his chest.

"My surname is Patmos, but you may call me Mathius."

Thadeus smiled to conceal the unease that the man's voice had planted in him.

"It is a pleasure to make your acquaintance, Mathius Patmos. Regarding your request for a quiet conference, I am always eager to speak with any well-intentioned visitor to Bastion. Although, I must first ask, as we all are quite curious, what do you know of the church bell that has graced these hills with its romantic resonance? It appears that its appearance has serendipitously coincided with your arrival."

Mathius returned his hands to within the shadows of his sleeves.

"The bell is the first of three blessings that the lord hath chosen to bequeath this land. For I am his conduit, and as such, I am to bringeth into this world that which he portends."

A stunned silence was all the crowd could muster. Thadeus, however, felt a sudden wave of inspiration as if he were being kissed on the cheek by the muse herself. Be him charlatan or prophet, it mattered not. Thadeus suddenly saw a means to an end in the man.

He turned about to face the hushed crowd standing in quiet anticipation. In their anxious and suspended faces, he saw a flock of sheep waiting to be told whether to dart from the wolf's teeth or graze in the shadow of their newfound shepherd.

"My friends. I dare not speak for our dear Reverend, for it is his place to best interpret the guidance of the lord, but what I can say is this: Bastion is, and will forever be, a bastion for all. And I for one cannot unhear the ringing of that bell!" He pointed to the hills. "I shall receive our visitor and hear his words. But I promise you this, dear friends. I shall speak in turn with your providence in mind."

He turned back to the black-robed visitor, gesturing warmly toward the courthouse.

"This way, new friend of both mine and Bastion."

Nine

Ginny Samson was attending to the refurbishment of a Trapdoor 1873 when the bell's unexpected clamor made itself known.

At the sound, she dropped her tools—something she never did—and fumbled outside and into the street. She was asleep. She was sure of it. She had heard the bells toll a thousand times in the restlessness of her dreams. But when the ringing finally stopped, she looked down at the mud and was met by the clarity with which the midday sun glistened in the avenue's puddles. She inhaled, and the lingering petrichor insisted—in its distinctive fragrance—that she was awake.

Has he truly come home?

Since the day that she had watched her only son disappear over the horizon, Ginny Samson traversed the many stages of her grief in a slow procession, a procession that she was beginning to believe would never cease. Only last month had she managed to clear her trunks and closets of his effects, a process that felt hauntingly similar to the abrupt departure of Frederick's father, years back.

But that was a different story entirely.

Ginny thought often of leaving town. To move somewhere that might offer her battered heart respite, or in the very least distraction. But a stubborn and festering hope that Frederick might, on some bright day, return with bell in tow lassoed her to Bastion forever.

On more than one occasion, she'd considered scampering across the wilderness in search of her only son. The cowardly sheriff refused to do so—stating a perceived futility—but the tales of bloodied scalps and the savage packs of Indians that littered the stories of her youth were sufficiently vivid to inhibit even the apathy of her flailing despair. Albeit desperate, Ginny was no fool. She knew well enough that to ramble into the wilds, particularly the Bighorn Mountain range that lay between herself and San Francisco, was akin to placing a rope about ones neck with a long way to fall.

And so, for months that bled into years, Ginny Samson simply put her head down and enveloped herself in her work in a hopeless attempt at keeping the red-hot tongs of her grief at bay. When the work dried up, as it often did—there were only so many firearms in Bastion, after all—she'd disassemble and re-assessable her own Winchesters time and time again until her oily fingers cracked and bled across the workbench. When that happened, she'd walk quietly next-door to the saloon to douse herself in whiskey. It was an engagement she often endured despite the bartender's awkward attempts at courtship.

He was cute enough, but no passion remained within her. Life was but a dull trudge forward lit only by the whispering flicker of hope's phantom flame.

But on that Sunday, a day that otherwise trickled past like all the rest, a bell rang in the northern hills turning what was moments before only a dormant candle into a forest's raging fire.

***

When Ginny arrived upon the church's plateau, she only vaguely noticed that the sheriff, Xavior, the reverend, and a tall stranger stood about in the landing. She failed, however, to notice the guns in their hands nor the tears welling in the reverend's eyes. She cared not that she'd never seen the stranger before, nor that his gaze was piercing and ghostly. All that she cared to recognize was that her Frederick was yet to be seem amongst them.

"Ginny," said Vale, holstering his gun.

"Where is he? Where is my boy?!" she asked with frantic bliss, tears cascading from her eyes.

Vale didn't know what to say. He had yet to see the boy, and his growing suspicion was that he had nothing to do with the arrival of the bell in the first place. He reached for her hands hoping to explain what he knew, but before he could do so, Ginny darted sharply from his reach to circumnavigate the building in a joyful jaunt.

"Frederick!!! It's mamma, where are you, son?!"

The upturned pronunciation of the statement's final syllable sank Vale's heart. The woman's call reminded him of the bleating he once heard from a lost bison calf, lost and alone on the prairie, calling for its mother through the night. The sound kept him up for weeks.

Ginny shuffled this way and that, endlessly searching for her son. But as she frolicked toward the graveyard on the opposite side of the building, Vale approached Reverend Gilroy, keeping a suspicious eye on the rider standing stoically beside him.

"Where's the boy?"

"One with the wind," spoke the rider, despite the question being firmly directed at the reverend. Without another word, the visitor then turned and walked to his mare grazing in the nearby grass. He mounted the creature with a swift and impressive swing of his leg, pressed his heel's bare skin into the creature's side, and loped down the hill towards town.

Xavior watched him go with dejection. He loosely held the grip of his pistol at his side, the weapon threatening to clatter to the floor at any moment. Noticing this, Vale moved swiftly to his side to disarm the man with a practiced sleight of hand. Xavior didn't fight it, but as Vale tucked the gun into his own waistband, Xavior looked up to meet the eyes of the sheriff.

"Flames," he whispered, his dejection now transformed wholly into that of a glassy stare. "Every night I see flame s... and his face..."

To Vale, his cheekbones seemed suddenly sunken to match the soot of his skin. He appeared nothing short of ghostly, a visage akin to those that had spent too long in the mines.

But before Vale could engage him in any sort of consolatory remarks, Xavior walked forcibly past him to begin a slow shuffle down the pathway on the trail of the rider.

"Don't ya go following him, now!" called Vale.

Xavior didn't respond, although Vale was unworried. The dejection in the man's eyes told him everything he needed to know. But just to be safe, Vale decided that he would wait to return him his pistol until the light of a new day.

Ginny emerged from around the broad side of the church, still calling for her son when Reverend Gilroy suddenly called to her in a blissful holler that rivaled her own enthusiasm.

"He's walked into the wilderness, madame!"

Vale was flummoxed, squinting at the reverend with incredulity.

"Now why in the hell would you say that!?" he yelled, quickly stepping to the man.

"He's gone west!" the reverend repeated as if it were obvious and evident to all. "You've just missed him!"

Vale closed the gap between him and the man to grab him by the white of his collar and lift him squarely from his footing. Despite the failings of his body, Vale was still a large man capable of manhandling others when necessary. "You know as well as I do that Frederick Samson is not here nor in those hills, John. Why in the hell would you say that!?"

The reverend clung at his collar and garbled what words he could.

"Because..." he choked, "it is...His will."

But before Vale could respond, he heard the trampling of Ginny's footsteps behind him, sprinting toward the rising cliffs that cradled the church's western perimeter.

"I see you, sweetheart!!" she called in a shrill exclamation. "Stay right there, Freddie, momma's coming!"

Vale dropped the reverend pitifully to his knees and raised his gaze to the cliff's peak, toward where Ginny appeared to be shouting. But when he did, Vale saw no one standing atop the cliff's looming ledge. He knew he had to corral her before she could hurt herself.

But when he started towards her, his chest abruptly convulsed in a violent and harsh contortion leaving him keeled over, coughing into the dirt with violence. He coughed so hard that he thought he might pass out right then and there, and for a fleeting moment, he was convinced that he would.

But when the fit finally passed, he wiped away the tears that coated his vision to see that Ginny had placed tremendous distance between them and was rapidly ascending the rocky and unhumbled cliff-face.

"I'm coming, Freddy!!" she called again, nearly at the peak. She climbed the flat rock like a spider racing toward its prey. When she reached the cliff's ledge, she spun about, as if looking for something that had been there, only a moment before.

"Come on down, Ginny! Frederick isn't here, darlin!" called Vale, fighting novel tickles in his throat between each word. "It'll be alright, but you gotta come on back down before ya hurt yerself!"

But Ginny didn't seem to hear. She just spun about in this direction and that, peering far off into the distant horizons that surrounded her. Vale's rising fear was that she might lose her footing and fall the terrible distance that separated them. But before he could attempt another warning, Ginny ceased her spinning and began waving wildly towards something, or someone far to the west of her.

"I'm coming, Freddy!!" she shouted, her words reverbing upon the surrounding cliffs. "I'm right behind you, sweetheart!" Before Vale could inquire, or do anything else of consequence, Ginny ran west atop the cliff's peak and out of his line of sight.

Vale rose to his feet and carried himself gingerly to the church's walls where he collapsed, leaning his back against the building's foundation. Hearing the nearby gasping wheeze of the reverend, Vale looked over to see the man clutching his throat as he stumbled awkwardly through the church's doors, shutting and latching them decisively behind him.

The distant echoes of Ginny Samson's calls to Frederick reverberated hauntingly through the hills. They grew quiet over the course of several minutes. Her voice seemed to ring out in a manner not unlike that of the very bell that had driven her mad and into the wilds beyond. Vale vaguely recalled hearing stories of mermaids that sang songs to lure sailors to their deaths on the high seas. He couldn't remember who told him the stories, and he sure didn't know if he believed them, but as the memory crossed him he felt a curious association with it and the circumstance before him.

Before many more minutes came to pass, Ginny's joyful echoes became only distant whispers on the wind. And then they were nothing at all. When that came to pass, Vale stood awkwardly to his feet to pound upon the door of the church.

"Open the door, John!" he called. Why had he told Ginny what he did? Gilroy knew more than anyone what despair resided within the woman. To give her false hope by ringing that bell, to direct her into the hills... well... it bordered on murder itself. Vale had half a mind to tie him up right then and there and drag him to the jailhouse.

What would his father do, he pondered, pounding again upon the cherry door.

But the door didn't open, and he hadn't the energy to kick it down himself. He'd be back and not alone, especially if Ginny didn't return and he couldn't find her.

All he wanted in the world was to sit on a quiet porch and smoke his tobacco. But with Ginny rambling into the wilderness in such a state, he knew that he was obliged to go after her. All the rest could wait, including Reverend Gilroy.

Vale spit a bloody wad to the floor, turned, and gently ambled down the hill towards whatever new developments were surely unfolding back in town. He'd get his audience with the rider eventually. He thought back to what the man had said, that he was "A messenger. A catalyst. A harborer of joys."

What in the world did that mean? And more importantly... what did it mean for Bastion?

Ten

Luke stepped back from the cells, the keyring dangling loosely in his hand. Despite having unlocked the cell doors, the two men within only continued lounging against the brick back-wall, perplexed.

"Well go on, then. Get out of here!"

"Bored of us already?" asked Shae.

"I'm just feeling forgiving, that's all. Now get out of here before I change my mind."

The two men stumbled to their feet and stumbled toward the jailhouse exit.

"Deputy," said Quinn in sarcastic reverence. Shae said nothing at all.

Luke sat back down behind the desk to fume in his indignity. What was he supposed to do now?

Nothing. That's what he would do. He would never again take initiative if it was to only earn him an ill-deserved lashing. No. He would sit and twiddle his thumbs until directed otherwise in bitter compliance. He tapped his fingers upon the desk, counted the black puddles of mold growing upon the ceiling, and revised the monologue he planned to share with his uncle regarding the whole ordeal.

The moments passed with drudgery.

He thought he heard the ringing of a church bell from somewhere outside, but the town had no such bell and he figured that it must have been Ol' Mcgroober trying out his newfangled dinner bell that he'd been going on about.

A few days back, while finishing a ribeye alongside the rest of the Hess clan at Sal's Eatery, Sal lingered a bit too long beside their table, rambling endlessly about the restaurant business and this or that venture. The Hess family was eager to get their check and take their leave but Sal was equally, if not more eager to keep the Hess's within the walls of his Eatery for as long as possible. He knew well that their patronage was the best advertising that one could expect in Bastion and he intended to take advantage of their presence.

"My new dinner bell, which should arrive any day now, is coming all the way from Denver! It will be truly impressive; I assure you that. You see, I've been told that it's made of the very same metal used in in the Maxim Gun. The Maxim Gun!! Can you believe that?"

Luke didn't even look up from his steak and only Thadeus feigned a polite and political interest in Sal's words.

"I intend to ring it near supper time every night to remind the town that we're serving their favorites. You see, I was inspired by Pavlov's latest work. In his research, he ..."

"Sal..." interrupted Penelope, Luke's mother. She extended a five dollar note into the air to dissuade any misinterpretation of her intentions to depart. "We can't thank you enough for dinner..."

Luke burst out laughing at the gesture.

When the family at last departed the establishment, his mother playfully placed Luke in a headlock and rubbed her knuckles across his skull.

"You need to be more tactful, my boy. Even when others are being silly, especially when they're being silly, we must always give everyone our respect. We are above no one, Luke."

But in his recollection of the story, Luke only chuckled as he ruminated on Sal's incredible lack of awareness.

Regardless, as the seconds carried on in the silence of the now empty jailhouse, he was beginning to find that his daydreams and passive observations were losing their potency to entertain him. The seconds were themselves becoming slogs that pulled at the limitations of his tolerance for inaction. He hadn't even brought a book to pass the time as he had figured that his time serving as the town's deputy would have been all but consumed with action packed patrols through town. He had witnessed—in more than one of his daydreams—a gold star upon his chest as he gallantly arrested miscreants, chased looting bandits, and took aim in shootouts! The last thing he was expecting was to be charged with monitoring the short hands of a clock.

A temptation to poke around the room rose in him. It wasn't exactly polite, he knew, but there was no harm in disrespecting someone that didn't respect him. Plus, it wasn't like he was going to steal anything. No harm. No foul. He was the deputy, and the jailhouse and its contents were as rightfully available to him as they were to Sheriff High-and-Mighty himself.

Luke pulled at the circular knobs of the long horizontal drawer under the desk's wooden top, a dry grating sound accompanying the action. Inside, he found three wooden tobacco pipes, a large bag of Prince Albert leaves, several boxes of matches, a jar of ink, a small pad of paper, and a steel-nib pen.

Luke closed the drawer, disappointed in the underwhelming nature of its contents. He had been hoping to find dead-or-alive arrest warrants or maybe even paperwork exposing the dark histories of Bastion's citizenry.

Surely, such things existed *somewhere* within the building. He just had to find where they hid.

He decided to try the shallow right-hand drawer of the desk. He pulled upon its knob but found that it wouldn't budge. He didn't see a keyhole around it and concluded that it simply needed some convincing. He yanked sternly upon it's weathered grain when it ripped away with a sharp crack.

Luke held the knob to his face with horror. It wasn't a clean break, its spine cut in a jagged sawtooth ridge that would make for a difficult correction. He'd done it now.

All would be lost if he were to allow the sheriff to regain the moral high ground in their relationship. It was imperative that he maintain leverage over the man, even in things as abstract as morality. *Especially* with such things.

But thankfully Luke wasn't entirely hapless and was handy with woodworking in particular. If he could just get his hands on some hide glue, he might be able to reattach the knob. With any luck, the dope might not even notice.

The general store typically had a bottle or two of such glue in stock, and he figured that it wouldn't take long for him to sprint over and purchase a bottle. If he was quick, he could have the knob fixed before the sheriff could return to notice his misadventures.

Without another thought, Luke jumped to his feet, placed the dresser knob into his pocket, and ran out into the late afternoon sunlight toward the general store. He sprinted through the ponderosa lined trail, finding it hard to ignore how aromatic the trees had become since their spritzing that morning. The fragrance nearly made up for the trite boulders that lined that pathway. What did "Higherosity" mean?

But when he emerged onto College, his pace skid to a stop as he approached an unexpectedly large crowd huddled about the intersection of the avenue and the path that led to the church. The throng stood motionless, all facing an approaching rider draped in black descending from the hills on the back of a horse.

Luke, unsure of what to make of the situation and pressed for time, resumed a quiet pace into the general store to the right of the crowd.

Luke found the store to be empty beyond Smelly Joe—the store's deaf bloodhound—napping soundly upon its straw bed in the corner. Maxine must be amongst the crowd outside, Luke reasoned, although it was a rare thing for the kindly southern woman to leave the store unattended during business hours. In fact, Luke wasn't sure if he had *ever* seen her counter without her standing behind it. Something truly remarkable must be happening outside to justifiably pull her away and Luke resolved to inquire on the matter once the knob was fixed.

Luke found the glue without much trouble and left a dime upon the hardwood countertop. As he pushed the door open and re-emerged into the street, he heard the unmistakable voice of his uncle, Mayor Hess, addressing the crowd. Luke could always tell when Thadeus was speaking in public by the way his vowels carried a hint of a drawl whose origin Luke couldn't possibly fathom.

On most occasions, his uncle's public facing voice was enough to conjure in him a pair of rolled eyes, but as he stood behind the crowd listening to Thadeus speak so vivaciously, Luke sensed a promptness in his voice that was altogether novel. It felt as if his uncle was legitimately inspired, driving his words from his lips from a position of passion rather than the typical reiteration of carefully curated literary devices.

He stepped nearer the crowd to hear his uncle's words with more clarity.

"I shall receive our visitor and hear his words. But I promise you this, my friends. I shall speak in turn with your providence in mind... This way, new friend of both mine and Bastion."

Thadeus's words were at first met by only a few isolated and hesitant claps. But as individual heads within the crowd began, one by one, to look around—as if to gauge the sentiments of those beside them—more and more palms took to applause. Before long, the entirety of the crowd produced a polite ovation in response to the mayor's words. Luke clapped too, although he knew not what he applauded.

Suddenly, the crowd parted before him, revealing the mayor and a tall man draped in red stoles striding toward him.

"Ahh!!! Providence has already smiled upon us, Mathius." Thadeus gestured toward Luke as they approached. "Allow me to introduce to you our town's newest lawman, and my nephew, Deputy Luke Hess. Deputy, this is Mathius, he comes bearing gifts for our humble town."

The Hess within Luke sprang into action with a gleaming smile and a confident handshake.

"Pleasure to make your acquaintance, sir."

The man that his uncle had introduced as Mathius extended a pale thin hand from the shadows of his cloak. He accepted Luke's handshake, and in his grasp, Luke thought he could intimately feel every minor bone within the man's hand. But when he raised his gaze to meet the man's eyes—as he had always been taught—Luke softly gasped at the sight of the milky left eye staring back at him. Mathius grinned in response, and in a flash of time no longer than the blinking of an eye, Luke could have sworn that he saw the burning of a tree in a suffocating darkness.

"It's nice to meet you, young one."

A seasickness lurched within Luke's gut as if he were aboard a vessel faring an angry sea. He had the sudden urge to vomit and it took everything within him to quell his stomach into a temporary knot of dryness.

"Forgive me...I...I've business with the sheriff... Welcome to Bastion, sir."

Luke shuffled quickly off before the knot in his gut could wiggle itself undone. He dared not look back at the crowd that surely watched him go, nor the white eyed man in black whose hand he felt gripping icily, still, upon his own.

Eleven

"Have ye always intended to tend taps, master barkeeper?" asked Quinn, squinting as he walked out the jailhouse doors.

Shae hadn't heard the question. His mind was away.

"Hmm?"

"Did ya dream of keeping bar, back when you were young?"

"Oh!" Shae chuckled.

Side by side they stepped from the wooden steps of the jailhouse porch and back onto the moist earth. Their trek back to the saloon would be a muddy one.

"I think I wanted to poke cows."

"Ya must not a grown up near the beasts."

"No. Mom died when I was young, and dad went off to join some imagined mob hunting down John Wilkes Booth. Never came home. So, I pretty much grew up in the saloon, back when it was still uncle Shilo's."

"And that didn't encourage ya to it?"

"No. I was more interested in the cowboys that would stop in from their drives, leaving dust and stories all about the place" Shae considering the boulders along the pine-tree laden path as he spoke. "There I was, day in and day out, staring out the same dirty windows, cleaning spittoons and enduring angry drunks—and uncles—when in would walk Johnny Rough-Rider spinning stories of stampedes and miles without end. More than once I thought real hard about taggin on with one of their outfits. Got real close one time, in particular. Packed my bags and everything! But when I stepped outside before dawn and looked down the long road—before it was named College—I just couldn't do it. Couldn't tell ya why. Just yellow, maybe. I don't know. Anyway, I turned back round and stayed put ever since. Just easier, I spose."

"Can't say I blame ya, master barkeeper. I've rambled long across this country and, although I can't say it's without its merits, I can't say it's without its troubles neither."

"What about you?? What did baby Quinn want to do with his days?"

"You're looking at it, master barkeeper! I'm a self-made man!"

"You're something!"

"Ahh shove that up yer arse and keep it there."

They shared a laugh as they turned from the tree laden path and onto the avenue. Their gazes locked onto the open country that unfurled beyond the eastern conclusion of the road, a thousand puddles glimmering upon its surface.

"Do ya ever regret not going?"

Shae gave him a curious glance. "Did your time in that cell twist your heart, Quinn?"

"I suppose that young lawman just got me feeling nostalgic, that's all."

Shae spit onto the dirt. "Don't know what he's doing."

"Ah, neither does anyone."

"But to answer your question, ya soft Irish bastard... sometimes... But when I do, I sip some good whiskey and fall asleep in my feathered bed. And before I know it, I don't."

Shae saw that Henry "Player" Johnson sat with his back against the saloon's doors, his arms crossed.

"And where have you love birds been off to?" he hollered, seeing their approach.

"Making friends with the law!" shouted Quinn happily.

"The law!?"

"Nothing for you to be concerned about, Henry," replied Shae before Quinn could. "I can't go allowing the talent, such as yourself, to be bothered by worry! A saloon with no whores needs an unbothered piano player to make up for the fact."

Shae unlatched the doors and gestured for the men to enter before him.

"Now go on and be unbothered for us all."

Henry obliged while Quinn proceeded to the back table where he sat and repeatedly shuffled a deck of cards. Henry hammered out some scales while Shae went about slicing oranges and preparing the icebox; each man engrossed in their distinctive preparations for the night to come.

But as Shae made his first cut into the produce, a peculiar, distant resonance dovetailed with Henry's keys.

It was the sound of a bell. A glorious sound with clean pitch and round reverberation. And as he listened further, it felt suddenly as if he were being coddled in a luxurious fur. He'd never heard a sound nor felt a feeling quite like it.

"AHH!!" he shouted.

The piano jarringly stopped as Henry turned to see what had happened. Quinn too paused his shuffling and looked to Shae.

"Are you alright?" the latter asked.

"I'm fine," admitted Shae, embarrassed. "Just cut my finger. A small thing. Everything's fine."

The men shared a chuckle and smart words before returning to their engagements. Shae looked down at the blood oozing from the slice that he had made in his thumb. A smear of blood painted the skin of the orange.

Had the Samson boy finally returned? If so, what a happy day it must be for Ginny. His cheeks stretched wide as he wrapped his thumb, thinking of the joy that was likely hers in that moment. He wished that he was with her, wherever she was, just to witness her expression.

On slow days, when there was nothing to do but sit quietly and wait for patrons, she'd sometimes sneak inside as if aware that the saloon was empty. She'd sit on a stool at the end of the bar, sipping quietly upon the brim of her glass. When she did, Shae would pour himself a matching drink and sit beside her to share in a silent moment of liquid warmth. They never said so much as a word to one another. She would merely point to the whisky rack when she entered and leave a coin upon the countertop when she left. But when they sat together in those silent moments, Shae felt more connected to her than he had any other person in the world.

In his mind's eyes, he did his best to recreate the soft folds of her face as he wiped his blood from the bar top.

Twelve

Upon arriving at the courthouse, Thadeus and Mathius ascended the building's stairs and entered the foyer within.

"Pie and coffee!" shouted Thadeus in the direction of the help.

Mathius remained stone-faced upon entering the hall, his arms swallowed in the folds of his cloak.

Clean white walls of plaster lined the room while cherry stained cornices of wood hugged at each crevasse and edge. Paintings lined the walls and the bright gleam of a chandelier hung above them. Three ornate archways led to various interiors of the building while the smell of fresh paint and tobacco wafted throughout. A tiled mural displaying a buffalo grazing on a golden hillside ordained the floor. A proud glint shone in the blackness of its eyes.

"This way, my friend," spoke the mayor, leading Mathius through one of the foyer's archways, down a hallway flanked by more paintings, and into a luxurious study.

Tall bookshelves lined the room while a servant fervently tended to igniting flames in a fireplace embedded in the far wall.

A pair of plush leather chairs sat facing the fireplace while a wide, glass-topped tree stump rose between them. Coffee and pie arrived just as the efforts to ignite the fire proved successful, leading the triumphant servant to take his leave, shuttering the mahogany doors of the study smartly behind him.

"Please, take a seat. Enjoy the pie," said Thadeus, walking to the gramophone. "The apples were nurtured in the Hess family orchard south of town. If you have time during your stay, I highly suggest you visit its curated rows. I'm likely biased, of course, as I spent my youth running through its grounds, but I am nonetheless proud to call the plot nothing short of spectacular."

He removed a disc from a nearby catalog and placed it upon the table of the gramophone. He turned the device's crank, sending the disk spinning on its top. A hanging steel needle was placed upon the peripheral edge of the disk, and after a few moments of brittle scratching, Brahm's Hungarian Dance No. 5 emitted from the device's bronze horn.

Mathius stood near the fireplace staring deep into its blossoming flames, his fingers laced loosely about themselves at the small of his back. As Thadeus approached, he saw that the man's eyes were closed as if in deep contemplation.

"So... You say that you have traveled far. From where do you hail, sir?" asked the mayor.

Mathius inhaled deeply before, at last, turning from the fire to face his host. He opened his eyes and smiled.

"You are without a doubt a worthy man. I see now why God has led me to your door," said Mathius with a lacquered tongue. The flickering of the flames illuminated alternating flashes of brightness upon his weathered and stern face. The sight ignited an unexcepted wave of subjugation and deference within Thadeus. But as quickly as it had arisen, he cast it away, amounting it to being nothing more than the approach of nightly melancholy.

"You must be a Godly man, to speak of Him like one might a close friend," he said carefully. "To what church do you attend?"

"Indeed," replied Mathius, ignoring the question. "We know each other well."

Thadeus turned away, chuckling. He felt guilty to laugh so openly at the words of a guest, but to insist that one knows God personally was to suggest vanity beyond respect.

"Well, then I must ask," he indulged himself, "what is he like?"

"He is patient..." Mathius said without hesitation nor humor. "And heavy handed.... He seems to see much in you, Thadeus."

Thadeus squinted in curiosity. He had yet to introduce himself as such, although upon a moment's contemplation knew that knowing the first name of a small town's mayor wasn't exactly Godly insight. Nonetheless, it struck him as peculiar.

Choosing to disregard the man's statement just as Mathius had disregarded his own question, Thadeus decided to shift the conversation to the practical.

"You come to Bastion blessing us with a bell and speaking of more gifts to come. To what do we owe such a privilege?"

Mathius faced his palms to the sky. "Only He knows. I am but a vessel to act upon his will. I am incapable of speaking on his reasons or intentions."

"Very well," said Thadeus with a growing fear that he had invited a delusional man into his private study. "And what are these further gifts that you have been charged with delivering?"

Mathius stared flatly into Thadeus's gaze as the overture of the Hungarian Dance reached its flailing crescendo.

"Do you ask this inquiry to quell an itch of suspicion? Doth thee not have faith in His works?"

Thadeus was taken aback by Mathius's insight into his growing apprehensions. Was he so obvious in his mannerisms? "Why, I've hardly just met you. You must agree that charlatans dance freely through society like leeches in wading waters. Without proof of something legitimate, without witnessing something manifest before my very eyes, I *must* be suspect, it is my *duty* to be suspect, for as the caretaker of this community I am charged with protecting its interests from...false prophets..."

Mathius's gaze remained flat and unbothered.

"I would be a fool to further dispose of my time without evidence to the contrary."

"Then why is it that you have invited me here, to your richly adorned hideaway, Mr. Hess? Could you not have demanded evidence of my mandate in the open air of the public? Or did you bring me to here in the hopes of claiming for yourself a *private* investment in God's will?"

Thadeus went to speak quickly in his defense, but before words could cascade from his lips, Mathius continued... "Do not fret, Mr. Hess, for my acceptance of your hospitality is equally bound to persecution, for neither I, nor He, seek the acceptance of the masses of Bastion. Not yet." He again closed his eyes and turned away from the mayor as he continued. "The flock is unprimed for that which will be revealed to them in time. But before such can come to pass, a duly endorsed contract between you and I must first be arranged. A contract of shared understanding, trust, and pursuit."

Prophet or not, Thadeus was beginning to accept that that he was not in the presence of a fool. He stepped to the globe that stood in the opposite corner of the room, pressed his palm to its face, and gave it a gentle spin. To a degree, what Mathius had said was true. Indeed, he did seek advantage. If the man was false and spoke from his nether regions, he would be but a useful tool in his hopes of enacting his own version of the Taiping Heavenly Kingdom. But...if Mathius spoke from truth...

"What sort of contract do you speak of?" he asked at last.

"A contract of mutual benefit. You get what you desire, and in exchange, this land is at last rewarded with a true bastion of purity, one worthy of those deserving."

"And what about the unworthy?" asked Thadeus reflexively.

"I am neither a statesman nor a planner. I am merely a..."

"A messenger. Right," said the mayor impatiently. His attention had drifted to the initial half of Mathius's previous statement.

"And what is it that I desire?" he asked, paying closer attention to his own mannerisms in the hopes of better hiding the growing intrigue that he had nurtured on the subject. "What is it that God claims that I so desire?"

"Power. Power unabridged by laws ordained east of here."

The crow's feet flanking Thadeus's eyes twitched.

"Mayor Hess, God sees glory in you and he sees the manifestation of grandeur in this land. In the visions that envelope my shuttered eye, he sees you and I standing side by side trumpeting a bastion of righteousness. Do not deny it. You are a great man. A great man awaiting a great opportunity. You are Alexander, watching the death of your father. You are Caesar, staring into the Rubicon's rushing waters. You are Bismarck, summoned to Berlin in the hour of crisis. Thus why I stand before you now, Mr. Hess. He sees into your being and whispers its truths to the inner of my ear."

"What's the catch?" Thadeus asked abruptly. "The way you pitch this, nobody loses. Suggesting a contract in such a matter implies an inherent risk of a signee to abandon terms. What, in this circumstance, might incur such a temptation?"

Mathius was quick in response as if expecting the question.

"The American government will be quick to respond to Bastion's abrupt dispatch from its grasp. As such, these designs will require a rock-solid resolve from all involved. The contract..." Mathius dug into his cloak to produce a finely bound scroll for Thadeus to examine, "ensures that all parties involved are equally bound to the ends that may come."

Thadeus grasped the scroll pensively.

"But do not harbor fear, Mr. Hess. If you remain true to the agreed upon terms, if you remain true to both myself and my guidance, the good lord shall prevent American flames from enveloping this town and its people. *You* don't have an army, Mr. Hess, but the lord, on the other hand, wields both shield *and* sword."

Thadeus unfurled the parchment and inspected its terms. The language was direct, forceful, and all encompassing. Several subscripts of the text lay beneath the main paragraphs of the arrangement outlining several *in which cases*, and *in such circumstances*. At the very bottom of the scroll lay three lines prescribed to signatories. One was assigned to *Thadeus Hess, Mayor of Bastion*. The second, to *Mathius Patmos*, while the third and final line simply stated *Witness*.

"And who would witness such a signing?" asked Thadeus, looking up from the document.

Mathius came closer to laughing than Thadeus assumed possible.

"Why, God, of course."

Thadeus nodded as if he should have known, although part of him wished to sign the document simply to see what it meant for God to sign such an earthly arrangement.

A thought then occurred to Thadeus. What would the repercussions be for breaking the contract's terms? Surely, the existence of a contract in itself implied an inherent punishment for neglect. He searched diligently through the document while Mathius, to Thadeus's surprise, took a seat in a leather armchairs and even took a sip of coffee.

At last, Thadeus found the subtext he sought: *Contempt of Terms.*

"If a signee is to turn from their obligations in the above stated arrangement, the punishment shall be that of reciprocal destiny."

"This wording is...odd," he said, handing Mathius the document and pointing to the line in question. "What does this mean?"

Mathius grinned.

"An eye for an eye, Mr. Mayor... An eye for an eye."

Thirteen

A crowd of whispering talk-a-lots hung about the avenue when Xavior Jenkins completed his trek down from the church. As he approached, more than a few of the gawkers separated themselves from the crowd to ask what he had learned of the bell and the mysterious rider that had seemingly catalyzed its song.

Xavior diverted his stinging eyes and dug his hands into his pockets to hide the persistence of their trembling.

"What did he say?" yelled one.

"Where did the bell come from?!" called another.

"Where is Frederick?!" shouted a third voice coated in worry.

Xavior pushed past the inquisitors to step inside the familiar confines of the smithy. With a metallic thud, he closed the steel door behind him to shutter himself within the heavy darkness.

"I shoulda done it," he whispered to the shadows. "I shoulda pulled that damn trigger."

With his back against the door, he slid to the floor, his heart still sunken by the sight of that milky eye riding past him in the clear light of day.

He closed his own eyes, finding the darkness behind them to be little different from the blackness of the windowless smithy. If only he could sleep. A silent, and restful sleep.

It was all that he wanted in the world.

Maybe after just one hour of rest he could think straight again. It'd been so long since his thoughts had been clear.

But, as had been the case for weeks, the very act that might lessen the weight of his troubles was that which delivered such misery in the first place.

What cruelty.

Most nights, Xavior would sit with Quinn into the thin hours of the morning to hide from his recurring nightmares. The Irishman was good company for those seeking thoughtless distraction, but to go out now, to endure the curious crowds and their persistent queries seemed an impossibility. He dared not endure it.

And yet, what was there to do? What could be done? Was he to continue enduring his internal terrors instead of the societal ones outside?

He quivered, feeling the exhaustion of his body. His tired limbs lay outstretched and languid upon the floor while the acrid scents of oil, burnt wood, and mildew lingered redemptively in his nostrils. The smells of a place familiar. He again closed his eyes and saw no difference in his sight.

He'd rest his eyes for only a moment to give his jumbled thoughts a chance to reorganize themselves; to give them a moment's opening.

Moments bled into one another and sleep soon arrived before he could sense its approach.

A starless night. A narrow column of trees. An orange glow flickering up ahead. An apple tree aflame beside a figure draped in black. A milky left eye, staring out from the darkness. Small humanoid forms hanging upon the tree like fruit, licking flames sizzling their skin. There's one of my vantage. I pull it from its limb. A cracking sound and the feeling of death. A long, empty cold. And then, nothing, nothing, and then nothing again. And again, and once more.

The sound of a shrill scream startled Xavior awake, the type of sound one cannot decipher to be real or that of one's dream.

"What words come to mind, when you look upon his gaze?" asked a voice in the darkness.

Xavior scurried to his feet and groped a nearby shelf holding a book of matches. He drug one against its striker.

In the burgeoning light, he saw none other than young Jebediah Lovely standing patient and still in the center of the room, a placid stare beneath disheveled hair.

"Jebediah?" Xavior asked, carrying the match to a waiting gas lamp's wick. The flame grew quickly upon the oiled tendril.

"It's a fruitless question, I know, but I'm helplessly curious, Mr. Jenkins... What words, thoughts, and feelings crop into your mind when you look upon the eye of the viper?"

Jebediah took a step toward the blacksmith.

"The viper?" asked the latter, perplexed.

"You know it well, the same that slithers in the flittering light. You know of whom I speak." The boy stepped a foot closer. "Now. What comes to mind, when you look into his eye?"

"What's going on, Jebby? Wha...Why are you here?"

The boy stopped his slow procession to turn to a nearby workbench. From it, he grasped a hefty smithing hammer and considered it carefully.

"Do you know what happened to my parents, the night that they died?" he asked.

Xavior did not.

"Well, let me tell you what happened, dear Xavior." He peered into the hammer's hard oaken handle, spinning it about.

"The moonless night of the third of July brought a bitter wind against the walls of our home. I opened the window. I let it in. And once inside, it swirled the drapes and tussled the linen. My parents tried to corral the wind. They tried to arrest it." He looked up from the hammer to meet Xavior's eyes. "They failed." Jebediah again took a step toward the blacksmith, this time with the hammer in his hand. "The wind cut quick and without quarter. Its old current separating their parts, returning them to a state more akin to the realities of existence than what their parts assembled imagined themselves to be. They were made holy in the wind's sight."

"Jebediah..."

A step closer was had.

"And then, I stepped forward under the moonless sky and found you in your slumber. You don't remember, but we walked together to the moonless orchard to saunter in dance between the sashaying trees."

The boy took another step closer, now only a few feet from the blacksmith. In his proximity, Xavior saw malice in the flickering reflection of his eyes. Abruptly, he grasped the hilt of a poker submerged in a nearby bed of coals to aim its end squarely at the still approaching boy.

"You speak as if you're in contract with the devil himself," he quivered. The pike trembling like the pistol he had aimed at Mathius in impotence. "Speak truth, Jeb. What is this?"

The boy stopped his approach, lowering the hammer to his side. A smile crept upon him.

"Truth speaks for itself."

All at once, Xavior grew heavy, as if suddenly swaddled in luxurious fur. To his slowly fading surprise, he felt his grasp loosen upon the handle of the poker.

It clattered to the floor.

Fourteen

Vale pushed open the door of the jailhouse to find the room—at first—empty and still. All appeared to be in place and Deputy Hess was nowhere to be found. That is, until the very same came casually strolling around the far corner, broom in hand.

"Sheriff," he said mildly.

Vale's instinct was to jokingly ask the boy if he'd made any further arrests since he'd last seen him, but something in the timid eyes of the boy held him back.

When he himself made mistakes while coming of age—as one does—his father made use of methods far less ambiguous than simple lashings of the tongue to correct him.

Vale collapsed into the sturdy armchair behind the desk to fill his pipe with fresh leaves of tobacco.

"I'm afraid we've got some work cut out for us," he muttered, attending to the pipe. "But I s'pose that's just what you've been hoping for, isn't it? A little excitement round here. Well, you've got it now... How acquainted are you with today's happenings, Deputy?"

"I saw a group of folks gathering around speaking with that rider. Mathius, I think my uncle... the mayor, called him."

Vale puffed a cloud into the air, nodding in affirmation. Luke continued.

"All I know is that the mayor and him went off to talk. As to what about, I'm not sure. But they seemed friendly enough."

"So I've heard," muttered Vale. "The doctor told me something similar, although, between you and I, I'm never too eager to trust that old drunk. What were you doing over on the avenue?"

"I went for a walk. Is that fine by you, or should I have waited here like a dog to be granted such liberties?"

Vale was tempted to respond in an escalating confrontation. It's what his father would have done. But at acknowledging the fact, he decided to instead let the boys sharpness go. He was going to need him in the hours to come.

He exhaled another cloud of smoke into the air between them.

"I need you to keep an eye on Xavior. He's hot and he might be hostile to our new friend. Could you make sure that he sticks to other matters?"

"I can do that. But... Why not you?" asked Luke.

"I'm riding after Ginny," Vale said in another puff of smoke. "She went rambling west on foot, out into the wilderness. Lost her senses I guess." Vale snarled his nose as he stifled a cough. "To be honest, Luke, I was really hoping that she'd be back by now. But being that she's not, I gotta go and get her.

"You want someone to come with you?"

"No," said Vale, trying to think of a metaphor that might resonate best with the mind of a child. "Sometimes, the knight can only swing his sword because he knows that the shield is held firmly in his other hand."

"Okay," said Luke, visibly confused. "But am I the sword or the shield?"

Vale didn't know the answer, but gave one regardless.

***

"Hellooo, Willie!" bellowed Vale in sarcastic reverence.

"Vale," responded Willie, rolling his eyes as he went about reinforcing one of the livery's load-bearing beams.

"Ginny heard the bell."

"So I've heard... No sign of Frederick?"

"No."

"Where'd she get off to, then?

"Somewhere west of here." Vale spit near his boot. "How fast can you get Lucky ready for me?"

"Give me three minutes." The man stood, abandoning his project to run toward the saddles that hung against the back wall.

As he waited, Vale noticed Jacob still standing in the very same corner as he had been before, still facing into the darkness of a corner's crevasse. He'd known horses to occasionally take to odd behavior after eating bad hay.

"Willie, ya gotta stop feeding these horses moldy..." Vale stopped his accusations mid-sentence when he noticed the midnight mare of the rider standing idly against an opposite corner, doing the very same thing.

Vale uneasily considered the sight as Willie approached, Lucky's bridle in hand.

"I'll be honest, Sheriff, I've never seen nothing like it. Might be horse flu. Might be coincidence. I don't know. But if, when you get back, you find me doing the same thing... well... just take me out back and shoot me, alright?"

Vale was in no mood for levity as he took the tack. "I should be back by tomorrow. If not, send the boy after me."

"The boy?" asked Willie in earnest puzzlement.

"Deputy Hess, Willie," said Vale with a chuckle, "Deputy Luke Hess."

Fifteen

Just as the sun dipped below the western horizon, Vale rode Lucky east in the search of Ginny Samson. It was the first time that he'd ridden beyond Bastion in years.

He had hoped to extend his streak of locality for many months further, considering that riding outside of town was generally associated with effort or tribulation. He'd much rather be spending his days lazily smoking on the jailhouse porch watching squirrels hug the branches of the wind tussled trees. Hell, he'd rather watch young Luke bumbling about his duties.

But such was, of course, the duty of being sheriff. He just wished that he had chosen a profession that better agreed with his growing sloth.

He'd done plenty of tracking in his younger days and figured that he could pick up on Ginny's trail before long. It'd been decades since he'd last done any serious tracking, but the process was well enough engrained in his memory. The hard part would be getting into the elevation and avoiding any unwanted interactions with grey wolves, mountain lions, or grizzlies. The latter were the inhabitants of many of Vale's more vivacious dreams. As he pondered the subject he reached into his side-saddle's holster to caress the long metal of his Winchester.

He knew that a rifle shot alone wouldn't be enough if the shot were placed anywhere but the beast's forehead or heart. Nonetheless, the heaviness of the metal offered a tangible covenant to quell his fears.

At the outset of the journey, Vale decided not to push the horse too hard. Instead, he let it carry him forward in a patient trot. He knew from experiences long past that he may end up requiring the horse to carry him further than the short distance of his original plans. It wouldn't do him well to exhaust the horse from the outset.

A consoling fact was that Lucky was a young and healthy colt known for its vivacity. Willie knew his lot and Vale was glad for it. He and the stable master had known each other for a long, long time, and as Vale came to consider it, he thought Willie might be the closest thing he had to a friend in Bastion. And if one was to be friends with anyone in such a town, hell, it might as well be the stable master. Why not add the gunsmith to the list?

"Where are you Ginny," he whispered aloud.

The plan was to ride further west than she could have already walked, then turn back to—hopefully—catch her head-on. He only hoped that she still tread due west. If she had instead wandered north, things would get harder by the mile. The country west of Bastion was timid. The land to the north was not.

But here, the ridgelines upon which he and Lucky tread spread out mildly from the true mountains in the west. The occasional patch of trees clumped themselves into cliques while the buffalo grass waved gently in the pleasant evening air. A sunset burned flamboyantly behind the jagged mountain range toward which he rode, the ethereal specter of Bighorn Peak rising straight ahead. The red phase of the sunset was particularly breathtaking, and in its swirling and distant swatches of illuminated clouds Vale thought—curiously—upon one of the few fond memories that he had of his father.

In it, he sat in a small fishing boat casting a flimsy line into the water. The old man sat beside him, silently surrounded by the gentle ripples of Jackson's Pond—a body of water south of Bastion near the Colorado territory. He couldn't remember if they ended up catching anything or not, but what he *did* distinctly recall was the bleeding sky atop the same eastern horizon, somewhere south, sometime ago.

"Red sky at night, sailor's delight," his father had said. And for whatever reason, Vale thought consciously to himself, "Remember this, Vale... Remember that."

And he did.

When darkness overcame the retreating light of the horizon, Vale figured that he'd ridden far enough west to outrun Ginny and pulled Lucky's reins to the right. The resulting trek north led him across the perpendicular ridgelines in an uncomfortable adjustment from the smooth ride that had taken him west. Now, he and the horse were forced to descend awkwardly into ravines of uneven footing before then rising into coalescing earth of the same. Three times, Lucky's hooves got caught in particularly dense wells of mud, forcing Vale to kick the beast's sides harder than he'd like to in order to spur the animal free of the earthy glue.

The moon was high and bright and Vale was thankful to see no further clouds rolling in to shade its light. That was the big bet. If the moon was obscured, his chances of finding and corralling Ginny would have been greatly reduced. But the face of the moon burned brightly across the night sky, readily casting a bright-blue hue atop the rolling landscape.

When Vale summited a hilltop rising distinctively higher than all those around it, Vale pulled at the reins to encourage Lucky to stop. He closed his eyes to reset the sensitivity of his vision—a trick he'd learned from an Indian scout a lifetime ago—and looked east in the hopes of seeing Ginny rambling towards him in the wide landscape.

"Share with me some of your luck, boy," he whispered to the horse.

But only the gentle swaying of the sagebrush met his eye; the only sound, the quiet sashaying of the same. In his imagination, Vale pictured Ginny dehydrated from her yelling, already prone and fading upon the earth. At the thought, Vale pressed his spurs into Lucky's sides, propelling the beast east to find her.

But just as he did, a tremendous headwind rolled over the horizon to blow his hat squarely off his head. Vale turned back to see that the old Stetson had come to rest at the base of a tall pine behind him. He'd worn the hat for as long as he could remember and didn't intend on losing it now. He swung his leg over Lucky's side, jumped down, and jogged over to retrieve the hat without a thought.

Vale plucked the hat from the base of the tree and slapped it against his denim.

Suddenly, he heard the fast encroachment of racing hooves from behind him, leading Vale to believe that another was riding briskly upon him. But when he whipped around, Vale saw instead, to his horror, that it was Lucky—carrying all of his provisions and protections—racing wildly past him in a spontaneous spook.

"Lucky!!!" he shouted, sprinting after the colt. He knew what it meant to be left without a horse in such a country, his voice disappearing into the vastness of the empty space all about him.

Vale went to call after Lucky once again, but when he made to holler, a familiar tickle in his throat graduated to a tight squeeze in his chest. With speed, the convulsion brought him to his knees. Soon, a sense of breathless panic and a piercing pressure overcame him. He hungered for breath, and with each missed inhalation, the lack of oxygen in his brain amplified a rising tide of anxiety.

As he heaved, he was sure that he was soon to die.

Vale slipped from consciousness and collapsed to the floor. Silently, he lay contorted in the grass beneath the looming and indifferent gaze of the moon. A slight breeze sashayed all things that were loose enough to dance, and nothing came or went for a duration irrelevant to the hillside.

Sixteen

Luke stood outside Maxine's General Store with his back pressed firmly against the walkway's pillar. His arms crossed his chest and the brim of his sun-bleached hat hung low about his eyes. A toothpick spun about his lip while he gazed across the avenue toward the sealed entrance of the smithy.

The doors had remained closed since Luke approached the scene some half-hour before.

With Vale off searching for Ginny, it wasn't lost on Luke that he was, until the sheriff returned, the sole representative of the law in Bastion. When he initially considered the fact, a tremendous wave of pride overcame him. It was all he'd ever dreamt of, after all.

But as the minutes passed and the sunset turned to darkness, a slow, persistent anxiety rose within him. What terrible things could happen under his watch? And, even more anxiety inducing, what would he be expected to do in response to such things? What if Xavior was to open the door, rifle in hand, and march to the courthouse? Was he prepared to draw and shoot the man? What if Shae and Quinn had grown smart that he'd been tasked with sole authority over the town and emboldened the saloon's contingent to spill their debaucheries beyond the confines of the saloon?! Was he prepared to quell their salacious riot? Could he possibly be expected to maintain order all on his own while the sheriff went off to God-knows where for God-knows how long?

What if he didn't return at all?

An elephant's pressure grew upon his chest, and as the darkness of the evening flourished and swallowed the street in entirety, a thousand worries inhabited Luke's peripheries.

The toothpick spun with ferocity between his lips.

With jolting immediacy, the door behind him ripped open, prompting Luke to jump into the air and produce a less than intimidating shriek. But when he spun about, he was only met by the maternal presence of Maxine Weathers exiting the general store. She dangled a keyring in her hand, presumably intent on closing-up for the day.

"Well, I'm awful sorry to startle you, master Hess. If I had known you was standing there I might have opened the door with more cushion."

Her voice was soft and consolatory like a morning rain. It made Luke think of his mother's embrace. He wished he could go off and find it. Tears quickly swelled beneath the green of his eyes and his lower lip began to tremble.

"Oh, there, there Master Hess," she said, approaching Luke with concave brows. "Whatever is the matter?"

But before she could cradle the deputy in her embrace—something that he both subtly desired and simultaneously disdained himself for desiring—Luke backed into the street to wipe the tears from his eyes with a swift drag of his blue cotton sleeve.

"All is well, Ms. Weathers. I have to go, though. I have business. Tasked by the sheriff himself... Good day." Luke spun about, and, feeling compelled to validate the statement, strode directly toward the still shuttered door of the smithy across the way.

Luke knocked on the door with authority, fearing that if he were timid in his actions, Maxine, surely watching him from across the street, might see further into his personified anxieties. Regardless, the sharpness of the metallic rap that his knuckles produced on the door startled him and the lagging seconds that then unfurled pressed mightily upon his growing, faceless dread.

Something suddenly occurred to Luke as he waited for the door to be answered. What was he to say if the blacksmith answered the door? Surely, he couldn't just come out and state his objective. Was he to lie and inquire on a different matter? Why had he knocked on the door in the first place?

He turned about, feigning boredom, and saw that Maxine Weathers was nowhere to be seen.

Had he, perhaps, placed excess emphasis on what others thought of him? It was something that had been drilled into his psyche from the day that he was old enough to be responsible for his actions. "Reputation is worth more than your skin," his mother would often say. But as he continued scanning the empty street in the merciful silence that persisted behind the smithy's door, he began to consider if the audience was indeed as interested in the performance as were the actors. The thought soothed him. Were his most ominous worries only reflections of himself? Specters of his pride? The darkness of the street seemed suddenly softer and less littered with danger.

A smile grew upon his face and he nearly chuckled. "Well, if I ain't yeller," he whispered aloud, boldness reclaiming his demeanor.

But then, as if in contest to his ease, the shrill sound of a deadbolt dragging against metal announced itself behind him. Luke turned about slowly to reluctantly address it.

Peering out from the propped open door was the smiling face of Xavior Jenkins. Blackness filled the space behind him. The man's eyes were vivacious while the unmoving nature of his facial muscles were nothing short of peculiar. Xavior said nothing.

"Xavior," quipped Luke, uncertainty again regaining a foothold within him, "I wanted to check in on you. To see that you're okay. I've been told it's been an eventful day."

Xavior's smile remained unchanged as a single tear welled in the pocket of his eye. There was something unplaceable and uncanny in the manner in which Xavior looked at him.

Xavior's mouth at last flinched to necessitate speech, its muscles doing so with such a start that its speed induced a sharp, reactionary twinge in Luke's own limbs. It was like watching a recently deceased cow suddenly speak perfect English.

"Hello, Luke. It's a joy to see you... Would you like to come inside... and see my wares? I've a bushel of merchandise... that I'm confident you'll envy."

Xavior didn't speak in such a way. Nor did he use such words. Luke again wished that the sheriff was there to act on his behalf. But he wasn't, and he had to make decisions for himself whether he liked it or not. He decided it best to prod no further with the man. As far as he was concerned,

Xavior could be as peculiar as an oriental suit so long as he remained in the confines of the smithy.

"No, thank you," he said, his gaze cast down. "I have to go."

He spun about and, unsure of where exactly he intended to go, stammered west along the avenue toward any destination but the company of the clearly distorted blacksmith.

He turned back to see if Xavior watched him go and, indeed, the blacksmith's toothy grin could be seen peering out from the smithy's darkness, cloaking him like a veil.

Unable to shake the peculiarity of the sight, Luke stopped and turned back to confront Xavior's observation of him in such a way. In response, Xavior patiently retreated into the swallowing darkness, closing the door before him.

In a metallic screech, the deadbolt slid back into its frame.

But before he could contemplate the peculiarity of the encounter, the sound of distant conversation in the direction of the courthouse captured Luke's attention. He turned to see his uncle emerging into the flickering light of the courthouse landing with Mathius at his side.

Just as Luke came to perceive them, the mayor shifted away from Mathius and called in Luke's direction. "Luke! Deputy Luke! Is that you down there?"

Luke considered not answering. To instead slip away and retreat into the darkness of any peripheral alleyway. But there was no escaping Thadeus Hess. Luke knew all too well that when his uncle's attention was set upon something, be it a plan of action or a person of interest, there was little that could be done to pull him from his vision when it tunneled.

"Uncle!" Luke called at last, approaching the courthouse steps with performative vigor.

"You remember Mathius," said Thadeus in his public facing baritone, gesturing toward the robed man standing beside him. "We were just discussing matters of policy. Mathius comes representing higher authorities, and, as it just so happens, your name was on our tongues only minutes ago."

"All lies," replied Luke addressing Mathius. He surprised himself with the quickness of his wit. "In what context did my name precede this serendipitous meeting, gentleman?" As he spoke, Luke took note of a southern twang mingling amongst his own vowels. He couldn't deny that his uncle held influence over him.

"The mayor and I were discussing coming improvements to this town," spoke Mathius. "As such, we will be requiring godly men, men worthy of trust, in the coming days. The mayor insists that this description suits you well. Would you agree, Deputy? Are you a godly man? Are you worthy of trust?"

If Luke had learned anything from his uncle, it was never to turn down an opportunity when it came knocking. "It's called 'Yes, and...'" Thadeus had drunkenly murmured at a dinner party once. "Just say yes to everything and make it up as you go. And if you smile wide enough and make people feel like they're being listened to, hell, everything else generally falls into place nice and keen-like afterwards."

"Yes," Luke heard himself say.

Mathius responded only with a flat expression, his eyes resting heavily upon the deputy. Something in the placidity of his face reminded Luke of Xavior's. It gave rise to a dissonance in his gut. He trusted his uncle, and he trusted his ability to make decisions on behalf of Bastion, but who exactly *was* this man... and what did he mean by "improvements?"

"Of course he is," offered Thadeus in a supplemental affirmation of his nephew's virtues. "He's a Hess! If nothing else, if no one else, we can rely on the Hess's in this town. I assure you that, Mr. Patmos."

Mathius offered a gentle nod, a gesture that Luke couldn't decide to mean one thing or another. The man then stepped toward him, holding a bony hand before Luke's face. A silver ring with a circular face clung to its middle finger. Inlaid on the ring was an interlocking web of lines as if three triangles were laid upon one another.

Mathius nodded again, this time in a clear indication that Luke was to kiss the jewelry.

Luke wasn't much of a church going man, but given the stoles upon Mathius's shoulders and the ethereal aura that he carried, he assumed the act to be of religious importance. And since he had only moments before insinuated himself to be a godly man, Luke disobeyed the protesting inclinations of his intuition, leaned forward, and placed his lips fleetingly upon the ring. Its metal stung in its coldness and the scent of unkempt flesh permeated the skin of the man's hand.

As he reset his posture, Luke gazed past Mathius's shoulder to see Thadeus nodding in a serious yet approving manner. The look in his eyes seemed to say that he was doing well in whatever circumstance he was now irrevocably involved.

"Come, now child," spoke Mathius. "Let us walk together so that we may become acquainted with each other's aspirations."

Without bidding adieu to Thadeus or waiting to see if Luke would follow, Mathius descended the stairs, away from both Hess's in a deliberate and careful manner.

At Luke's hesitation, Thadeus gave the deputy an affirming nod of confidence to descend the stairs and catch up with the man walking from the steps and into the darkness.

"We'll convene tomorrow then, Mathius. As agreed upon," called Thadeus. Luke could sense in his tone a hint of chagrin at not being formally bid adieu by the visitor. Mathius didn't respond and only tread forward into the night.

At reaching Mathius's side, Luke found his solo presence to be unsettling in ways that he couldn't wholly place. In all honesty, he desired to be doing just about anything other than walking alongside the man. But Luke wished to do well by his uncle and make him proud. He wouldn't abandon his uncle's confidence in him now, not after such an endorsement of his character.

"How would you describe your relationship with God, young one?" asked Mathius, treading slowly upon the avenue. With each step they increasingly became engulfed by the darkness beyond the courthouse's flickering lights.

"I'd say it's a... personal relationship," responded Luke following a ponderous moment.

"Are not all relationships, particularly those with God, personal?"

"I suppose they are..." said Luke. He wasn't sure of where the man was headed with his words nor footsteps.

"And yet any relationship, be it with a friend, father, neighbor, or God, cannot ultimately flourish without the kinship of others. Does community not perfect one's personal relationships? Would our relationship with God, too, not be complete without proper constructs in our organized communities and governance? For only in our shared yet simultaneously personal relationships with God can we approach the epitome of our earthly salvations. Do you not agree, deputy?"

"I do," said Luke, not so sure that he did.

"Then you would be in favor of actions taken by this community's leadership to support such ends?"

"Indeed," said Luke, not so sure that he would.

Mathius stopped and remained eerily still. They stood at the juncture of the avenue and the path that led north into the hills. Luke suddenly worried that the man might confront him on the insincerity of his affirmations and considered offering a preemptive excuse for a sharp exit from their conversation. But before he could construct a reasonable alibi, Mathius pulled a deep and raspy breath and turned to face the young representative of the law.

"Very well, Mr. Hess. If such is the case, I trust you'll join us tomorrow atop the courthouse steps. For when the sun reaches its peak, the people of Bastion will come to know their salvation at last. It shall be as was written in Acts 2:44: '*And all that believed were together and had all things common.*'"

Mathius turned from Luke to embark upon the moonlit path toward the church. As the man's footsteps grew distant, Luke stood alone amongst the darkness to contemplate much in silence.

Seventeen

A glass shattered near the back of the saloon. Quinn, dancing a hearty jig atop a table's God facing surface, had accidentally kicked his own drink to the floor in a jubilant flailing of his limbs. A cheer rang out through the brightly lit crowd while Henry "Player" Johnson continued his rendition of Maple Leaf Rag without interruption.

"Awe shite!" Quinn sang out, deflating into a resigned acknowledgement while still standing atop the table.

"That's alright, ya crazy bugger!" called Johhny Hilbo, another frequent albeit less ambitious patron of Shae's saloon. "You'll do better tomorrow!" Johnny then turned about to collect a silver dollar from a despondent patron sitting beside him.

For some months, many of the saloon's most frequent customers had begun placing bets amongst themselves as to whether Quinn would get himself kicked out by the end of the night, and if so, at what hour it would occur.

The betting suited the old Irishman just fine as the betters of the early hour wagers would happily slip him drinks beyond the watchful eye of those betting on a late-night ejection. Some found that half the fun came from either trying to sneak Quinn drinks or in the prevention of it.

It was like chess except the king was Quinn's liver.

Other betters had long running games on how long it'd take for Shae to have enough and finally banish Quinn outright from the establishment. Some too suspected that the pair shared an odd Irish kinship that complicated the situation. Regardless, the frequency of Quinn's drunkenness incurring damages and fines upon the saloon had increased as of late and several dollars were risked in the matter.

All this to say that Quinn's shattering of his glass wasn't a novelty and Quinn knew the drill. Right on cue, Shae emerged from around the bar wielding a broom, dustpan, and a paternally disappointed demeanor. Quinn took the broom with a frown and attended to his self-inflicted duties with a practiced sway.

From afar, it nearly appeared as a dance.

When the last of the shrapnel was corralled into the trash barrel, Quinn drug a chair to a corner to stand atop its cushion. He extended his arms wide in reception to all that were present. At seeing this, Henry stopped his playing, and a hush fell over the saloon as Quinn began to sing:

"Drink, my friends, it's all that ye can,
The earth dulls thy feet and dry work culls thy hands.
Stupors they guide thee to the first morning light,
To quell the ambition of death cold and blight.
So drink for me now, friends, I head for the door
I've drunk my heart full, I'll see you no more!"

A rapturous applause saw Quinn stumble out into the evening.

Shae was glad that it was only a glass that had received the brunt of Quinn's inebriation that night. He could never anticipate when the Irishman might fall against the piano or damage the saloons other furniture. He would have likely seen to it long ago that the man never step foot into his bar ever again, but the lobbying dollars that lined his pockets to not do so more than offset the costs of the damages. And, in all honesty, Shae recognized Quinn to be, at the very least, well-intentioned. He never became violent or surly and had become a sort of fixture that would have rendered the saloon an entirely different place without him.

And so, with Quinn's departure from its walls that night, the saloon proceeded to take on a quieter, more reserved nature for the remainder of the evening.

"I swear to ya, here and now, that man is the devil incarnate," said a voice near the end of the bar. The statement pulled Shae from his contemplations of Quinn, intriguing him just enough to pick up a rag and shine the bar nearer the conversation to eavesdrop further.

"Oh, come on!" exclaimed another. "Just cause he was wearing black and had a bad eye don't mean nothing. He's probably just a Veteran, which leads me to suppose that you, sir, support the prejudice of cripples!"

"A false dichotomy if I've ever heard one," laughed a third voice that was unquestionably Doctor Stevenson. "And a red herring to boot! But regardless, my concern is this: from where did the bell come? From my vantage, it could have only arrived in one of two ways. One, the bell was carried over the unpaved and soaking wet hills before being lifted into the belfry—without assistance of machinery, I might add—all by persons unseen and unheard, *and* within a matter of singular hours. Option two, the man is as he says he is, the acting hand of god, facilitating the bell's materialization at the bequest of the almighty. Now, if those were the choices, I wouldn't blame Hess for, at the very least, taking company with the man."

A mixture of agreement and low grumbles met his words while what was at first a casual eavesdrop had become a locked-in attendance for Shae. Did the doctor say, "hand of god?" What had he missed?

The conversation continued, leading Shae to look up and see the prominent voice of the crowd to be that of Jules Mackenzie, a one-time cowboy that broke his leg on a cattle drive years back, stranding him in Bastion without a realistic alternative.

"Option three," proposed the cowboy, "the rider's actually the devil *masquerading* as the hand of God. You all saw him whisper to that horse before it walked into the stables like an obedient child. It practically let itself in without a worry in all the world! I'm telling y'all, something unnatural is afoot and the animals know it! They always know it before us humans do. Tell me this, can any of you's recall seeing a single bird fly overhead all day long? I sure as hell can't, and I shouldn't be the only one here bothered by it."

Not even the doctor could think of something to say in response and in the resulting contemplation, the crowd seemed to notice—all-at-once—Shae attentively listening in.

"What about you, barkeep?" asked the doctor. "What are your thoughts on all this?"

Shae raised his eyebrows and shook his head with a snort. "This is the first I've heard of any of it, if I'm being honest. I heard the bell earlier but just assumed that the Samson boy had finally come home with our tax dollars in tow. You mean to say that that's not the case?"

The group collectively shook their heads.

"Where's the sheriff?" he asked. "What's he got to say about it?"

"Well, I've nearly forgotten about Ol' Kingsbury," said Jules. "Him and Xavior walked up the hill shortly after the rider arrived. But afterwards they came down separate and neither shared much in the way of answers. Xavior didn't say a word and just went into the smithy, locking the door behind him. The sheriff, on the other hand, came down and, hearing that Mathius and the mayor were meeting in the courthouse, threw up his hands, had a coughing fit, and walked back to the jailhouse. However, before he did, he let on that he didn't see no cart, no tracks, and nothing at all to imply Frederick Samson's return. And then there's Ginny..."

With the mention of the gunsmith's name, the group turned from manic curiosity to a collective sadness. Benson Jones, the town's lone poet, collected his hat in his hands, turned, and walked out into the night without a word.

"Best to let him go," said Stevenson. The table jointly shook their heads as the doctor looked toward Shae, assuming that he hadn't yet heard the story.

"According to the sheriff, she ran up to the church, dead-set on reuniting with her boy. Can't say I blame her after all she's been through. Anyway, when she got up there and found no Frederick, well, she went mad and ran off into the hillside in search of him."

"Okay... Why didn't that lazy son of a bitch go after her?" asked Shae in a sudden fury that surprised all who heard his words. He was rarely one to raise his voice and none present had ever once heard him curse.

"Said he'd come down in a coughing fit," said the doctor with hesitation. "I can attest to the validity of such. He's been dealing with a mighty congestion of..."

"Well then I blame this goddamn town for trusting an invalid with our safety," interrupted Shae, reaching down to produce a bottle of bourbon and soon pouring himself a glass of the honeyed liquid. He tilted his head back to accept the dose not a moment before a second was poured. He then turned and walked to the back door at the end of the bar.

"Watch over things, Henry," he called to the piano player in a wavering holler, pushing open the door and emerging into the night. Before he could finish his subsequent drink, he collapsed to the dirt. The sobbing that came overwhelmed him. He had never shared with anyone how much he had come to adore his gunsmithing neighbor. Hell, he might not have even shared it fully with himself until that very moment.

Maybe she had been his cattle drive, he thought suddenly. Maybe she was what had held him so tightly in place among the otherwise unremarkable slow drift that was life in Bastion. And now she was gone, likely left abandoned to the elements to wither and die alone because the duly elected sheriff had a cough.

Goddamn him. Goddamn Hess for deeming that sloth worthy of employment. Goddamn Bastion. In a white-hot anger he hoped for Willie's dark prophecies to be true when, to his surprise, an arm caressed his shoulder in a swaying embrace.

"There, there master barkeeper. I'll work off the cost of the glass. I promise you that."

Eighteen

Shae placed a glass of whiskey with a submerged apple slice upon the top board of the piano's back to await its player. It was among the first things he did every morning, save for Sundays, of course.

He unlatched and pushed open the saloon's mahogany doors to let in the bright light of the morning. But to Shae's surprise, Quinn was absent from the exterior walkway. That was a rarity. More often than not, the Irishman would be present to greet him "good morning" as he did so. Instead, from around the corner Shae heard the drunkard's snoring reverberating against the brick of his alleyway abode.

It must have been a long night for the Irishman.

The air was warm and Shae already longed for the rain that had dappled the dirt the day before. If they were lucky, it might be the first of a string of storms to pass through the area. It wasn't a blind wish, either. He'd lived in the Buckshaw Valley long enough to know that summer monsoons rarely arrived individually.

When he returned to his dutiful position behind the bar, the doors behind him swung open. One by one, in walked a trio of men, each engrossed in separate attentions entirely. Henry Johnson led the threesome and thus initially pushed open the doors to enter the saloon. Behind him, Dr. Stevenson caught the door before it could close in his face. Henry was evidently too eager to sit at the piano and sip at his morning dew to notice the doctor walking briskly behind him. In turn, Dr. Stevenson was equally blinded by the slight, and in his vinegar failed to notice Glenn Flowers—one of the mayor's orderlies—walking briskly behind *him*.

Glenn was a wiry man filling a suit clearly purchased with someone else in mind. In fact, such was a description that did well to describe him in general. Although he was born and raised in Bastion, Glenn never quite found his niche amongst its citizenry. He'd tried his hand at being Xavior's apprentice for some time, worked as Maxine's helper for a handful of months, and even offered his services to Reverend Gilroy. He was ultimately rebuffed by all. His latest endeavor was being Mayor Hess's errand boy, although only the errands deemed impossible to be bungle were handed to him.

Glenn entered the room with a dumb expression.

Sitting at his stool, Henry wasted no time in slurping from his glass of apple slice whiskey while Dr. Stevenson wiped at his brow with a flowered handkerchief.

Red River Valley began to play.

"Gin and Tonic, my man," said Stevenson, pulling out a stool with a slight waver. As he sat, Shae noticed a stain on the doctor's lapel leading Shae to further notice a flask sized bulge in his trouser pocket.

He was still drunk, it appeared.

It was a rare occasion when Shae was forced to escort the doctor out of his doors but that was exactly what had happened only hours prior. Stevenson had taken to embracing shots with those equally disturbed by the day's events and, before long, was shouting openly about the devil being among them. Thankfully he didn't appear to remember much of it. Shae might have even been impressed at the man's endurance—still being upright and all—had Shae not known that the man was likely to see patients soon.

"You drank the last of my gin last night, doc. That tonic's no good anyway. How's a whiskey cocktail sound?"

"Like the spit-up of a cowboy, but it'll do."

Shae went about collecting his bitters as Glenn Flowers stood impatiently near the end of the bar, clutching his hat near his groin. He cleared his throat, hoping to get the attention of the men, but considering that neither Shae nor Dr. Stevenson appreciated his passivity, both simply ignored him until he spoke up. If he had something to say, he could say it. Furthermore, both knew him to represent the mayor, and while Shae outright despised Thadeus, Dr. Stevenson only respected him to his face. He had little desire nor patience to entertain the sensibilities of his lackies.

"Gentlemen," Glenn spoke at last. Shae looked up to see that the man had raised his chin as if recalling a script.

"Today at noon, a new Bastion holiday is to be announced upon the steps of the courthouse. All are asked to attend at the bequest of the mayor, Thadeus Hess."

Glenn smiled and nodded in agreement with his words, as if he were satisfied at recalling the sentence sufficiently.

"Good day, gentlemen," he then said, exiting the saloon.

Shae scoffed—not giving the proclamation much credence—and immediately returned to the crafting of the doctor's drink.

"A new holiday?" slurred Dr. Stevenson with a loose grin. "I suppose the mayor has at last decided to proclaim the first of August as a celebration of his reign." He burped. "I'm surprised that it's taken him *this long* to see himself akin to Augustus."

Shae poured a carefully measured ounce of whiskey atop the waiting bitters, muddled orange, and water. Shae knew from experience that any lack of precision would be worthy of the doctor's wrath. It was much too early in the morning for Stevenson's lamentations, and he intended to get the drink right the first time. As always, the doctor would be looking for excuses to complain.

"Don't you think so?" Dr. Stevenson asked.

In his intense effort at perfecting the drink, Shae hadn't processed a word of the doctor's previous statement. He didn't much care for the man.

"What?"

"I was expressing my condolences for this town," he slurred, gesturing all about. "Hess and his ego. Blaah."

"I thought you were a friend of the Hess's," said Shae, presenting the cocktail before the man.

Stevenson raised the glass and examined its contents, carefully sniffing its aromas with closed eyes. He sipped the drink, and to Shae's relief, smiled as he spoke thereafter.

"I *am* a friend of the Hess's. Anyone that's smart ought to be. But if I know anything of the Hess's, it's that their designs," he burped again, this time raising a fist to his sternum in acknowledgement, "on power are rarely limited. And that one," he said, pointing in the direction of the courthouse, "that one's got plans."

***

The hours passed slowly as more and more customers wafted into the saloon to exchange theories as to what the announcement at noon was to be.

And with each new face demanding liquid courage to quell their unease, something in Shae sensed that what the doctor said was true. Hess was up to something.

He thought back on a story that he once read in a book left behind by a transient cowboy. In its pages, the story told of a man that sat on a throne beneath a sword dangling by a thread.

Nineteen

Thadeus stood in the courthouse's foyer gazing into a painting that lined the circular room. It was his favorite by far. The piece hung upon the wall between the building's front entrance and a passageway that led off toward the orderlies' quarters and the kitchen beyond. Its oiled face depicted a butte jutting from a ponderosa lined hillside while a kaleidoscope sunset set the backdrop of the scene ablaze. Engraved into the brass nameplate along the frame's bottom border read: *Mato Tipila; Bad God's Tower*.

The painting's visage was a welcome distraction from the rising murmur of the crowd outside. He switched his attention to the wreathed face of the grandfather clock nearby. Eight till noon. He had hoped that Mathius would have arrived by now but understood that there was no point in bestowing the present moment with undo worry. Mathius would arrive when he arrived.

He returned his attention to the painting's finer details.

As ethereal as the butte appeared, it was indeed a real place; one that he had visited on more than one occasion. His initial visit to the monument was on his sixteenth birthday when his grandmother had hired a pair of Lakota guides to take him, his sister Penelope, and their father to the site. The guides rode their horses while the Hess's traversed the landscape in a horse drawn carriage crafted by Xavior's father Benny, rest his soul.

On their approach, Thadeus recalled seeing the tower rise majestically from the surrounding earth like the trunk of a California Redwood—of which he read extensively about in his studies. He envisioned it once being the base of a tree so large that its branches might have brushed the moon. What monstrous saw had decapitated its top, who could have possibly wielded such a tool, and where had the wood of its limbs been carried off to?

As they drew nearer still, one of the guides, a man that had introduced himself as Red Feather, pulled his steed alongside the carriage to lope beside it. He must have noticed the glittering amazement in Thadeus's eyes. He addressed the boy directly, albeit softly, while both Thadeus's sister and father slept soundly beside him.

"Long ago," Red Feather began, "seven girls were playing in these hills when they were chased by a group of bears. The beasts drew near, and fearing for their lives, the girls prayed to the great spirit to save them. The spirit, Wakan Tanka, heard their call and lifted the very ground they stood upon high into the air, far from the reach of the bears below. Do you see those lines in its walls?"

Thadeus nodded that he did.

"They were scratched into the face of the rock by the claws of the beasts. They tried to climb its edges but it was too steep and the girls were safe atop the plateau. Do you know what happened to the girls?" he asked.

The door of the courthouse creaked open, lifting Thadeus from the depths of his memory. With the portal open, the volume and breadth of the crowd outside was jarring in its contrast to its muted nature when the door was closed. The tone of its many singular voices seemed to coalesce into that of a single vexed song; one of baited curiosity.

When his orderlies had gone door to door that morning summoning the town to the courthouse's steps at noon, they hadn't provided details.

"Tell them that a new holiday, a Bastion holiday, is to be announced," was all Thadeus had asked for them to share.

But the distrust in the crowd's tone was obvious and a flicker of anxiety flashed within him. Had he been a less experienced speaker, or less resolute in the irrevocable actions that he was soon to embark upon, he might have even entertained the flicker. But anxiety had no fertile soil in which to lay roots in Thadeus Hess. He'd salted that plot long ago.

It was Mathius that had opened the door, stepped into the room, and shut the door gently behind him. To Thadeus's surprise, the man had abandoned the black garb that he had worn the day before. Instead, he wore a neatly ironed navy-blue suit; unmistakably Father Gilroy's. His beard was trimmed to a civil degree and a white clerical collar peaked sheepishly out near his collarbone. The red stoles that adorned his shoulders were the only remaining garb from the previous day.

Had Thadeus not raised his sight to the man's eyes and become immediately swallowed in his enrapturing gaze he might have thought him a different man entirely.

"You clean up quite nicely. How are you this day?"

"Well," replied Mathius, walking slowly about the space with his head down, carefully examining the tiles that made up the wise bison of the muraled floor. "The crowd is eager. They sense a change. The masses can always tell sooner than the individual when a tide shifts. But they will do well in accommodation. It's a cloudless day and the sun will provide much in the way of hampering any trepidations that may arise."

Thadeus nodded in agreement.

Mathius continued, "Deputy Hess... is he among us?"

Hearing his name spoken, Luke emerged from the passageway that led to the study. He wore an uneasy expression to match the canted pinning of his badge upon his chest. A toothpick spun tirelessly between his lips.

"Have you seen any sign of the sheriff?" he asked Mathius. "I was hoping that he would have arrived by now."

"No," said Mathius curtly. "But he shall arrive soon. Do not fret, young one. All is, and will continue to be, in hand."

Mathius turned to the door that he had emerged from just moments before and pulled it open. The high chatter of the crowd outside suddenly hushed as the opening of the door seemed to imply that their curiosities were soon to be dissolved.

"It's twelve O'clock, Mr. Mayor. The flock awaits its shepherd."

But before Thadeus stepped out onto the landing to address the waiting crowd, he first moved to his nephew. He knew that if he were to have any success in convincing those prone to skepticism, he would first be required to dispel the trouble lingering on Luke's face.

Thadeus rested a sure hand on the boy's shoulder, gripping it tightly.

"What is it that troubles you so? He might not look it at times, or even act it for that matter, but Sheriff Kingsbury is a capable man. Soon, he shall re..."

"What's happening, Uncle?" Luke asked abruptly. A shimmer of tears welled in his eyes and he looked unambiguously as if he were on the precipice of sobbing. "What *is he* talking about?" Luke pointed at Mathius. "Who *is* he, and why is he telling us what to do? But to answer your question, Ginny Samson troubles me. The bell, appearing out of thin air troubles me. The fact that he's wearing Reverend Gilroy's clothes troubles me. But most of all, I'm troubled by the ambiguity of your words mingling with such severity in your eyes. What is happening?"

Thadeus shifted his gaze to Mathius, still holding open the door. Sunlight streamed openly through its portal. Mathius eyes betrayed an appearance of disappointment. Both men had discussed and agreed upon the value of having a representative of the law beside them when sharing their intentions with the crowd. The law gave credence and implied consequence. Both would have been valuable attributes to aid their coming proclamations.

But it wasn't to be. Luke was a Hess and was therefore stubborn. It would take more than colorful words to dispel his untimely worries.

"Go on," spoke Thadeus, gesturing toward the study. "I'll send in some pie, and when we're finished with the announcement we'll sit together and all will be made clear."

"Don't treat me like a child."

Thadeus slapped Luke as quickly as the boy's syllables left his lips.

"Then don't act like one."

Luke dropped his gaze to the floor while a moment of stillness passed. Then, without a word, Luke brushed past his uncle and into the blinding heat of the day. Thadeus closed his eyes and ran a hand through his hair. He called a deep breath into his lungs. There would be time for reconciliation later.

As for now, the crowd awaited his elucidations.

And, so, as if a switch had been flipped, Thadeus smiled, opened his eyes, and strode confidently through the doorway that Mathius continued to hold open for him. As his eyes adjusted to the brightness of the scene before him, he saw that a surprisingly wide crowd stood expectantly at the base of the courthouse steps. More than a few lingered under the shade of peripheral trees while a handful held umbrellas to shield themselves from the sun.

He saw the dismissive posture of Shae Mackenzie, his arms woven across his chest, distantly tapping his boots upon the shaded walkway. In the further distance he saw Luke walking dejectedly away upon the length of the avenue.

Thadeus closed his eyes, pulled in a breath of warm air, and used it to speak.

Twenty

Vale walked upon the endless sea of the plains, thirsty and afraid. Of what exactly, he hadn't the initiative to ponder. He looked into the sky in search of the sun but saw no ball of fire overhead. When he returned his gaze to the horizon, a distant, hulking grizzly could be seen galloping toward him. He tried to run but felt no legs nor earth below him. He tried reaching for his pistol but received no sensation from his hands. The grizzly grew closer with each of its terrible strides, its encroaching presence queerly paired with the squeaking of a wheel. The juxtaposition of the sound upon the terrifying sight was peculiar, peculiar enough, in fact, to bring about a moments contemplation that thrust him from his unconsciousness and into a fit of coughing.

When the fit finally passed, Vale opened his blurry eyes to look about—in consciousness—at the brightness of his surroundings. In the developing clarity of his sight, he saw the patient approach of a mule-led cart, a young man at its helm.

The shrill creaking of its wheels had indeed awakened Vale from his dreams, but as his eyes became accustomed to the sight before him, he was forced to reconsider if he was in fact awake and not still dreaming. For as he sat awkwardly up and looked toward the sound of the encroaching wheels, he saw that it was none other than Frederick Samson, not only alive, but contentedly smiling atop the driver's seat of the cart. Although it had been years since he'd last seen the boy, it looked as if he hadn't aged a day. Was he wearing the same grey button up shirt, pearl snaps and all, that he had worn on the day of his departure? Surely not.

The mule that labored at the front of the cart was the very same that had taken Frederick west, a reliable beast named Sammy. By god, the joy that will come to Willie when he sees it.

Frederick appeared comfortable and at ease holding Sammy's reins. With a confident pull he subdued the beast's momentum and brought the cart to a halt but a dozen feet from Vale. The sheriff remained on the ground with one hand propping him up from his previously supine position.

"Now, what's the sheriff of a town as proud Bastion doing all the way out here?" asked Frederick.

Vale was still working to overcome both the disorientation of his slumber and the shock of Frederick's appearance.

"I was looking for... Where have you been, Freddy?" In the back of the cart, Vale noticed something hulking hidden beneath a canvas tarp. Given its size, he was surprised at having not noticing it until just then.

"It's been a long road," said Frederick with a knowing smile, patting the empty seat beside him. "Climb aboard. We'll ride into town together."

Vale hoisted himself into the cart and was glad to sit upon a seat meant for sitting. He was sore, surprisingly so, particularly in the muscles of his abdomen. The frequent violence of his coughing fits were beginning to take their toll. But having no desire to consider what his abrupt unconsciousness implied, he instead turned his attention to the miracle of Frederick sitting beside him, gently whipping the reins.

Vale was astonished at the perfection in the boy's skin. It was as if his knuckles had never once seen a ray of abusing sunshine. The fact was all the more perplexing given the length of time that he must have spent under the sun during his travels. In his face he saw more of the same.

"Freddy..." he began, struggling to find the words that he knew he was obliged to convey.

"If you're worrying about my mother, don't be."

"What?!"

"I came across her this morning before the sun had risen. In fact, she found you before I did. She pointed me in your direction. She was weak and thirsty, and so after we sat together for a long while, I left her with a band of soldiers that had made camp nearby. They'll look after her and promised to bring her into town when she's back on her feet. When the time is right."

A tremendous relief overcame Vale. "Thank God," was all he managed.

Frederick wasn't forced to do much to keep Sammy on a level path toward town. It was as if the animal itself knew the way while Frederick only loosely held the reins in his upturned palms.

It was a pleasant day and the yellowed grasses frolicking this way and that. As the cart passed through the shade cast by a thriving thicket of cottonwood, they traversed a gentle shower of dispatched cotton falling diagonally from the tree's branches, riding the breeze.

"How long have you been gone now, Freddy?" he asked. "Has it truly been three years? California must have treated you well..." A flicker of resentment floated on his words—something that he was not initially intending but subsequently stood behind as the words lingered in the open air.

A long moment passed without a response by Frederick, and as it did, Vale sat in an uneasy limbo between a rising anger toward the boy's abrupt appearance and a shy guilt for having expressed it in a manner so poorly disguised.

"I'm sorry such sorrow has come to nestle itself within you," Frederick said at last. But as relieved as Vale was to hear the silence broken, the manner in which Frederick spoke, and the words that passed his lips, both seemed wholly removed from his memories of the boy. He turned to validate that it was indeed Frederick that sat beside him.

"There is something I must share with you, Vale. Something of importance. Something that will require much from you," said Frederick, retaining a forward gaze. "As we speak, deception takes root in the bedrock of Bastion. A false prophet speaks through the mouth of your mayor leading your home, your people, and your lives along a path that ends in destruction."

As Frederick spoke, Vale began to wonder what drugs the Samson boy had discovered in the city by the bay. But as his prophetic words continued, he suddenly recalled the dark-clad rider and all that was so confounding back in town. But... how could Frederick have known any of that?

"...He promises salvation through falsities and hollow words, wishing only to toy with the whims of man. He does it only to ease his curiosities, to play with the question: to what extent will man fillet itself in the pursuit of meaning."

Vale was not hearing the words of Frederick Samson. That much was becoming clear.

"Who are you?" he asked, carefully eyeing the "boy" sitting beside him.

"A messenger on high. But that is not important. What's important is this. You must do what I cannot, for I am unable to intervene so directly in the matters of men. Yes, such an act would make things simpler, but simplicity is rarely, if ever, conducive to what is right. Fate must take its own path. You know this."

Vale hesitated in his response as he internally repeated the words back to himself in the hopes of understanding what had just said to him. He ultimately nodded in response.

"Before the eyes of the crowd you must refute the claims of the false prophet. Then, you must raise the cargo of this cart in place of the bell that the snake has produced. Its resonance will poison the minds of the town if left to ring unabated for too long."

A glimmer of tears coalesced in Vale's eyes. Had he at last come to meet his life's ultimate purpose? Had Susy's insistence of him making a good impression on the lord finally paid dividends?

"Will you do this? Will you do this for your very soul and for the souls of your kin?"

Vale nodded with fervor. He was enraptured, fully engulfed in his sudden role in the grand narrative unfurling before him.

"Good. Much depends on your shoulders, Sheriff Kingsbury. More than I can share with you now." The presence appearing as Frederick Samson then pulled back on the reins, prompting Sammy to cease her momentum and rest idle.

He turned to face Vale, his immaculate skin suddenly making all the sense in the world.

"Step down and examine our cargo, Sheriff."

Eager to show servitude to what he was beginning to suspect to be an angel, Vale spun himself from his seat and marched to the rear of the cart. The tarp that covered the cargo was a hardy tan, nearly mimicking the soil's color. He reached for one of the many ties that bound it taught and begun to unravel its bindings. Then the next, and the next.

At last, a sufficient number of the bindings were undone and Vale lifted the tarp to examine the bell underneath as he was instructed.

But in the instant of the tarp's rise, Vale's perspective shifted instantaneously. He was now sitting atop the cart's seat holding Sammy's reins in his palms. The cart stood idle in a field facing the western façade of the courthouse's gaudy architecture. Frederick was nowhere to be found.

From the other side of the courthouse rose the reverberating sounds of Mayor Hess pontificating.

Twenty-One

At ten till noon, Shae locked the doors of the saloon and strolled the long plank walkway toward the courthouse. When passing the storefront of Ginny's gun shop, he bit down hard upon his lip.

The metallic taste of blood was to accompany him for the remainder of the day.

Through the warbling heatwaves that oscillated his vision he saw a wide crowd milling about the courthouse's bottom steps. He was impressed at the wide breadth of spectators that the mayor's invitation had enticed. It seemed that nearly the entire town was present to hear that which was to be declared.

He leaned against a post along the walkway to observe the scene further. Maxine Weathers hovered near the back of the crowd, Smelly Joe sleeping soundly in her shade. She wore a white, floppy hat that was quintessentially hers. She'd tell anyone that inquired that it was hand-made in Marseille, France.

The Hess's, meanwhile, huddled tightly near the center of the crowd. More than a couple turquoise and lavender ostrich feathers jutted from *their* caps. At the center of their milling, Doctor Stevenson boisterously conversed with Penelope Hess in a clearly performative manner.

Beatrice Valentine sat under the shade of a nearby ash tree, surrounded by her flock of students. The ages and demeanors of the students ran the gamut. Most of the elder students sat around Beatrice casually talking with one another while the younger of the brood danced about and dug in the dirt. Beatrice, oddly, looked longingly in the direction of Willie Boyle who stood beside Jules Mackenzie. Both men awkwardly held their arms across their chests, scanning the rooftops of the buildings. Shae recalled Jules's observation from the night before, that he hadn't seen a bird overhead in over a day. Shae raised his gaze himself and indeed saw no indication of meadowlark, sparrow, or warbler.

Not even a hawk traced the eyelet of the sun.

As he lowered his chin, he was surprised to see deputy Luke Hess striding briskly through, and past the crowd. His gaze was downcast while a look of frustration engulfed him. Shae nearly made to holler at the boy, to tell him that he wouldn't need to walk all the way to the saloon to arrest him again, but the dejection in Luke's face was pitiable and Shae elected to let him be. Whatever it was that was burning him up was doing a good enough job of it already.

The murmur of the crowd maintained a steady buzz until a sudden hush overcame it. Shae raised his gaze to the courthouse steps to see the confident stride of Mayor Thadeus Hess traverse the open doors of the building to look over the crowd with a bold proclivity. Behind him walked who Shae first assumed to be Reverend Gilroy, but with a second glance saw that it was someone else entirely wearing Gilroy's navy-blue suit, clerical collar, and draping red stoles of ceremony. The man stepped forward to stand only slightly behind the mayor on the courthouse landing.

Thadeus addressed the crowd.

"Ladies and gentlemen. Proud sons and daughters of Bastion. Thank you for choosing community, day after day. Even as the sun pours down on us with the scolding weight of its August rays, you voted, by the simple yet deliberate act of attendance, in favor of our shared asso ciations... In favor of Bastion... In favor of one another. For our institutions cannot stand, nay, they cannot exist, without your continued vote of attendance and kinship. Yes, my friends, we all know it to be true, that the price of community is inconvenience. And to my proud eye, Bastion continues to embrace the latter to be worthy of the former. And so, on this day, the first of August, eighteen ninety-eight, I stand before you to speak of both.

"Hear me now!" his voice began to rise with sharp inflections. Shae thought his words increasingly akin to the pontifications of a sermon. "We are bound to one another not by blood, obligation, or accidental association. Nay! We are each other's keepers by our daily votes of neighborliness, our shared understanding of the soil on which we stand and have erected our lives. By the very same argument, I could not, and would not, argue myself to be a brother of he that lives on the eastern coast of Maine, nor in the swamps of Louisiana. Neither would I dream of dictating to such men what is to be deemed important and thus taxed and enforced in *their* lands. Matters of Bastion should be dictated by those familiar with this land and not by those distant. Not by those likely to see this town as little more than a peg upon the contour lines of a map."

Shae felt his brow coalescing into contour lines themselves, astonishment rising within him. Were the mayor's words truly going where he increasingly suspected them to be?

"Let us not forget, my friends, that in the Declaration of Independence published on the fourth of July 1776, that our forefathers unambiguously wrote that it is the obligation of the government to ensure life, liberty, and the pursuit of happiness for a people that consent to be governed. And found in this very same document, written by Thomas Jefferson, John Adams, Benjamin Franklin, is the clear insinuation that when an erected government fails to support these aims, it is the right, nay, the *obligation* of the people to institute a new government to better support the happiness that they define for themselves and themselves alone. And so, on this day, people of Bastion, in the words of Thoman Paine, I say that we have it in our power to begin the world over again! I say it to you plain. Bastion shall see itself unburdened by the chains of the American Union!"

The crowd, all at once comprehending the crux of Hess's argument, erupted in a cacophony of shouting and uneasy glances toward their neighbors. Some stood mouth agape in utter puzzlement while others immediately raised their fists and screamed in the direction of the men atop the courthouse landing. The words "treason" and "traitor" were exclaimed openly. But Shae also saw a surprising number of the crowd eagerly curious as to what their neighbors' reactions were to be so as to inform the direction of their own. From what he could assess, the prevailing sentiment of the crowd, at least for now, was that of cautious anger, as such seemed to be the most appropriate response to the argument being posited before them.

"My friends!" exclaimed Thadeus, his arms defensively outstretched. "This concept of action is far removed from mine, for I would never, not in a hundred-thousand years construct such a plan without guidance from hands on high."

Shae scoffed aloud as the man wearing Reverend Gilroy's clothing stepped forward to stand equally beside the mayor. A hush returned to the crowd, and before long, not a whisper could be heard amongst them. No birds were heard above and even the prevalent neighing from the stables fell eerily silent. The man's voice brought the same associations to Shae's mind as did the crackling of flame.

"My name is Mathius Patmos. God has sent me here to see to it that His will be done. I hear His words in the hoo-ing of the barn owl. I see His limericks in the dancing of the grass. I feel His love in the presence of you all, here and now..." His voice began to rise. "I am here to dictate terms on behalf of God for he has deemed this land to be worthy of his providence."

He paused as a breeze swept through the crowd as if to emphasize his words. It wasn't until the wind fully departed did he resume his soliloquy.

"Now hear these words, for they are the lord's. Bastion is to be known as The Kingdom of New Jerusalem and any that see to a separate path are opposed to the will of thy God."

Stevenson was right. They've lost their Goddamn minds. Shae might have erupted into a fit of anger himself if not for his confidence that the crowd would soon—on their own—depose of the delusional men atop the landing in quick order. And sure enough—right on cue—an angry murmur again rose from the crowd as the mysterious man wearing Reverend Gilroy's clothing spoke in a rising candor. Shae even saw a flash of legitimate fear cross the face of Thadeus, a rare sight indeed. The sight made Shae smile. Serves him right. This was America, a kingless land, and Thadeus was soon to be reminded of the fact.

But just as the fervor of the crowd was on the verge of boiling over, the shrill squeaking of ungreased wheels approached from somewhere unseen, cutting through the growing frenzy of the crowd.

"BLASPHEMER!!!" called a familiar voice.

All present looked to the right, towards a sight obscured by Shae's present perspective. He stumbled into the street to see beyond the storefronts that had previously blocked his vision to witness Sheriff Kingsbury sitting atop the driver's seat of a mule led cart, holding the reins. In the back of the vehicle rested a tall mound covered in a tan canvas tarp.

"Your lies will come to light!" shouted the sheriff, dismounting from the cart. "I was left to a dry death, out there amongst the hills. But God, the righteous and true God, came and shed on me a light of mercy! Citizens of Bastion! The true God of light has gifted us a bell all his own! A bell of righteousness, one that we shall raise in the stead of the one hoisted by this demon!"

The sheriff ambled unsteadily to the straps that secured the tarp, snapping each free with the slice of his knife. "Behold! See before you the glory of God's love!"

The sheriff grasped the edge of the tarp and pulled it sharply back to expose its cargo for all to see. For what the sheriff had hauled into town, atop a cart eerily similar to the one piloted by young Frederick Samson three years prior, was a tall mound of buffalo bones crowned by the contorted corpse of Ginny Samson.

Twenty-Two

A gasp erupted from the crowd as Vale himself stumbled backward, aghast at the sight that he'd unveiled for the entirety of Bastion to witness. The sight alone was enough to horrify Vale, seeing Ginny's skin mottled and shallowed so. But to hear the horror so loudly expressed from all those about him, to know that the sight of his abrupt terror was so equally shared, a worse hell he couldn't imagine.

A pitiful whimper leaked from his lips as he unevenly spun about to meet the petrified gaze of his wife, Susy, standing nearest him in the crowd. A single tear fell from her eye. He suddenly recalled that he hadn't checked in on her after they had separated so sourly the day before, outside of the church. She must've been up through the night drenched in worry.

In a flash, his previous moment's torment was replaced by the unsalvageable sorrow in seeing such pain in his wife's eyes. He stepped toward her, intending to do whatever he could to console her anguish, but his approach was met only by her equal retreat back into the crowd, her eyes wide in horror.

The faces of the crowd too told a story of equal parts disgust and rage. They surely thought him mad.

"It is clear, people of New Jerusalem, that the sheriff has been corrupted by the devil himself!" declared the visitor atop the courthouse steps, the very same man that Vale had been convinced—only moments before—to himself be evil incarnate.

Vale was no longer sure of anything.

"He must be cleansed in the light of the lord!" continued Mathius in an accelerating pitch. "Allow me to eradicate the evil within him. It is now his only hope at salvation. Bring him to me!!"

Vale returned his gaze to Susy to see her backtrack further into the crowd, soon swallowed by it entirely. The anger that had existed beside horror in the crowd's collective stares had since come to monopolize their faces. Mathius's words had, apparently, been received with warmth.

Johhny Hilbo, a man Vale had arrested on more than one occasion, was nearest him in the crowd. He extended an arm toward Vale, palm upturned while stepping evenly toward him.

"Come here," he snarled.

Johnny wasn't alone. Several others of the crowd inched toward him, eager to satisfy their thirst for justice despite not contemplating what "justice" Mathius had offered them. Neither had they had time to process the tectonic proclamations that had been ordained to them but minutes before. All they knew was that their sheriff had gone mad, killed the town's gunsmith, and presented her corpse to the town with ceremony. Thus, when their mammalian desire for retribution was offered, the crowd became an organism all its own and the questions and ambiguities of the situation dissolved into a collective desire for vengeance.

The anger in the crowd's encroaching eyes rapidly posed Vale a choice. A choice that would need to be answered in immediacy. Give himself to the mob, or resist. He hadn't time to consider the ramifications of either but the words of the man draped in stoles echoed in his mind.

"He must be cleansed in the light of the lord!"

Something deep inside Vale knew that such a process would involve neither light nor the lord.

He hastily pulled his revolver from his hip and aimed its barrel at the crowd, sweeping its gaze from side to side, stepping carefully backward.

"Let's all calm down, now. I don't want to shoot nobody, especially none of you. I can see that you're upset, and rightfully so, but I didn't do this!"

Vale continued backtracking while doing his best to keep the crowd that crept toward him at bay.

"You know me. Billy! Sam! Thomas!" called Vale, hoping to nudge the men that patiently pursued him toward a remembrance of their long associations. "And you know that I couldn't have done this! Something evil pulled a veil over my eyes! Benjamin! Tacitus! Are you really going to trust the words of someone that rode into town just yesterday?" He pointed his free hand to the landing of the courthouse where Mayor Hess and the visitor stood, unflinching. "Can't you see? It's quite clear now, isn't it? You're rotting from the top step down!"

Before anyone could respond to Vale's appeal, Thomas Beckers, a laborer at the apple orchard, snappishly broke from the crowd and lunged toward Vale.

"YOU BASTARD!!!" he screamed.

Vale felt the heavy metal in his hand recoil as a ringing followed the thunder that it produced. It was an instinctual act. It mattered not. The encroaching crowd paused, as did Vale, to see Thomas stutter to a stop, grasp the crimson that manifested upon the white of his shirt, and collapse face-first into the dirt.

Things were no longer ambiguous.

Vale spun about, sprinting from the crowd with a speed that he was surprised he still possessed. He felt tears welling in his eyes and did what he could to see through the resulting ripples of his sight. He heard the roar of the crowd chasing closely behind when the crack of a gunshot rang out, its bullet disturbing the air but an inch from his right ear.

His only chance was to be fast, focused, and lucky, and to his widening eyes, the latter seemed to manifest itself before him. Twenty feet ahead, the distinct white of Sylvester Hess's quarter horse, Benevolence, was hitched to a post outside of the livery. It was likely his only chance.

Another crack of a gunshot rang out from behind him, this one finding the dirt near his feet, spraying sand in front of him like shrapnel. His only potential saving grace, it seemed, was that most in town were poorly acquainted with their sidearms. He skid to a stop, flipped the lead rope from the hitching post and spun himself onto the horse's saddle. With a start, he kicked his heels into the sides of the beast and gripped tightly upon the horn. The animal neighed and pulled him briskly down an alleyway just as another bullet snapped itself into the wood of a nearby wall.

The horse was agile, so much so that Vale was nearly ejected from the saddle as it angled its corners, carrying Vale into the obscuring hills north of town. As he hugged the horse's flanks with his thighs, intermittently kicking to spur the horse ever faster, a tickle in his throat matured into a violent bout of coughing, speckling the white crest of the horse's mane in a shower of crimson blood.

Twenty-Three

Luke didn't know where he was headed.

All that he knew was that he didn't intend to stand beside Mathius—and that bastard uncle of his—as nothing more than a mute symbol of credibility for whatever it was that they were plotting. He kept his eyes to the dirt as he pushed through the crowd and even ignored the inquiring holler of his mother from somewhere amongst its rabble.

He walked until he reached the eastern conclusion of College Avenue as it dissolved into the wilderness unraveling beyond it.

Nearby stood Bastion's rectangular welcome sign, a plank tightly nailed to a decapitated aspen trunk rising from the crevasse of three obsidian boulders. Upon the sign, bold letters of the town's namesake were chiseled into the eastern face of its pine. Below the name, the population was listed as being 47, although even Luke knew the number to be wildly outdated.

Luke climbed upon the boulders and sat cross legged, staring east into the rolling plains beyond. He crumpled his nostrils in an attempt at stifling his tears.

What was to be made regarding this whole mess with Mathius? Something about it just felt...wrong. Meanwhile, he was beginning to recognize just how little influence he had in the situation. It was as if he were helplessly flailing in a river's current that pushed unyieldingly against him. Maybe if he could...

The crack of a gunshot awoke him from his contemplation.

He turned his gaze to look back down the length of the avenue to see, in the far distance, a figure sprinting toward him and away from of a closely pursuing mob!

Was that the sheriff??

Luke stood and quickly ambled toward the action. As he made his way past the saloon in the crowd's direction, he saw that the figure indeed was the sheriff, now mounting his cousin Sylvester's prized quarter horse.

But before he could make any closer observations, Luke's vision abruptly evaded him. An intense pressure pronounced itself upon his skull and he felt as if his face was being coated in warm honey. A blanket of calm wrapped itself snuggly about him and everything that ever was became a dream's whisper in the darkest depths of the ocean.

All was nothing.

Until, that is, a wobbling reverb of sound approached Luke's perspective from somewhere at first distant. The sound drifted patiently nearer in a wet, echoing swirl that was initially difficult to interpret. It sounded as if a thousand sucking drains in the sump of a terrific basin, each in competition to inhale more liquid than their rival. But as Luke's awareness increasingly dislodged itself from the cocoon of its surrounding blackness, he discovered that the sounds were, in fact, that of people speaking, shouting, and lamenting.

And then, just as he began to recognize the voices surrounding him to be individuals familiar, the blackness that surrounded him languidly atrophied into sight once again. Gradually, small pockets of light appeared and then merged until his entire field of vision returned.

He found himself standing beside a terribly saddened crowd. Why were they so distraught?

His memory soon returned, although the last thing he remembered was racing toward the crowd to see what had driven the masses to chase after Sheriff Kingsbury. Why was he running from them? And then—unceremoniously—came blackness.

Did he trip and hit his head?

Luke meandered toward the crowd in the hopes of inquiring, its masses calling out in a cacophony lacking clarity. Whatever it was that had impacted them must have been a truly awful thing based on the despondence that seeped from them.

The crowd seemed to be huddled over something that lay at the center of their collective feet.

As he drew near, he saw that a pitch-black mare, saddled but without rider, ambled casually past the crowd in the direction of the eastern conclusion of the avenue. No one seemed to notice the horse moving past them; so enraptured were they by what they looked down upon in the dirt.

Luke reached for the trembling arm of a man near the back of the crowd—intending to get the man's attention—but found, to his astoundment, that his hand went right through the man's sleeve.

Just as he raised his hand to examine his extremity with incredulity, a woman removed herself from the crowd and stumbled away, covering her sobbing face with her hand. In the void that her departure from the crowd left, Luke could finally see what it was that lay on the ground. In the dirt lay... *his* body, his head covered in a sea of liquid red while his forehead was marked by the unmistakable cavity of a bullet's entry wound. His eyes were open, staring flatly into the sky.

Luke stared at the body with a shattered mind. He went to draw nearer but tripped on his own feet and cascaded through the bodies of several of those that huddled about. Just like when he reached for the sleeve of the man a moment before, he fell *through* a dozen legs, leaving them undisturbed.

It was as if he were the wind and they the indifferent blades of buffalo grass on the prairie.

He caught a closer glimpse of his lifeless body and, in seeing the unending stare of his very eyes, regretted doing so. He looked away and saw that the woman that had stumbled from the group—to provide him with his initial vantage of the body—was his mother, Penelope. She was being consoled by several of his uncles and cousins against the cleanly wiped windows of the saloon.

Nearby, Luke noticed Quinn looking on from the shadows of the alleyway between the bar and Ginny's Gunsmoke. For a moment, Luke almost thought Quinn was looking right at him. But just as he contemplated the fact, Quinn's gaze caught a glimpse of something separate, stealing away his attention. He wasn't alone. Soon, the collective wailing of the crowd hushed and a pathway to the body was made. Mathius stood at the end of the opening; his hands clasped solemnly near Reverend Gilroy's belt-buckle.

Mathius walked slowly to where the boy's body lay, and with a graceful crouch placed his hand upon the bloody forehead. Without moving his hand nor rising from his low proximity to the earth, Mathius lookup up to the crowd that huddled around him.

Luke watched with an air of discombobulation.

"My friends. The lord has tasked me with blessing this land with miracles thrice. The first was the bell that swings freely from your northern belfry. The third is yet to come. But the second, my friends, comes henceforth. See upon thy works as a testament to the validity of my words and the words of your mayor. See upon thy actions as a blessing from the Lord himself; a reassurance of your faith in his will. See upon thy blessings..."

"Liar!" screamed Willie Boyle from the edge of the crowd. He looked around at the surrounding masses, horrified and perplexed. "Have you all so quickly forgotten what he has said up there on the steps? He and the mayor intend to succeed from the union! He calls himself a prophet! Are we so quick to forgive blasphemy?"

"Willie..." sobbed Penelope, still leaning against the windows of the saloon. "My boy... My Luke..." Luke could hardly tolerate hearing his mother in such pain. "Let him try, at least, whatever it is that he intends to try." She then broke down entirely, requiring three men to carry her away.

A wind blew through the crowd, ruffling the feathers of their holiday hats.

"… and know that this land," continued Mathius as if he hadn't been interrupted at all, "this Kingdom of New Jerusalem, is the righteous will of the Lord our God!"

Mathius then collected a heaving breath. A vein on his forehead pulsated and Luke might have mistaken the zeal of the zealot for anger had he not heard his words. Mathius returned his intrusive gaze to the dead body over which he knelt, his hand covering the pit in its flesh. He leaned in close and whispered words into the ear of the corpse.

With a curiosity that bordered on apathetic abandon, Luke carried his hollow perspective closer so as to hear what was being spoken. But so soft were the utterances that Luke was forced to lower himself to the ground, uncomfortably close to both the faces of Mathius and his own departed visage; closer to Mathius's sun-weathered face than he had ever wished to be. The dappled lines of the man's cheeks were layered in leathered pits and discolorations that spoke to years more numerous than Luke cared to fathom.

The words spoken were not English. If they were, their pronunciations were undeniably of a foreign nature. He leaned in closer still, when Mathius suddenly halted his words and shifted his sight from that of the body to stare directly into the eyes of Luke's new perspective.

Luke shuttered and might have shrieked had he not already reached the limits of his emotional capacity. Regardless, the abruptness—and nature—of the man's howling stare sent a cold terror deep into whatever remained of Luke's psyche.

A grotesque moment passed until Mathius's gaze mercifully shifted, as if he were looking for something that was not there. As if he didn't see him at all. He looked about for a moment further until relenting to return his focus to the corpse; to continue speaking into its ear.

Luke retreated into the increasingly curious crowd watching with bated breath. They looked on, ever curious as to what promised miracles were about to unfold before them.

In the corner of his eye, Luke noticed Shae Mackenzie exiting the saloon with a peculiar demeanor. He turned east and walked beyond the occlusion of the crowd. But Luke's fleeting curiosity of the bartender's glassy stare quickly evaporated as he returned his attention to Mathius tending to his corpse.

Luke began to hope that he might, in a flash, be pulled back into his body. Was he about to be delivered from the edge of death? He thought back to his initial sensations of darkness and quaked at the realization of what the sensation truly was.

But, as it turned out, Luke's budding hopes at drawing fresh breath were dashed as quickly as they had arrived. Thoroughly bewildered, he watched as the corpse that lay before him—his own corpse—suddenly pulled a deep and guttural breath from the air. A gasp of amazement swept through the crowd while Luke looked on in horrified incomprehension. Mathius removed his hand from the body's forehead revealing a smooth batch of skin still stained in blood but lacking the hole that had induced its mortality.

The body let out a terrible cough and jarringly sat up to aid in the process of clearing its clotted lungs.

All the while, Luke looked on, still separate from his flesh.

Once the body had emptied its lungs of mottled liquid, it opened its eyes and looked about the scene.

"I have seen the Lord!" it shouted suddenly. "And he hath given thee breath!"

Mathius stood tall above the body, raising his hands devotedly to the sky.

"Glory!!! May it live forever in New Jerusalem!!!"

Twenty-Four

Quinn awoke to the grinding sounds of conversation reverberating against the bricks of the alleyway. He reached behind him to produce the bright yellow earmuffs that he kept nearby for such occasions. He put on the muffs and tried his best to gather up the slumber that was quickly abandoning him. He had been sleeping off the remnants of the late-night bender that he had shared with the doctor the night before.

But as he continued grasping for the sleep that continued to leak through the sieve of morning, he noticed a heaping lump pressing against his side. He rolled over and reached for it, discovering a rotting apple resting under his bedding.

His mind began to wander, and, suspecting that his sleep had succeeded in evading him, tended to collecting the scattered fragments of memories from the night before. Much of the evening remained elusive although half recollections of him and Dr. Stevenson gallivanting through the late-night streets slipped through the cracks, each memory a key to unlocking the next. He recalled the doctor showing him how to dance the Prisyadka, both men attempting to ride the donkeys in Willie Boyle's stable—a feat that was primarily defeated by the animals' refusal to leave the corner in which it dumbly stared—and a vague recollection of walking through the long corridors of the Hess apple orchard. That explained the apple that lay beside him, at least.

He looked about the brick walls surrounding him, trying, in vain, to ignore the muffled voices rambling on in the street.

At least the high brick bookends of the alleyway lent him comfort. They've always been reliable in doing so. There were few places in town that provided such comfort to Quinn as did the alleyway between the saloon and Ginny's Gunsmoke.

In it, there was an inlet that cut into the brick of the latter's face where he nestled beds of hay, or even discarded cotton bedding when he found them. It was a blissfully shady spot in the summer, and in the winter he corralled into the corridor pallets of wood that retained a modest degree of heat. The commute to and from the front doors of the saloon wasn't terrible and he and the sheriff had come to an understanding, long ago, that if he kept to himself and didn't bother anyone too much, he could stay right there and make it homely. Ginny didn't mind none, neither did Shae, thus Quinn became quite fond of his modest nook between the structures. It was the closest thing he'd come to consider a home since traversing the Atlantic in 1851 at the age of six.

Second to the inside of the bottle, of course.

But just when he nearly fell back into the warm embrace of sleep, the ongoing squawking of the voices in the street rose to a further level of intensity, prompting Quinn to remove his earmuffs. To his surprise, he discovered that the voice was that of Doctor Stevenson himself, rambling to an unseen ear regarding a holiday of some kind. There was a certain foreboding in his tone that, in turn, summoned the memory of the doctor going on and on the night before about a disaster that was soon to befall the town.

Apparently neither a sea of liquor nor the morning sun had been enough to stifle the doctor's trepidations.

Quinn listened out of a passive curiosity, but when he heard that an announcement was to be made at the steps of the courthouse that day at noon, Quinn's only anticipation of the event was for it to pull the talkative masses, and doctors, from his front stoop so that he might again find rest in the resulting silence.

And indeed, when they at last departed to walk towards the courthouse, Quinn again found sleep and drifted into its depths.

He found himself standing before a cottage set ablaze, his feet upon moist Irish grass. Then came the calling screams of his mother; screams all-too familiar.

Help.

Help.

Help.

But, instead of helping, he turned around, finding the ocean's edge immediately before him. He stepped forward and entered its everything.

It filled his lungs.

***

The sound of gunshots ripped Quinn from his slumber. He was glad for it, considering his nightmare.

He rolled onto his chest and raised his gaze to look out the narrow corridor of the alleyway and into the avenue beyond. He heard running footsteps approaching from places unseen when a triplet of further shots rang out. The footsteps fell silent, followed quickly by a dull thud.

Quinn continued looking curiously into the avenue—with his limited perspective of only hard packed dirt and the storefront of the florist, across the way—when something peculiar appeared in the narrow window of his sight. A shimmering pocket of air moving slowly from the obscuring bricks of Shae's saloon and into his perspective. It appeared like a vertical, almost humanoid rendition of a horizon's mirage on a summer day; fluttering the air and glistening transparently in the sun's hot gaze.

He might have missed it, had he not been limited to such a narrow window of perspective.

Before long, a rueful crowd of saddened and horrified faces began to trudge through the street toward things unseen and obscured by the brick of the saloon. Indifferently, they overcame the space that the glistening shimmer of air occupied, apparently unaware of its presence. For its part, the shimmer did nothing to indicate a dissatisfaction with their doing so and only continued to hover in a formless writhing wiggle.

The sounds of collective wallowing poured out from the places unseen, although Quinn's attention remained enraptured upon the glimmer continuing to hang over the street so delicately.

He crawled to the edge of the alleyway to get a closer view, but in doing so, found that the crowd had congregated nearby over something lying in the street. It was the body of Luke Hess, blood pouring liberally from his forehead.

Poor boy. Quinn had no true qualms with the newly minted deputy.

In his periphery, Quinn saw that the glistening shimmer of air now moved gently toward the crowd writhing about the body. It reached its edge, lingered, then seamlessly traversed it. It moved toward its center before finally halting beside the bloody corpse.

In a manner that was impossible for Quinn to define, he became overwhelmed by the feeling that the shimmer was somehow looking directly back at him. It was an odd sensation to say the least.

But his attention was again pulled away, this time noticing the faces of the crowd suddenly looking west in the direction from which they'd come themselves. A look of pitiful hope draped their eyes as if they were looking to a salvation they feared was but a mirage. A cloud of respite, soon to pass.

Quinn himself turned to look at which they stared, finding a curious looking man in a navy-blue suit and red draping stoles. His presence was undeniably imposing, if not outright frightening.

He'd never seen the man before, and yet, the crowd lowered their heads submissively as he drew near, parting to allow him a clear path to the lifeless boy upon the floor. He kneeled at his side and placed a gentle hand on his forehead. The man then spoke boldly to the crowd in a regal tone. He spoke of God's will, blessings to be given, and some place called New Jerusalem when Willie Boyle suddenly erupted from the edge of the crowd.

"Liar!" he screamed. "Have you all so quickly forgotten what he has said, up there on the steps? He and the mayor intend to succeed from the union! He calls himself a prophet! Are we so quick to forgive blasphemy?"

"Willie..." sobbed a woman from somewhere unseen, "My boy... My Luke... Let him try, at least, whatever it is that he intends to try."

A wind blew through the crowd, ruffling the ridiculous hats more appropriate for celebration than the macabre scene before them.

The curious man resumed his proclamation to the crowd in a manner Quinn thought to be pious and self-assured. He then lowered his chin and whispered into the crimson painted ear of the boy.

As this happened—and apparently unbeknownst to most of those looking on—Shae brutishly stepped out the front doors of the Saloon and walked curtly east, toward the edge of town. Quinn had never seen a man move in such a manner, so eager to take each step further. Quinn thought he walked with the gait of a man wronged. A gait unlike the bartender.

Quinn shifted his gaze back to the crowd where the enigmatic figure continued whispering into the ear of Luke's body upon the ground. The shimmer of air that had so enraptured his curiosity remained beside them both. Quinn suddenly had the urge to vomit—a fairly common sensation for the seasoned drinker—but before he could turn back to his rabble and oblige the urging of his quivering stomach, a final development presented itself to swiftly mute all else, his nausea not excluded.

The body that lay so still upon the dirt, its head covered in the crimson of death, pulled a rasping breath from the air. It coughed violently, then sat up to consider the crowd that equally gasped in equal parts terror, relief, and astonishment.

"I have seen the lord!" Luke shouted. "And he hath given thee breath."

The man that had whispered into the body's ear then stood and joined Luke's proclamation with one all his own.

"Glory!!! May it live forever in New Jerusalem!!!"

Luke stood with a confident steadiness that Quinn thought peculiar considering his recent condition upon the floor. Rarely did he himself rise from stupors with such stability.

Luke and his revivor then strolled slowly, side by side, toward the courthouse. The crowd followed behind them in silent fealty.

And yet—in their stead—Quinn saw that one remained, if it could be considered a "one." He was beginning, for whatever reason, to believe that it was.

In the air above the blood on the dirt, blood that had flowed so eagerly from Luke's forehead but minutes before, floated the formless shimmer of air.

Quinn again felt compelled to believe that it was staring right at him. No. More than that. It seemed... to beckon to him. But before he could move toward it himself, to his surprise, it began to move toward *him*.

Quinn rocked onto his bottom and shuffled slowly backwards in a reactionary retreat. He leaned onto his elbows to prop himself up against the grime of the alleyway's floor. As the floating shimmer drew near, its rippled air became more defined yet no less peculiar. Quinn's skin rose in prickled goosebumps; in subconscious acuity.

The shimmer halted its approach only a foot before Quinn's strangled gaze.

A moment of terror initially crosses Quinn, but when no harm befell him, curiosity become the predominant sensation within him. He drew a deep breath, leaned onto his left elbow, and ever so gently reached out with his right hand to traverse the shimmer's glean.

As his fingers met the shimmer's space, he felt nothing but a slight and nearly undetectable tingle upon the skin of his hand. It was almost as if were placing his arm into a cloud of heavy mist, tickling his fingers with its hollow touch.

He retracted his arm and sat himself upright into a proper sitting position. His suspicions of the shimmer's sentience grew.

"Hello?" he asked in raspy Cork.

There was no initial response from the shimmer languidly hovering before him, until, suddenly, Quinn felt a single word forcefully pronounced within the confines of his mind.

Luke.

As soon as the word came to pass his perception, and before he could inquire further, the shimmer broke off to traverse the brick wall of Ginny's Gunsmoke, leaving Quinn to ponder more things than one.

Twenty-Five

The mob swarmed past Shae on the heels of the fleeing sheriff. The former stood still like a riverbed's boulder, the river's current carrying past him. His gaze remained locked upon the cart—and its cargo—still pitifully unveiled and open to the punishment of the sun.

Shae walked solemnly toward the cart intending to return the tarp to its merciful place atop the remains of Ginny Samson. With each step, he came woefully closer to the blotched and crumpled corpse laying atop the bed of bones; helplessly entrapped by the sight. Even the frightful sound of gunshots behind him sending the crowd into a fervor beyond even that of their initial pursuit did little to undo his attention upon Ginny.

As he stood over the corpse examining the permanence of its decay, its mottled skin, its hyperextended and twisted joints, a part of Shae Mckenzie was pulled away by the breeze, never to return.

He replaced the tarp upon the cart's ghastly mound, although the body maintained its outline in the surface of the tarp now resting upon it. He stood over it, burning the sight of its ridges into his retinas before eventually—and mercifully—turning back to begin a slow walk to the saloon.

In the fogginess of the daydream that he'd suddenly found himself in, Shae saw that, up ahead, the frenzied crowd had taken to furiously congregating about something on the ground outside his establishment. He couldn't care less. All that he desired in all of the world was to retreat into the confines of his bedroom above the bar, lock the door behind him, and drink enough whiskey to escape the memory of Ginny's mangled corpse.

He strode past the crowd, vaguely hearing the distraught calls of its participants. He looked neither at their faces nor whatever it was that had so rapturously drawn their attention at the center of their collective feet. He pulled open the saloon's door, ascended the creaking stairs, and pushed open the door to his bedroom.

But as he stepped inside, Shae was startled to find the short silhouette of a person, no, a boy, looking out the window, gazing at the crowd below. The light pouring in through the drapes made identification of the figure's slender frame immediately impossible although the size of its body and the untamed dishevelment of its hair implied it to be Jebediah Lovely standing before him.

"What are you doing?" Shae asked meagerly.

"Watching..." said Lovely. "Watching the congregation."

Shae stepped into the room, the old floorboards pronouncing his advance. He only wished to be alone.

"Jebbie... I need you to..."

Something in Shae's peripheral vision decapitated his previous train of thought. The sheets upon the bed appeared to be concealing something beneath them. Something mangled. Something terribly familiar.

"They squirm about so frivolously," said Jebediah, still looking out the window. "Never quite sure of whatever to do, or not to do. There's one now, pacing and unfurling herself into the dirt. It's all so... ugly."

Shae didn't respond. His gaze remained locked upon the sheets of the bed so poorly concealing the outline of a twisted heap beneath it. Another creak of the floorboards announced a further step in its direction.

"It's all so... fruitless," continued Jebediah from the window.

Shae reached for the sheet's corner with a shaking hand. There was no leaving such a thing to a moment's further concealment. He had to see it's grim contortions again.

There was no choice. Let him see her mottled skin once more. With swiftness, he yanked back the sheet to find nothing but a stained mattress beneath it.

"So full of nothing."

Shae lowered himself to sit upon the edge of the bed, sinking his face into his open palms. His limbs buzzed in vibrant inconsolability. His eyes stung and his heart burned as if ablaze. He felt suddenly confident that he had loved her. There was no question about it. In her wordless presence she had given him more than anyone else ever had, could, or ever would. Was she to now be nothing but a faceless wraith of his feeble lacking, howling wordless insinuations to him in the coldest of nights? Would his heart's orchard forever be filled with trees barren?

He had forgotten that he shared the space with the Samson boy until he felt the weight of another sitting upon the mattress beside him, returning Shae to the present moment.

"Do you know what the swarm attends to, just outside your window?"

In his stupor, Shae hadn't cared enough to assign a theory to the assembly. But now, pressed on the matter, it seemed rather obvious.

"I s'pose they shot the sheriff," his hands still encaging his face.

"Indeed, they shot *at* the sheriff," spoke Jebediah in his high-pitched juvenile voice. "But they missed. One of their bullets struck young Luke Hess in the forehead. The boy is dead."

Shae slowly raised his face from his hands to stare blankly at the flaking wallpaper across from him.

"Are you telling me…that the sheriff…"

"Yes…"

A long silence would have reined in the room if not for the wailing of the distraught surveyors outside, painting the subsequent seconds in thinly muted dirges.

"Not one pursues him," continued Jebediah in an even tone. "Not one stalks the fiend responsible for the death of this town's young deputy. Not one seeks to hold Ginny's axe-man to the stone."

Shae felt a flare in his nostrils. A warmth upon his face and a shaking in his limbs. He felt Jebediah lean in close to whisper into his ear, feeling the boy's breath as he spoke. "She waits for you at midnight's boulders."

Shae turned to see that the boy had produced an ebony pistol, offering him the leather of its grip. The matte of the metal implied its purpose.

Shae hesitated, as one does when offered a gun without context. But the insinuation was clear and Shae ultimately reached for the grip and grasped it. The moment he made contact with its leather, three visions flashed before his eyes in quick succession. A black mare standing against a cloudless sky—the town's welcome sign rising beside it. Vale riding a white horse into the narrow cleft of a large granite face. And finally, a top-down perspective of Ginny and Luke lying side by side in the yellowed grass of a field—their eyes covered with pennies. Their mouths filled with dirt.

"Not one," reiterated Jebediah, returning Shae's attention to the musky room.

Contemplation abandoned him. As did uncertainty, fear, and passivity, each replaced by an all-encompassing rage that drove him from the room without pause. With the pistol tucked into the band of his waist, he descended the stairs, pressed into the street, passed the suddenly hushed crowd, and strode boldly beyond the few buildings that stood east of the saloon before the cavernous plains beyond.

True to Jebediah's words—and just as his vision had foretold—a black mare, saddled in equally dark tack, stood idly beside the obsidian boulders that held the town's welcome sign aloft. He approached the beast without the traditional gentleness that one gives an unfamiliar horse. Something intuitive within him knew that such cautions would be superfluous. He jumped upon its back and before he could settle into the seat, the mare took off into the wilderness like a shot. Soon, he and the horse carried steadily southeast in a breakneck gallop.

The second of the visions that had come with his touch of the pistol's leather was unmistakably that of Vale riding into Butcher's Pass. The spot was iconic to most of those native to Bastion; a gigantic stretch of granite that erupted from the landscape with a crooked crevasse—not four feet wide at its widest point—traversing the rock.

Butcher's Pass was both distant and close enough from the town to offer those uninspired by the familiar sights and sounds of Bastion a destination that was within the reach of a single day's ride. It would be a reasonable destination for Vale given the circumstance. Pairing that knowledge with the vision of the sheriff approaching its distinctive face, Shae felt confident that riding to Butcher's Pass would be his best chance at finding Vale and bringing him to justice.

Beyond being a quality location for a day trip—or an instinctual destination for an escaped murderer such as Vale—Burcher's Pass was also an ideal first night's camping spot for those embarking upon the fortnight-long journey to Cheyenne. Shae had to assume that if the sheriff was indeed headed for Butcher's Pass that his final destination could very well be the capital city. He'd much prefer catching up with the man long before then. The prospect of a dozen day journey upon the plains held no romance for Shae—even in the red of his vision.

Shae was forced to do little in steering the mare and he quickly began to suspect that he would be required to do little of such throughout the remainder of his journey. The horse knew where it was going, that much was clear. The fact further reinforced a growing suspicion in Shae that it was not Jebediah with whom he had spoken to in his bedroom.

And yet, he didn't care. It didn't matter. The only thing left that did was giving himself an opportunity to place a bullet sized hole in the chest of Vale Kingsbury. All the rest was a train past the station.

All that mattered was Vale's blood upon the soil.

Twenty-Six

Shae had—at first—assumed the rapid pace of the mare to be anomalous. Surely, the animal would be forced to slow at any approaching moment. But as the minutes turned to hours and the ride pressed ever onward, Shae was surprised to find that the horse's pace wavered little, if at all. If anything, it might have even increased its clip making the journey atop the violently jostling horse a test of endurance.

The muscles that he was forced to employ to remain upon the mare approached a painful fatigue while his bottom begun to rub raw from the unceasing violence of the horse's canter. And as the endorphins of his despondence—at last—began to entropy, a trickle of uncertainty made its way into Shae's thoughts.

Was he prepared to kill a man? He was but a saloon keeper, after all, not a bounty hunter. Even the shit-kicking cattle hands that drifted into town every so often made him feel sheltered and yellow when standing beside them.

Sure, he had long romanced the idea of a bolder existence but as the miles continued on and the beating sun refused to waver, he began to question more things than one. Not that he nurtured designs of turning back. The sight of Ginny's corpse in such disrepair left him irrevocably shattered in ways he hadn't previously known possible. And because of it, he refused to acknowledge any future where justice wasn't served.

If the sheriff was the perpetrator, and the deputy was dead, *someone* had to enforce retribution on behalf of the wronged. It might as well be him.

Ginny and Luke deserved at least that.

The journey to Butcher's Pass was a familiar one, a journey that begun in the higher hills surrounding Bastion, a landscape littered with capricious gulleys and ravines filled with tall trees and dense shrubbery. Shae knew it well.

But as he traveled further and further southeast, he and the horse descended into the more scarcely littered prairieland that lay beyond. Here, a sea of yellowed grass swayed in a western wind that seemed all encompassing. The sight of such grass made him increasingly uneasy as it invoked the third of his visions, that of Ginny and Luke lying disposed in its wavering yellow.

It did well to reinvigorate the fervor that had driven him so far from his home in the first place. And soon enough, he was again biting at his lips with a renewed lust for Vale's undoing.

The plains were only occasionally accompanied by tight thickets of trees, solemn jutting rocks, or other oddities to break up the monopoly of the unending fields of yellow. Shae gave long bouts of attention to such monoliths when they came as they did well to distract him from the burgeoning pain in his legs that resurged with each jolt of the horse's stride. One such distraction was riding past Ol' Reacher, the colloquially known ash-tree that rose into the sky atop a particularly high knoll. Shortly after that, the hulking carcass of a bison was seen lying in a dried pond. Three turkey vultures picked at its flesh.

The hours passed slowly, leading Shae to doze in and out of daydreams both confounding and strange. At one point, he could have sworn to have seen saw Quinn dozing lazily against the trunk of a lonely cottonwood. The heat of the day was making itself known.

Shortly thereafter, he pulled mightily at the reins to convince the mare to finally stop and rest at a stream flowing beside their trek.

Shae descended from the saddle to find his weary legs tardy in the recollection of their primary duties. He fell to the floor.

Shae regained his composure and lifted himself back onto his feet. He carried himself to the nearby stream and drank greedily from its water. He might have sat beside it for an hour's time had he not turned back to see the mare standing but feet from him, staring expectantly in his direction. He reached out to pat the muzzle of the beast, hoping to ease its evident impatience, but the animal stepped back before he could contact its skin. It neighed brutishly and dragged its front hooves against the dirt. It was becoming all the more obvious that he was not the dominant party in their relationship.

At the acknowledgement, Shae considered the pistol still wedged against the skin of his waistband. A sliver of uncertainty again arose from within him

Before the horse could protest further, Shae hoisted himself back into the saddle to endure the final leg of the journey. He only hoped that it wasn't for nought. What would he do if Vale wasn't at the pass as his vision had foretold? Would he track the man across the plains like the rangers of old? The prospect of spending further time in the jostling saddle seemed inconceivable.

"You best be waiting for me, Sheriff," he whispered aloud.

When the sun fell low enough to flirt with dusk, Shae and the beast traversed a slow hill to reveal the granite rock-face known as Butcher's Pass upon the horizon. From his distant perspective, Shae pulled at the reins to bring the mare to a halt. This time, the animal obliged with no argument.

The crevasse that traversed the rock could be seen from his vantage, but there was no sign of the sheriff. If he was indeed there he was either in the crevasse or on its far side. That was good. He was well aware of the discrepancy that existed between he and the sheriff when it came to gun-fighting.

If he was going to get the drop on Vale, he would require the element of surprise to be in his favor.

On the proximal side of the pass stood a wide and thinly populated thicket of cottonwoods. The breeze was working hard to separate wads of cotton from their limbs. As a result, a thousand pockets of wafting cotton casually drifted past Shae as he and the horse rode through the grove.

Shae dismounted and thought to tie the horse's lead rope onto the trunk of a nearby tree but ultimately decided that the horse—with its curious sentience—was of no risk to run off. He let it linger casually amongst the trees.

Shae breathed heavily and pulled the pistol from his waistband, gently cocking back the hammer. He crept toward the entrance of the pass with darting eyes.

The face of the rock rose some thirty feet into the air, its cragged walls thoroughly coated in the golden rays of the setting sun, the only variation being that of the cottonwood's outlining shadows.

A cool air emitted from the crevasse and he paused to listen before stepping inside. No sounds emitted from its corridor save for a thin, howling wind that came to know the wisdom of the cragged split. Shae looked to his feet and saw the stains of bay rum upon his shoe. Was it only yesterday that he'd cleaned the saloon so thoroughly? He suddenly missed Quinn and the sounds of Henry tickling the ivories. He missed the glean of the wood and the absurd acts of thirsty men. But then, he thought of the empty stool at the end of the bar, forever destined to remain so. Things were to never be the same, no matter how desperately he wished them to be.

He closed his eyes, and in that darkness saw the mangled corpse of Ginny Samson crowning a pile of bones.

He would either be the hand of righteous revenge or die in the pursuit of such. He was content with either fate, as inaction seemed the only choice to be intolerable.

He then heard himself whisper something surprising, as he was the furthest thing from a religious man.

"Glory."

There was no conscious intentionality behind the word, but it—for whatever reason—was soothing to his ears. It reminded him of the church bell's call; a warm embrace, like that of a luxurious fur.

He felt no fear.

He raised the pistol in his outstretched hands and spun about to aim both its sights and his own down the narrow length of the granite corridor.

Twenty-Seven

When the sheriff interrupted Mathius's speech with accusations of blasphemy, Mayor Thadeus Hess was filled with a wordless, shaking rage. When the man unveiled what his cart was bearing, he was confounded. But when he saw his young nephew crumple to the dirt with the immediacy of a severed branch, he experienced something he hadn't the words to explain.

"Luke..." was all Thadeus could muster in his paralyzed stare. He recalled with clarity the final words he'd spoken to the boy and even more so the slap that he had given him only minutes prior.

He made to step toward where Luke had fallen, toward the coalescing crowd that had since abandoned their chase of the sheriff in lieu of collective mourning, but was held back by the outstretched arm of Mathius, still standing beside him.

"All is well, Mr. Hess. All is in hand. New Jerusalem shall have its lawman yet." Mathius then stepped forward in his stead, a soothing smile across his face.

Beyond him, Thadeus noticed the saloon keeper, Shaemus—*was that his name?*—stumbling awkwardly from the cart in an uneasy gate. The tarp had been replaced atop Ginny's remains, presumably the saloon keeper's doing.

Meanwhile, Doctor Stevenson drug the limp body of Thomas Beckers to his nearby office adjacent the general store. The ranch-hand seemingly forgotten by the crowd—their attention quickly replaced by Luke's misfortune.

Halfway down the stairs, Mathius paused and turned back to face the mayor.

"Retrieve the helmet. It is past due for this town to know who it is that leads them."

How did he know of it? Thadeus had yet to tell Mathius of the heirloom. And furthermore, surely the town already knew who it was that led them. He was their only mayor, after all.

And yet, the idea of brandishing the helmet upon his head, to allow it to glisten in the sun like the triumphant warriors of his ancestry was undeniably seductive. If nothing else, its glean would certainly serve as a useful prop to instill further credibility—and authority—to the arguments still to be given. Kingsbury had interrupted their proclamations at an admittedly fortunate time. The crowd was beginning to lose all sense. Luke's misfortune would delay it further, but the matter of whether the town would accept their designs still hung in the balance. The helm would be useful in reinforcing their arguments. He suddenly pondered why he hadn't thought of it sooner.

He retreated into the courthouse to retrieve the helm.

When Thadeus re-emerged, the ornament in hand, he looked down the length of the avenue to see a sight that startled him so terribly, that he failed to notice the helmet's refined brim escaping his grasp. He only became aware of the fact upon hearing the sound of its metal clanging to the floor. For, along the avenue, the crowd marched silently back toward the courthouse behind the steps of Mathius... and Luke. The latter's head and chest drenched in blood.

The clearly stunned masses followed closely behind them. Some walked with tears flowing down their cheeks. Others prayed openly.

The crowd stopped just short of the courthouse steps while Mathius and Luke ascended to meet Thadeus staring blankly at his blood-soaked nephew.

The helm lay discarded at his feet.

Luke approached the mayor, stopping only a foot from him to gaze into his eyes with the intensity of flickering flames. To Thadeus's enduring incredulity, the entirety of his face and the majority of his shirt were drenched in rapidly congealing blood. It would have been a truly terrible sight if not for the insinuation of worse fates—somehow—avoided.

Thadeus reached out to touch the boy's cheek with a gentleness that was rare of him. The scent of wet iron hovered about them.

"How?"

Luke raised his hand to gently grasp his uncle's fingers, lowering them from his blood-stained skin. He then bent down to collect the helmet that lay tamely at their feet. Thadeus had forgotten its existence.

Luke examined the helm carefully before raising his eyes to meet the trembling stare of his uncle. He held out the helm, offering it to him.

Thadeus grasped it with distraction.

To his further surprise, the boy then turned, stepped to the edge of the landing, and boldly addressed the crowd that stood watching with bated breath.

"I have spoken with the lord beside the dark lake!" he shouted. "His voice, tender rays of morning on the frozen plains; His presence a gentle song. I'll never know doubt again, my friends, and I'll never be the same." His voice abruptly quieted. "And as I lowered my head and pleaded with my God to take me, to carry me into His arms, to whisk me away into his shimmering tower, He implored my silence and spoke clearly. He said that my purpose had yet to fulfilled on this earth. That I was to be the sword of His blessed land." Luke's voice again rose in both tempo and intensity. "That I was to be the blade to cut through the wicked that deny His Kingdom's cometh. For New Jerusalem, the words that he used, is to be His land upon this earth, *His* kingdom." Luke's head lowered, his voice returning to a soft murmur. "He promised me peace, when His land was settled. He swore me comfort, when its borders secure. But until that day, that blessed hour for which I so joyfully yearn... I shall be His blade."

A familiar breeze caressed the crowd.

"But beyond this, there was one final command that He asked me to share with you all, here and now. One specific instruction to profess to his flock. He said, that he that bares the helm of the eagle shall be thy kingdom's Presider."

Luke pivoted his weight to his back foot to return his gaze to Thadeus. Mathius followed suit, as did all others in attendance. Thadeus looked down at the heirloom in his hands, catching a reflection of sunlight shining upon the cross grasped in the eagle's right talon.

He placed the helmet upon his head, and after a momentary pause filled only with the tussling of a gentle breeze, the masses erupted in jubilance.

Luke looked on, coated in blood, grinning.

Twenty-Eight

By the tears in their eyes and the fervor of their applause it was clear that the masses were invested. Most of them, at least. There were sure to be holdouts of course, but such detractors would be addressed in time.

Following Luke's soliloquy to the crowd, he, Thadeus, and Mathius retreated into the confines of the courthouse's study to contemplate their subsequent steps in governance.

"We must not forget that God does not act in half-measures," spoke Mathius, his eyes again staring into the flames of the study's fireplace. "God's empire on earth should follow such an example."

"I couldn't agree more," said Luke, turning to his uncle. "For in the voice of the lord, there was no insinuation of gentleness. We must be decisive in our actions. We must ensure that the Kingdom of Jerusalem is one of action and not pity for those unworthy of its basking light."

Thadeus paced slowly about the room, his ancestral helmet still adorning his head, his gaze lowered in musing. His steps brought him to the foot of a bookshelf whose backing pressed against a muraled atlas of the world. He reached to the bookshelf's highest shelf to grasp the spine of a book intermittently laced in crimson. A gold latch insisted its pages shut.

He undid the latch, opening the book to its initial pages, turning to address the room's company as he did.

"Only weeks ago, this book, this terribly fascinating book found its way to me through providence. I was strolling through the orchard in the first light of morning when a sparkle of sunlight reflected upon something metallic near the base of a tree. What shone was the golden clasp of this tome's cover." He flicked the latch with his finger. "But what struck me as peculiar, even before I had a chance to crack the book's spine was the realization of what that sparkle of light was forced to overcome to capture my attention in such a way. What odds could describe the flight of such a guiding light? First, it had to escape the sun, then zoom a hundred million miles through space and atmosphere, coast along the earth at dawn's narrow angle, elude the hundred surrounding tree-trunks of the orchard, reach the metal glean of the book's clasp, and then, and only then, reflect in such an angle that might capture my retina's attention... Providence, my friends, absolute providence."

He resumed a patient pacing about the room.

"The book is titled, '*The Taiping Rebellion in China*', and it chronicles an independent nation's pursuit of utopia. It inspired me immensely and quickly, implanting in my imagination dreams of pursuing similar pursuits, right here in Bastion. But practicality left me restricted, and despite my strong aspirations, I came to fear that my dreams would remain just that."

He raised his gaze to look unambiguously to his nephew.

"But having heard your recounting of the lord's words, Luke, I believe now, I *see* now, that providence had met me with intention on that early morning stroll through the orchard. I believe that it was the lord himself that had left this glorious tome of example for me to find; leaning it against that tree's trunk at such an angle to become a candle to be lit by His fire, a candle to light me the way, to prime me for the revelation of His blessing. And as such, I believe that this New Jerusalem, this kingdom over which I shall preside with privilege, is to be the lord's subsequent attempt at achieving the same worthy ideals pursued in the Taiping Heavenly Kingdom.

"Nephew... The lord has chosen us. Let's not let Him down."

***

The trio quickly agreed upon a series of policies that were thereafter implemented with matching swiftness.

A single bell's toll rang out in the hills when Luke descended the courthouse steps to meet the crowd still milling about the western conclusion of the avenue. An eagerness to contribute to God's will pervaded them.

"Who amongst you would raise thy hands to join the ranks of this kingdom's militia?"

Nearly every hand was raised. They were to be his "saints," Luke proclaimed.

The first order dictated to the saints was to wrap Ginny's corpse in spotless linen, carry it up the hill, and give it a proper burial in the graveyard behind the church. Upon their return, the late gunsmith's shop was then raided by the same arms that had laid her to rest. The resulting influx of arms and ammunition were itemized and cataloged before being carried to the courthouse to join the armory to which the jailhouse had already contributed.

The deputy was a resoundingly imposing presence since his revival. In everything he did, whether it be the organization and delegation of his saints or in dutifully announcing the proclamations handed to him from his uncle, he acted without hesitation or even the slightest hint of contemplation. He was seemingly autonomous; a perfect fit for the nature of his quickly developing role in the kingdom.

There was plenty otherwise to keep one's attention occupied at the time, so it was forgivable that the only person to fully recognize the severity of the boy's shift was his mother, Penelope.

She had hardly recovered from the whiplash of her son's dying and revival when she placed herself before him while he trounced about the avenue barking orders at his saints like a seasoned officer. His face and chest were still coated in dried blood when she demanded his attention by touching his face, just like his uncle had done upon the height of the courthouse steps.

"My sweet, sweet boy."

"I'm fine, mother. In fact, I feel... wonderful." He smiled a queer smile that appeared nearly menacing. "You, on the other hand, appear as if you should eat something. An apple perhaps? It would calm thy nerves."

Penelope was, admittingly, not terribly close with Luke. Being the matriarch of the Hess clan afforded her little time to socialize. But a mother knew her son, and something was undeniably different in the boy's tone and choice of words.

"Would you come with me? After what you've been through... maybe you could use a quiet moment too."

"I have matters to attend to."

Her gaze descended to the dirt between them. Be him Lazarus, he was still a Hess, ever reliant on hyper-activity to quell everything from ennui to the emotional turmoil that surely came from...

"Did you really meet God, Luke?"

"I have a role for you." He announced suddenly, completely ignoring her words. "A position of highest importance. Would you see to the orchard at once, Mother? My saints will be waiting for you there. They await the Mother of Bread."

"*The Mother of Bread?*"

"*Someone* must ensure that the kingdom is adequately fed, or shall we starve?"

"I don't understand."

"The lord will make things clear in time, Mother. Go. I'll come and visit you soon."

***

That night, the saints went door to door, led by Luke himself, facilitating the compulsory confiscation of arms and ammunition from all denizens of the kingdom formally known as Bastion. Only one resisted, Veriticas Samuel, the town's most notorious fence.

The saints had received word that Veriticas wasn't intending to comply and saved approaching his shack near the outskirts of town for last.

When the darkness of night was as complete as the waning moon would allow, the posse approached the building in a wide arching semicircle, each saint with a pistol drawn. The plan was to get into position and call out from the darkness demanding that Veriticas come out without a fight. But as the group drew near, a boot snapped a twig. A gunshot and a flash of light emitted from the shack, followed shortly by the dull thud of a saint's body hitting the dirt. A cacophony of gunfire erupted in reply, dicing the shack with seven half-dozen bullets.

All was silent, after that.

Twenty-Nine

The following morning, once all of the town's weapons had been collected, Presider Hess, as Thadeus had dictated he be called by all, made a decree through Luke's mouth atop the courthouse landing.

"There shall be no more hunger in thy God's land, for all means of satiating thy bodies shall be provided by the lord through the generous hands of the chosen!"

For most, confusion was the prevailing response to the proclamation. But there were some that saw no ambiguity in his words. At hearing the statement, Maxine hurriedly made for her general store nearby. At pushing open its wooden doors and stepping inside, she found three rifle bearing saints already emptying her shelves into crates.

"Orders of the presider, Ms. Weathers," spoke one, a middle aged and dumb Hess named Jeramiah.

"Damn your orders. This store's my life Jeramiah. My livelihood. Would you deprive me of that?"

Jeramiah postponed his efforts to look up at the silver-haired woman. The others continued on without pause. "Can't you see this as a blessing, Maxine? You don't gotta work no mo! The lord will look after you from here on out."

"He's looked after me just fine already."

She stepped around the men to stand behind the counter. Where was Smelly Joe, she fearfully pondered. At reaching the register, she groped under the counter's wood for the grip of her shotgun. Her fingers found only air.

"Ya shoulda turned in yer arms when we came asking for em yesterday," spoke a separate saint, a young man she couldn't recall the name of. Only then did she recognize her shotgun slung across his back as he bent down, continuing to slide a shelf's contents into a crate.

"Where's my dog?"

***

In all, and in short order, the Saints sequestered Maxine's General store, Hilbo's Slaughterhouse, and all periphery cattle pens, chicken coops, and yielding crops that fell within the jurisdiction of what the presider deemed to be the borders of New Jerusalem.

An impressive display of logistics oversaw the operation, with saints—men and woman, old and young—scurrying this way and that to accomplish the directed feat. The presider insisted that the order of sequestering all means of nutrients be accomplished as soon as possible. Being that the presider had been appointed by God's instruction, many of the saints received his proclamations as if it were the words of the lord himself whispering such commands into their ears.

They moved with fealty.

All means of nutrients that could realistically be transported were carried to the Hess orchard and its surrounding acreage. The crops that couldn't be harvested were burnt and the animals that couldn't be transferred were culled. Saints took their shovels to the dirt surrounding the wells of private homesteads to fill their depths with earth. The only wells that were left alone were the several of the Hess orchard and the old well in the graveyard behind the church; the latter having been deemed unfit for drinking several years before.

The afternoon was hotter than the day prior, and only the billows of black smoke that rose from the burning crops gave shade to the kingdom's occupants. Those that had been present to receive Luke's sermon were largely apathetic to the sight. It was the will of God, after all. But there were also those that had not been present to see the revival of their deputy and were therefore left blindsided by the sudden happenings.

Before long, an initial wave of those that had refused to submit were soon dragged before the courthouse steps to receive their judgement. A wide swath of those that were similarly tempted pooled nearby, concern draping their faces.

The initial three to be brought forward in such a way were Johhny Flynn—an alfalfa farmer that had refused to set his crop ablaze, Blake Underhill—a wild haired shepherd unwilling to hand over his sheep, and Jules Mackenzie—the one-time cowboy whose crippled leg had stranded him in Bastion, all those years back. The latter told the men that had arrived to sequester his chickens that he would kill their mothers if they touched his flock.

With a pair of goose eggs decorating his face and a thick bundle of string conjoining his wrists, Jules hobbled before the steps of the Courthouse. He joined the two other aforementioned men that had too chosen their independence over whatever fate awaited them.

"Benny!" spoke Jules, seeing that a nearby saint—holding Johnny Flynn's arresting rope—was a close friend of his. Their homes shared a backyard and they cordially coordinated the drying of their clothes upon the yard's singular clothesline. "This is madness, Benny, can't you see it?"

"I can see just fine, Jules," said the saint. A look of both sadness and condescension filled his face. "I saw a man brought back from the dead. He spoke with the lord, with God, Jules. That's not something I could unsee if I tried."

Benny looked heavily upon Jules, waiting for the latter to respond. But seeing that he only looked back at him with a heated and hateful gaze, continued in his defense.

"I ain't no spotless character. You know that. But if we is to accept the lord into our company, I s'pose we're gunna need to do things that are hard for us to do. Things that don't feel easy. But I trust in the lord, Jules, and if he wants things to be as they're being, then I'm here to make em that way."

"But God ain't talkin to ya, Benny! It's a boy crowned by nepotism, a delusional mayor, and a wanderin zealot! That ain't God."

Benny handed another saint the tail end of the rope arresting Johnny Flynn's wrists to approach his former friend, fervor blazing in his eyes.

"There was a bullet in his head, Jules! Now, I know you weren't there. Don't know where you was. But I saw it. I saw the blood flowing from the hole in Deputy Luke's head. There was pieces of his brain about, all covered in dirt while his eyes were rigid, watching the sky—flies landing unbothered upon them. He was dead as dead, Jules. And then, like he was guided by words on high, that wanderin zealot you mentioned came on up to him, whispered something miraculous into his bloody ear, and Luke sat on up like it was Sunday morning and he was late for church. Now, if that ain't God talking, Jules, I don't know what is."

Their attentions were pulled away when the doors of the Courthouse were pulled open by a pair of finely dressed saints, each wearing their Sunday's best—the saints had yet to be dictated a formal uniform, although it was assumed by many that such a development wasn't far off.

Through the open doors walked Mathius and Presider Hess, the golden helm resting squarely upon his head.

At their approach, Luke similarly arrived from the direction of what used to be Maxine's General Store. He curtly instructed the poor sinners to stand side by side, facing the Courthouse steps. Mathius came to rest near the back of the landing, looking on as Thadeus stood upon the front ledge, his hands clasped behind him.

When the sinners were in place, Luke ascended the steps to provide the presider with a detailed report of the transgressions committed by each of the men below. The presider appeared unsurprised upon hearing the words whispered into his ear.

At last, he spoke.

"Blake Underhill. Step forward."

The named obliged the order with energetic defiance. He gnawed upon his lip, his nose gnarled.

"You have been accused of defying orders holy. What say you, in your defense?"

Blake smirked, nearly erupting in laughter.

"That you ain't God. That all this bullshit that you and yer goons are pullin ain't nothing but..."

The sharp crack of a gunshot accompanied Blake's body crumpling to the floor. Luke stood over Blake's lifeless body, his pistol outstretched in the direction of where Blake's head once stood. Without a flinch, Luke bent over and grasped the legs of the man. He carried him across the dirt and into the open doors of what was once Maxine's general store.

A saint patiently held the door open in expectation.

Both Johnny and Jules stood with mouths agape. But before either man could process the scene, the presider again spoke, this time with candor.

"Johhny Flynn. Step forward."

The named hesitated, a fresh pool of blood resting on the dirt directly before him. Was he expected to step into and splash Blake's still warm blood?

As if conjured by his hesitation, Luke suddenly reappeared from the general store with a wildness in his eyes that lent courage to Johhny's decision.

A light splatter was heard as he stepped into the crimson puddle.

"You have been accused of defying orders holy. What say you, in your defense?"

The presider's helm glistened in a bout of sunshine that, for only a moment, shone through the black plumes of smoke that otherwise blotted the sky. The air reeked of burning pine, a sweet and acrid scent of things approaching ripeness, crudely turned to ash.

"Ignorance, ma lord. I hadn't yet known the depth of your.... persuasion."

Another shot rang out into the afternoon air. No birds scattered from the sound as none were present upon the eaves of the surrounding structures. Johnny fell to the floor, his shoulder splashing into the same puddle of Blake Underhill's blood that he had been so hesitant to disturb.

In a similar fashion as had been done with the corpse prior, Luke lowered himself to collect the legs of Johnny

Flynn and dragged him into the still open doorway of the former general store.

Jules had seen enough to know what had been written on the wall. Writ before he'd even arrived. Jules lowered his head, dropped to his knees, and closed his eyes. He thought of the open plains, the soothing silence of its empty sea.

Darkness came swiftly to the one-time cowboy.

Thirty

The things he would do for a smoke, pondered Vale as the miles crept past him. He'd wrestle a water moccasin if it meant he could pull from the pipe that he'd left upon the seat of that damned cart, back in Bastion. His bag of tobacco mocked him, pressing itself into his thigh like a tumor.

He figured that he was being followed and thus had no time to stop and makeshift a means of inhaling its combustion. He had good reason to suspect it, too. After all, rarely was one chased out of town by an angry mob not pursued thereafter. He had no choice but to assume that he was.

When he reached the arboreal landmark of Ol' Reacher standing atop its rising knoll—a knoll decisively higher than all the others in the surrounding landscape—he awkwardly scampered up its limbs to gain a vantage of the hills that lay between himself and Bastion behind him. The branches were old but sturdy; not yet ready to succumb to age nor the wind of the plains. He reached a height he deemed high enough to offer a sufficient vantage and saw that, sure enough, a rider galloped at a tremendous pace in his direction, some miles back. It was little more than a speck in the far distance, but the sight was impossible to misplace.

Details of the speck were sparse, but the color of the approaching steed appeared to be black. Could it possibly be the town's new zealot riding on his trail?

There was no time to waft nor wonder. Based on its pace, he'd surely be overtaken in less than an hour if he continued on a steady path toward Butcher's Pass. Likely less. Maybe it was folly to have chosen such an obvious destination. He knew the pass was a risky choice for his initial destination, but he had figured that if he could make camp in the crevasse of its granite, he could defend himself well enough within it. He was familiar with the spot more than most other candidates on the surrounding emptiness of the plains.

And when it came to defense, familiarity was everything.

But it was now clear that he wouldn't make it in time. He would be forced to pivot. He looked about the area for anything that might provide advantage to an improvised defense, but saw nothing but cascading hills in all directions. His best chance—he began to suspect—was to ride perpendicularly from the path that he was on and hope that whoever it was that followed him didn't pick up on his change of direction.

Vale lowered himself carefully, unhitched his rental steed, and raised himself back onto its saddle. He extended his arm to a nearby branch and plucked a leaf from its tendril. He brought the oval greenery to his lips, gave it a kiss, and tossed it into the air directly above him. The leaf, at first, drifted to the west. But just before it met the ground, it was caught by a sudden breeze that carried it several feet northeast. At once, Vale kicked his heels into the sides of the quarter horse and took off in that direction.

He resolved to move as quickly as possible, hoping to gain the occlusion of the distant rolling hills in case the trailing rider sought perspective, just as he had. He gripped the leather reins of the fine Hess tack and encouraged the beast to overcome the hillside at as fast a clip as it could endure. He felt terrible for pushing the animal in such a way. It wasn't the horse's fault to be in such a situation, after all. But Vale equally knew that animals involved in great-plain shootouts rarely escaped such encounters any better than their riders. The horse would be better suited to endure a punishing sprint than a bullet.

The day was scorching and unshielded by even the faintest wisps of clouds. Soon, he knew that he would be forced to give his animal rest. A dead horse was worse than a slow one. So, when he came upon a meager stream after a hard gallop to the northeast from Ol' Reacher, Vale led the animal to the stream's gentle bank and dismounted. He hesitated, however, in letting go of the lead rope, still scarred from when Lucky had abandoned him the day before.

How long ago that now felt.

But the animal only tread wearily to the water and appeared without the energy to bolt. Despite this, Vale continued to hold tightly upon the reins as his eyes remained trained in the direction from which he had ridden.

For now, only the swaying grass of the hillside met his gaze.

When enough time had passed, he would retrace his steps back toward Ol' Reacher to—with any luck—ride on the heels of he that trailed him. To pursue the pursuer.

He sat upon a meager boulder resting beside the stream. Had it only been yesterday that he'd gone off in search of the gunsmith? And was it that very morning that he had sat upon the cart beside someone that he was so utterly convinced to be an angel? Was the glaring sun above him the same that saw him pull back the tarp before the entirety of Bastion's eyes, revealing the distorted corpse of Ginny Samson atop a pile of bones? Every moment from that until this one seemed to be but a series of timeless eternities of thoughtless action and reactions. There was no time for contemplation when hunted in such a land; in such a country. Not if he wished to survive it.

And yet, as if in revolt to his determination to remain focused, the memory of Susy standing amongst the crowd occasionally slipped into his mind's eye. When it did, Vale removed the pistol from his holster to check the fluidity of its spinning chamber; a futile attempt to bring his attention back to the necessary and emotionless present.

The only other introspections that arose in Vale while he sat idle was an appreciation that his lungs had given him respite throughout the majority of the day. He wasn't sure what would have come of him if a coughing fit had taken him while escaping the mob, back in Bastion.

He only hoped that the lull in his chest would continue.

When he deemed that he'd given his tail enough time to unknowingly ride past him, he remounted the horse and began trotting back towards the ash tree upon the knoll, his eyes ever diligent as he did. When he reached the tree, he was glad to see no waiting steeds or gunman at its trunk. He pulled the reins southwest and resumed his trek to Butcher's Pass. As far as he could tell, he'd successfully claimed the initiative in their game of cat and mouse.

And yet, despite his optimism, he kept a hand upon the hilt of his pistol for the remainder of the ride. He had to assume that whoever it was that was tracking him knew what they were doing. He'd learned, long ago, that it was best to not underestimate a situation, especially one harboring so many unknowns.

***

When the jutting wall of granite at last emerged on the horizon, Vale left the horse hitched to a boulder. He approached a hill on his hands and knees to scout out the scene. From his perspective, prone along the grass, he saw no midnight mare lingering amongst the trees that precluded the granite face. But at the same time, without question, he saw the distinct profile of a man walking cautiously through the trees toward the crevasse, pistol drawn.

The figure was still too distant to be surely identified, but it wore what appeared to be checkered, pleated pants below a long-sleeved white t-shirt, its sleeves rolled a quarter of the way up the arms. Shae Mackenzie was known to adorn such an outfit, but there was no way that *he* was his tail. What business would the saloon keeper have in following him all this way? What motivations could have possibly possessed him to do such a thing?

The verb lingered at the forefront of his mind. Nothing was beyond question. Not after the cart. Not after what he himself had pulled so surely into town that morning.

Then, just before he made to crawl carefully back towards his horse, a large raven flew brazenly overhead. It swooped within a dozen feet of Vale before doubling back to swirl over him once again in a tight circle.

"Caw! Caw! Caw!" it called into the brightness of the day. It was going to give him away! Vale turned his sight back to the pass, fearfully confident that the man amongst the trees might hear the bird's call. But after several long moments, the figure remained dissolved within the trees, hopefully now within the quiet confines of the rock's crevasse.

After what felt like minutes, the raven at last gave up its encirclement of him and flew off in the direction of Bastion.

Peculiar was a mild word for the circumstance, but there would be hours plenty later on to consider it further.

Hurriedly, Vale returned to the horse, unhitched its rope, and climbed back upon the saddle. His window of opportunity would close quickly. The figure would be searching for him within the pass for the next several minutes, after which he would be forced to assume that Vale was elsewhere and begin searching backwards for his presence. Vale would be best suited to confront the man before his rival's perspective had broadened.

And so, as quickly and quietly as he could manage, Vale rode into the swath of trees that proceeded the rock's crevasse. When he reached their dancing cover, he smartly dismounted from the horse and hitched it to a pine's rising trunk, all while keeping a steady eye on the opening in the nearby granite. He removed the pistol from its holster and approached the opening with its sights firmly set on the rock's open maw.

A soft breeze blew from it, troubling the leaves overhead. That was good. He hoped that the sound of their shuffling would be sufficient to cover the sound of his approach.

A thought occurred to him. What if the figure was indeed Shae Mackenzie? Sure, Shae had always been a thorn in his side, ever eager to play devil's advocate in this situation or that, but he was hardly worthy of a bullet. He again thought of the raven and the absence of the horse that had surely carried the man to the pass. He thought of the sureness in which he himself had carried Ginny's remains into town and the veil that had obscured his own vision—dousing him with righteous conviction. If something similar had befallen Shae, was he prepared to put the man down? He knew, of course, that the answer depended on how eager Shae was to point his arm in his direction. If the question was to be Shae or himself, Vale had no qualms in deciding that conundrum, but he nonetheless hoped that such a choice wouldn't come to be had.

With his weapon drawn, his finger already half pulling upon the heavy resistance of the trigger, he faced down the long, cragged corridor of the crevasse.

Nothing stood in the initial twenty feet of the passage before it veered to the right, its high, winding walls obscuring whatever lay farther inside. Vale paused to listen intently, hoping to gain insight into the location of his pursuer but heard only the cool, whistling wind blowing from its confines.

Cautiously, and with a slowly rising ache in his trigger finger, Vale stepped into the twisting corridor. He knew the passage well, but in the hypervigilance of his senses each yard of the surrounding rock seemed foreign and mocking in their obscuring proclivity.

Stepping around the bend of a particular sharp angle, Vale froze. Standing fifteen feet ahead of him stood the back of Shae Mackenzie. The man walked away from him, his arms raised in the support of a gun all his own.

Vale steadily held the sights of his pistol upon Shae's back; the trigger half pulled. He knew the answer that he would give, if the question were to be raised.

"Don't make me shoot you, Shae."

The named slowed his cadence to a stop before gently lowering his arms, and the gun, to his sides. Still facing away, he began to chuckle.

"In all the years I've known you, Vale, I've never once pegged you as sneaky."

"You didn't know me back when I had to be. And now, because of you, I had to be. Drop the gun and we can both walk outta here."

A wind's trembling whistle traversed the crevasse, providing an overture to the silence that then lingered for several moments. Eventually, with a measured slowness, Shae turned about to face the sheriff, his gun still dangling at his side. Both men knew that if he raised it at all, even an inch, that the revolver in Vale's outstretched hands would make a tremendous noise.

"Why'd ya do it?" asked the barkeeper. "Why'd ya kill her?" A flat exhaustion draped him.

"Would you believe me if I told ya that I didn't?"

"No."

"Then don't ask questions you're not willing to hear the answers to. Now drop that damn gun and go and get out of here! I don't wanna put a bullet in ya, Shae. Just let me be and..." A cough interrupted Vale's words. By sheer will alone, he managed to maintain his composure enough to keep Shae's weapon at his side until he could clear his throat.

"I gotta have yer gun, Shae. I need you to drop it to the dirt. And if you're not willing to do that, then I'm gunna have to do something I really, really don't wanna do."

"It couldn't be *that* hard for ya, to put a bullet in me and all. I mean, you already mutilated Ginny. Presented her like a goddamn Remington painting..."

"I didn't kill her, Shae!"

"... and then, you went and got poor Luke killed like it was nothing."

Another silence permeated the space between them.

"That's right. Got yer deputy shot in the head by a bullet intended for yours. So what's another body in the dirt today, Sheriff? I already signed over my warrant. Ain't nothin worth nothing to me no more." A tear slid from his eye. "So make my goddamn day, Vale. Make a trinity outta this mess."

The news of Luke's death was unexpected. The kid was innocent as they came, and the thought of him in the dirt as a result of his actions was another specter that he knew he'd be forced to reckon with in quieter hours.

But he had to reckon with the situation before him first. He noticed Shae's demeanor shifting slightly as he spoke. What was initially a white-hot anger had, within a matter of moments, unraveled into a despondency that he'd never before seen in the bartender. He again recalled the raven and the veil that had been pulled over his own eyes.

"What prompted you to come all the way, Shae? To chase after me like this? And... whose pistol are ya holding there so tightly?"

Shae again chuckled. "Now it's my turn to distrust *your* belief in *my* words."

"Well, unlike you, I don't ask questions that I'm not willing to hear the answers to."

Vale lowered his gun, softening his finger upon the trigger, although not entirely removing it. He opened the door and hoped desperately for Shae to walk through it.

From somewhere far off, the song of a western meadowlark reverberated through the granite walls.

"Have you ever felt the whisper of the devil on your ear?" asked the barkeeper with a tremble.

Thirty-One

The hours that followed the deputy's revival blew over Quinn like the clouds of an all-too familiar storm.

Quinn listened to the speeches given from afar before retreating into the saloon. He had his own key, something Shae didn't need to know.

The bartender was no-where to be found, and not even Henry came by to play the piano.

The townsfolk that passed by the tall windows of the saloon carried a look of fanaticism that he hadn't seen in many long years, not since the great famine that had driven him to America in the first place. In their wild, darting eyes, he recalled the madness that had taken the countrymen of his own native land. In that circumstance, their madness had been a symptom of the lack of food in their mouths, the sickness of their mothers, the bodies in the streets. But here...now... how quickly his neighbors had changed.

Quinn retrieved a bottle of rye from behind the bar, sat upon the third step of the stairs, and patiently waited for his only real friend in the world, Shae Mackenzie, to return from wherever it was that he had gone.

The hours passed slowly, marked only by the wild-eyed packs that walked briskly past the saloon, their shadows growing long in the approaching dusk. Some intermittently stopped to point toward the saloon and sneer.

Quinn suspected their intentions just fine. From what limited conversations he'd overheard immediately following the speeches, before his retreat into the saloon, he'd heard enough to know the direction with which things were heading.

"It's about time if you ask me," said an unseen voice amongst a crowd. "Gluttony and greed have driven this town into the grips of the devil for far too long."

"Did you see his eyes when he sat up?" spoke another. "There's no denying it, friends, he held council with the lord. There's no denying it at all!"

"Burn the sinners!" bellowed Dr. Stevenson from somewhere in the crowd.

Shae knew well enough that before very long, maybe before the day would reach its end, that a posse of men would enter the saloon with weapons and fire to destroy that which they deemed to be beyond the worthy sight of the lord. They'd done it in Ireland, he recalled, in wandering packs of vigilante mobs seeking to appease a God that had abandoned them, violently demanding reverence to scripture so that their sons may eat once more.

"No" was not an answer that was received with empathy in such circumstances. It was instead, more often than not, met with fire.

He thought he'd never see such madness again in his lifetime. Despite the many evils that were prevalent in the new world, he long suspected—maybe hoped was a more appropriate word—that such reactionary flames were an evil native only to Europe and its antiquity.

But alas, as the packs continued to march dutifully about the avenue outside, he began to suspect that he was mistaken.

The hours ambled past while the bottles eagerly emptied in the darkness that soon filled the saloon. From somewhere in the distance, the rabid banging of Xavior's hammer repeatedly fell upon the anvil. A gunshot was heard from somewhere not so far away.

In his stupor, Quinn thought back on his escape from his childhood village set ablaze by the mob as he escaped in cowardly desertion of his family. An act of self-preservation, but cowardice nonetheless. Should history repeat itself, here at the end of the world? Would he run away, once more? Was that who he was? The runner?

The thought of instead finishing the bottle in his hand—and many more—in the coming hours approached him and lobbied its position. Quinn listened intently to their arguments, each supported by corresponding swigs of the bottle.

It wouldn't be long now, he knew. Alcohol would be the first of many culprits to be strung up when enemies were required in days of upheaval. Maybe he ought to beat the righteous to the punch. After all, if they came for the drink, they were sure to quarter him too. None in town so personified the sins of the bottle, after all. If he wished it, he could burn the building to ashes himself, right then and there. He could steal from the righteous their satisfaction.

He'd heard long ago that the smoke killed ya before the flames could get to licking your skin.

But then, just as his thoughts began to linger toward action, a shimmer in the darkness emerged from the mahogany of the bar, heading directly towards him. Without question, it was the shimmering pocket of air that he had seen earlier that day in the alleyway.

The old Irishman let out a bellow of laughter. His belly of whiskey thought the sight marvelous.

"Where ya been off ta, ya buggar? I got ya a glass but ya never came to drink from it! Even in these end days, *especially*, in these end days, one can use a drink."

His laughter trailed away, his joviality soon replaced by a sincere consideration of the flickering apparition floating silently before him. Maybe it was the boy, after all.

"Luke?" he finally asked.

The specter at first gave no answer and only continued to hover before him in the saloon's growing darkness. But then, a single word abruptly manifested itself in the forefront of Quinn's mind.

Follow.

The shimmering body of air then drifted from Quinn in a gentle and silent slide toward the saloon's back door. Quinn hesitated only briefly. What had he to lose, after all?

The specter continued on out the back door and into the hills that unraveled beyond. Quinn followed closely behind, trekking into the uneven landscape while intermittently pulling from the bottle that he had taken with him for the road.

Maybe he'd lost his mind, he considered as he and the specter overcame a third hill. He'd long debated whether the drink would come for his brain or heart first, and a part of him was relieved that it might be the former. It would be easier to dissolve if one wasn't aware of their disintegration, he reasoned with a chuckle.

But just as he did, the shimmer ascended a final hill and stopped. Quinn joined the shimmer in rest and saw that his present perspective overlooked a quaint glen of aspens down below. To his surprise, three figures huddled quietly amongst the trees.

A voice called to him in a defensive and fearful tone. It was a female's voice, the voice of Beatrice Valentine, Bastion's schoolteacher.

"Who is it!?"

Somewhere near her, a rifle's cocking hammer pronounced itself.

"Easy, loves!" called Quinn happily. "It's Quinn!"

"And what is Quinn doing here!?"

"Following a ghost!" he responded, quickly falling into a liquored laughter that lasted several seconds.

When his merriment finally subsided, he heard the figures faintly whispering amongst themselves. Eventually, a second voice, that of Willie Boyle, called up to him.

"What love have you for our new savior, Quinn?"

Quinn couldn't help but chuckle once again at the question. "I haven't the stomach to love another as I'm still drinking my last."

More whispers followed as Quinn did what he could to corral his amusement. It was a lovely thing to be so tickled, he thought. What a lovely thing indeed.

"Quinn!" called Beatrice, once more. "Won't you come down here and join us?"

Thirty-Two

The night was a dreadful affair. Vale had insisted upon the lack of a fire in case "that devil", as he had taken to calling Mathius, had sent further followers on his trail.

"A quiet dark will make for hearing footsteps easier," he had reasoned.

But as the night drug on with Vale snoring boorishly beside him, Shae thought the accompaniment of flames, and the reassurance that came with it, would have been worth the risk. Not to mention, they rested in the center of the long crevasse with makeshift drawstring tripwires placed on each entrance. No one was entering the crevasse without their knowledge.

But Vale was in charge—apparently—and in their abundance of caution, Shae endured the evening in darkness. The only thing that accompanied him was the narrow sliver of stars overhead, Vale's coarse snoring, and the occasional howling of coyotes in the distance.

But what haunted Shae the most, as the night drew on, was the memory of what had driven him so thoughtlessly into the wilderness with murder on the forefront of his mind. He was the furthest thing from a violent man. Never in his life had he even thrown a punch. The fact that he could be so easily persuaded to track a man across the wilderness to put a bullet sized hole in his chest chilled him.

"It was Jebediah's words," he insisted to Vale when they had descended from the brink of violence and sat side by side against the crevasse's granite. "Something in his presence... it was like a snake had slithered into my brain."

Vale had nodded as if understanding. Not that he could. Even he himself could hardly make sense of it.

"Even now," he continued, "bright flashes of malice cross me. I have sudden urges to..." he paused, seeing the sheriff's eyebrows raise. "They're not strong enough to blind me anymore. They're not as strong as they were earlier. But... I'd be lying if they weren't still there."

"When I pulled the reins of that cart into town," began Vale in consolation, "I felt something similar. I was so sure... so convinced that I was about to confront the devil himself. That I was the righteous hand of God, coming to smite down evil." He chuckled. "Now, I'm left wondering who, or what, I had shared such pleasant company with on that cart."

"Was it Jebediah?"

"No. It looked like Frederick."

Both men stared off, equally perplexed by their similar albeit differing bouts of illusion.

But as Shae stared up into the stars with Vale snoring beside him, he was just glad that Vale had confronted him in the manner that he had. His longstanding apathy of the man notwithstanding, he knew that he owed the sheriff his life. If he had reached the sheriff within a mile of Bastion, with those wicked words still worming about in his mind with fresh intensity, he had no doubt that at least one of them would have been left upon the yellowed grass to be picked at by the vultures.

He turned his head to look over at Vale, lying on his back in the muddy grass, his large belly peeking out from under his shirt. A gruff, deep rattle accompanied each of his heaving breaths.

So much for being undetectable.

The coarseness of Vale's snoring reminded Shae of the ruthless coughing fits that he had witnessed the man endure on several occasions throughout the lateness of the day. And yet, despite the consistent and ominous interruptions, he watched the sheriff nearly whimsically construct a pipe from a thick branch of cottonwood to suck down a half bag of tobacco. Even then, as the lingering smoke of the tobacco hung about them, the man would, out of nowhere, be forced to double over and cough streams of bloody phlegm into the dirt.

Vale concealed it well, but as they sat about discussing the predicament that they'd found themselves in, Shae could have sworn that he saw a shimmer of mortality swimming in the sheriff's eyes. He'd seen the look in men before, and more often than not, those that adorned it weren't long for the world.

A pack of coyotes raised their collective call from somewhere unseen. They must have killed something.

The plan, as had been agreed upon before Vale had slipped easily into slumber, was to ride to Cheyenne over the coming days and see what allies they could find in the city. Vale made it sound like he would have no difficulty in convincing the federal agent there to join him in confronting whatever it was that was happening back in Bastion.

"Should we find ourselves a priest or something?" Shae had asked while the light dwindled in their narrow space.

"You saw the mob that chased me out of town," said Vale, resting awkwardly on the dirt, pipe in hand. "I hope that I'm wrong, but my fear is that the timing of my arrival with Ginny was intentional. If this darkness... this evil... whatever it is... if it could get into yours and my head so easily, who else could it be manipulating? Let's not forget, Shae, that that man, Mathius, or whatever he calls himself, was standing awfully close to the mayor up there on those steps. If he can..." Vale paused to cough into the dirt before wiping his mouth with his sleeve. "If he can get into the mayor's head, and let's be honest, we both know that it wouldn't be all that difficult of a feat, then the mob will similarly follow. And mobs don't listen to priests, Shae. They listen to guns. It's only after the guns go off do they seek the guidance, and forgiveness, of God."

Shae closed his eyes and tried, in vain, to sleep. He let his mind wander and imagined what the city would have in store for him. It'd been years since he'd last seen the streets of the capital.

It was a necessary distraction, for in that darkness he sought anything to mute the memory of Jebediah's breath still dancing across the lobe of his ear.

Thirty-Three

When Quinn descended the hillside to stand amongst the small circle of figures congregating in the darkness, he found that its participants included storekeeper Maxine Weather, stable master Willie Boyle, and Beatrice Valentine, the schoolteacher. What gentle company, he thought. The only one from the group that he'd previously spent any real time with was Willie on the rare occasions when the man would mingle in the bar—most often on his birthday. As for the others, he'd only met their acquaintance in brief passings, both women being two of the very few in town to give him a smile or a nod when they did.

"Quinn," began Maxine in a stern tone, her figure shrouded in the pale blue of the moonlight, "should you agree to hear them, the words that I'm about to tell you, what we're about to share, is information coated in death. If you decide to stay by our sides after hearing them, there are people that will dice you bloody for doing so. On the other hand, if you hear these words, and then decide that you don't like what we have to say, well, we cannot accept such a risk... and believe me... I'm a mother of five, I'll know if you agree or not. But if you walk away now, stumble yourself back up that hill and forget we were ever here, then we never saw you and all is molasses. But I need you to choose for me, here and now. Do you want to hear these words?"

Quinn swayed onto his back foot and patiently scanned the surrounding darkness for his shimmering guide. It was nowhere to be found.

"Where'd ya get off ta, ya buggar?"

"We're wasting our time with him, Maxine," spoke Willie in a short and anxious manner.

"No, beast keeper, you're not wasting your time," responded Quinn, at last. "I've seen strive like you'd never imagine. Ya see, famine... it places horns upon the heads of men once holy. Mothers sell their children for apples. And all the while, the mob, it grows tendrils and sustains itself by the very decency it absorbs. But that's not to say that all a God's goodness gets swallowed by such woe. No. There always be the few bold enough to stand and die, even in the face of the hot red eyes of da devil. There are always those who'll hold their ideals to be of more value than their blood, their bravery sustaining the very humanity of our collective souls. For when the waves recede, and yes, they'll recede, when the beast deflates into the hollow shell of fear that it always was, it'll be the bravery of the few and the swords that they die upon, that the resurgence of civility will base their hopes, aspirations, and theologies upon. All this to say... Yes, I'll join your little rebellion, beast keeper. I've turned my back on bravery once. I shan't again."

With that, the four dissidents swiftly huddled to discuss the minutiae of their budding insurgency. It was decided that Quinn, with his unassuming position in society would serve their designs as a fox in sheep's clothing. If he could convince the saints of a dependent, new-found salvation, he could conceivably be placed into tight situations with an underlying assumption of ignorance to protect him. Most of the town would be quick to overlook the wit of the town drunk, after all.

On the other hand, Maxine was on the top of the list of those likely already deemed to be an 'enemy of the state'. After she had attacked, with her fists alone, the saints that came to acquire her general store, she'd have likely joined the likes of Johnny, Blake, and Jules in execution had she not been nothing but a kind-hearted acquaintance to all for so long. But goodwill wouldn't endure in a situation such as this. All amongst them knew that, soon enough, the tide would turn, and safety would abandon her. It would be best if she left town now in the search of help from places elsewhere.

"I s'pose I'll make for Gillette, first thing. I can take Penny, assuming they haven't locked down the stables. Willie, do you think they've made for the stables yet?"

"As of twenty minutes ago they hadn't," said the nervous, skinny man, "but twenty minutes ain't as short as it used to be."

Maxine exhaled heavily. "I guess I'll go tonight then."

For Willie and Beatrice, the group decided their roles to be relatively nuanced, at least at first. The group hadn't yet the resources nor manpower to make any real impact on the situation, despite their disdain for its developments. The short-term plan was for Willie and Beatrice to quietly inquire with those that they trusted to see where they might find allies in town.

Meanwhile, Quinn would work to develop the reputation of a repentant and changed man, enlightened by the light of the lord. The three would then reconvene in three days' time, in the same hidden valley in which they now stood to re-assess their footing and make plans further.

Maxine would attend if she could. If not, it would be assumed that she was working on plans grander in Gillette.

She was a brave one, thought Quinn. Braver than he.

"Maxy," he asked with a sudden flash of morosity, "Smelly Joe?"

Maxine's mouth turned up while her eyes collapsed into sorrow.

"He's off somewhere better than here." A tear fell from her eye. "I'll be seeing him soon enough, though. I suspect that he's waiting for me."

Thirty-Four

The following days were among the most grueling that Shae had ever known. Not only was he forced to endure the wildly uncomfortable position of riding behind Vale on the back of Benevolence, but the convex blue of the sky remained without even a hint of cloud-cover.

The yellow of the grass became axiomatic and the trees grew ever the more sparse the further they traveled from their home, a home that seemed to be intoxicatingly close to the mountains from their current perspective.

It also didn't take long for Shae to further fear for the health of his companion as he soon realized that killing game on the plains was much more difficult than it was in theory. By noon of the second day, he and Vale stalked a trio of deer for nearly three hours to no avail. Of course, if they had proper rifles, the process would have been exponentially easier. But the crude accuracy of their six shooters proved to be poor help in snagging the flesh of the agile creatures grazing upon the hillside.

Vale's routine coughing fits didn't help, either, and with each missed shot, the deer would scurry off, further and further over the horizon.

They made camp that evening with only empty bellies, frustration, and worry on their minds.

"We'll be quite the sight stumbling into town if we keep this up," chuckled Vale.

But Shae wasn't in the mood for jokes and only rolled over in famished fatigue. At least they had a fire to keep them company this time.

"Why are we going all the way to Cheyenne, Vale? Couldn't we just go somewhere closer? Gillette maybe? I don't get it. What's in Cheyenne that's not in those other places?"

"Representatives of the United States of America, my friend, that's who. Do you really think some lowly sheriff from Gillette is going to give half a donkey's hide about what's going on in Bastion? Not a chance. We gotta get those interested in collecting our tax dollars involved if we're gunna get the help I suspect we'll be needin."

It seemed like quite the assumption, thought Shae, closing his eyes. "Whatever you say, Vale."

Upon the light of morning, the two men mounted the gently demeanored Benevolence and continued their trek in a southeastern direction. To both their relief, they quickly approached a sunken valley that held a wide stream with a lengthy stretch of cottonwoods straddling its banks. No deer were seen along the water's edge, but it nonetheless appeared worthy of a mid-morning rest.

"Are you a trout man?" asked Vale from over his shoulder, encouraging the horse toward the glen. The thought of fishing the stream hadn't even occurred to Shae, but the idea of digging his teeth into some freshly smoked cutthroat watered his tongue. He was growing ever more appreciative to have Vale guiding him. If he were to be left to his own devices, he was quite sure that he would, quite unceremoniously, be as good as bones on the prairie.

They ambled patiently into the valley and approached the noble cottonwoods hugging the stream. As they did, it occurred to Shae that he hadn't seen a single tree the whole day prior, a day that had encompassed a wide swath of miles. The thought boggled him.

On each bank of the stream, which itself appeared to be only a stone's throw wide and no more than a few feet deep, grew tall, happy grasses and western coneflowers; their pinecone-like heads rising out of the earth in summer jubilance.

It felt as if they'd crossed into another world in their approach to the water's edge. Despite his lingering fatigue and the void in his belly, the soft rhythm of the stream and everything that accompanied its chorus brought a sense of reprieve to Shae's mind.

The men dismounted from the tired horse, that in turn, promptly made for the water to drink from its edge. Vale produced his pipe and began to fill its makeshift bowl with tobacco leaves, fighting back a cough as he did. Shae thought he looked quite gaunt; an uncanny juxtaposition to the ever-present optimism of the man.

He desperately hoped that his assessment of Vale's vigor was wrong.

Shae marched eagerly toward a pile of nearby driftwood in the hopes of finding a wooden spear to fish with. His stomach ached terribly, and even the pressing necessity of emptying his bladder came secondary to filling his stomach. He could pee in the stream while spearing a fish, he compromised.

But as he prodded through the water-logged refuse of the river, something in his periphery caught his eye. He looked up, and to his slowly processing dismay, watched as a pair of brown bear cubs, not three feet off the ground each, ambled slowly toward him.

It suddenly became clear as to why the stream was so empty of dear or other prey. They had unknowingly filled the vacancy.

Each of Shae's auxiliary concerns abandoned him as adrenaline flooded his veins. He stumbled slowly backward, back toward Vale and Benevolence, each unknowingly drinking from the stream.

"Vale," he stuttered in a hushed tone. "Bears."

Shae kept his eyes on the tree line, praying to not see mama bear emerging from the underbrush. He'd heard stories of over-protective mother bears closing with hunters and separating their various parts within seconds. Vale must have heard similar stories, for Shae—still walking backwards—heard a brutish cough emit from the sheriff's lungs before hearing the man stuffing his pockets and hurriedly running to the horse.

Shae turned about to witness Vale mounting Benevolence when he heard the unmistakable sounds of tremendous feet trampling fiercely behind him. He sprinted to the horse and nimbly bound onto its back just as the horse reared back in a terrified whinny, taking off in the way they'd come. Shae held tightly to the sides of the sheriff and looked back to see a sight worthy of nightmares. A colossal grizzly, massive and angry, bounding toward them with bad intentions. It was gaining on them quickly.

The horse was pulling them forward at a full tilt, and had it been just one of the men upon its back, it might have been able to outrun the approaching grizzly. But with each passing second, it became increasingly clear that they wouldn't escape the animal.

"Vale!!" called Shae. "It's gunna catch us!!"

Vale leaned to the left and, while still gripping the reins with his left hand, looked back, past Shae's left ear. He grimaced a fearful grin and looked as if he were about to say something when he suddenly squeezed his eyes shut and coughed into the air. Vale pulled himself back into the standard riding position and coughed aggressively into the mane of Benevolence. Even amongst the commotion of the moment, Shae thought he could hear the flat splatter of liquid upon the nape of the horse's neck.

But just as he was sure that Vale was blatantly out of commission, the man whipped around in the same fashion that he had before, his left hand gripping the reins to lean past Shae's left side. This time, however, as he looked back, Vale brandished his pistol in his right hand and aimed it at the closely pursuing grizzly, not ten feet behind them.

Crack!

There was only one shot fired from Vale's pistol, and Shae looked to Vale's expression for hints of effect. The latter only stared flatly behind them. For a moment, Shae was afraid that the look in Vale's eyes was that of resigned fatalism. But then, the slight curves of a smile curled upon his lip. Only then did Shae notice the blood dripping liberally from the sheriff's mouth.

Vale relinquished his grip on the reins and fell from the horse still galloping forward as quickly as it could manage.

Thirty-Five

Over the coming days and nights, Quinn spent his hours writhing at the foot of the courthouse's steps convulsing, rolling about, and perseverating in long soliloquies directed at the sky. He made sure that a King James was clasped in the tight of his grip for the duration of his performances.

"Lord, oh lord, let your holy fire scorch away these liquid sins!"

He knew, of course, that by causing such a spectacle he ran the risk of inviting the open scorn of those that most desired his undoing. He most certainly remained a moral fugitive to many for his well-known romancing of the bottle. On the other hand, he wagered that by performing his repentance so publicly before the saints had a chance to formally arraign him, that he could convert their ire into reverence.

If he were lucky, he might just become a symbol of the transformative nature of their god. That was his hope, at least.

By the end of his second day of performative repentance, he began to foster a growing confidence that his wager had paid off. Intermittently, saints and ardent passersby began placing supportive hands on his shoulders while he shook with the passion of his transformation.

It helped that he hadn't had a drop of alcohol in days.

As such, with every hour that passed, Quinn was forced to traverse the desert that stood between the lake of his previous saturation and the mountaintops of an authentic sobriety—one he hadn't known in years.

As he twisted, shouted, and contorted himself in the cloudlessness of the blighting Sun, his skin became coated in a sheen of sweat while his muscles ached and clinched themselves into inconsolable cramping. The resulting sight was one that surely enhanced his performative repentance

At times, he dreadfully sought water to quell the dryness of his being, but he refused to relent, even when presented with cupfuls by those concerned for his health. He understood that a degree of legitimate suffering, of legitimate repentance, would be required if he was to be believed for the show being put on.

Another day of frightful hollering and writhing came to pass. Come midday—Quinn lost track of what day it was—he noticed Maxine's general store being converted into the kingdom's distribution point for all food and drinking water. Before long, a winding line of dreary townsfolk protruded from its door, each carrying a steel pail in their hands. Every few minutes, he at the front of the line would emerge from the back of the building with a meager bag of items, their buckets sloshing with water.

Saints milled about the street buzzing in one direction or the next, each engrossed in individually prescribed pursuits with ardent attention. They were now easily identifiable by the red cloth ribbons hanging loosely around their necks; previously the red stripes of the American flags that had been—once upon a time—proudly displayed outside their storefronts and homes.

But in that late afternoon of Quinn's third day in the street, he looked to the landing of the courthouse to see the presider, in his glistening golden helm, peering contemplatively down at him. Quinn thought he looked like a Mayan god examining the sacrifices that were soon to be had.

After a pause, the presider descended the steps toward the one-time drunkard lying pitifully in the street. Luke followed closely behind him. As of that morning, Quinn's physiological shaking had at last receded, replaced only by convulsions of a purely performative nature. But as happy as he was to be abandoned by the symptoms of his detoxification, he wished that its grip had still been with him for his approaching audience with the only man whose judgement truly mattered.

When the presider stepped near, Quinn rolled onto his knees to bow, his forehead pressed upon the dirt.

"Presider Hess, only through the light of your kingdom have I come to see the depths of my depravity. You have given me life anew, great Presider. I owe all to..."

"Can you stand?"

"Yes," Quinn said, rising shakily to his feet.

"What can thee contribute to this kingdom of God?"

Quinn was prepared for the question and did his best to conceal his relief at hearing it.

"Before the devil took me by the way of the long drink, I was a speechwriter, believe it or not. I prepared statements for many a statesman across this country. I was darn good at it, too! I'd be happy ta offer my skills in such a manner, as, I imagine you'll be giving plenty a speech in tha days ta come. It could be valuable to have one, such as myself to..."

The presider held out a hand, imploring the man to stop talking. He turned to Luke to whisper a word, prompting the one-time deputy to turn and ascend the stairs back toward the courthouse behind them.

"We shall see if what you say is true. The wisdom of the elderly shall be appreciated in this kingdom of God. I shall give you a chance to prove your honesty. I must say, too, that I have much respect for one that so willfully turns themselves from evil. It is my hope that you shall inspire many to follow such a path." He raised his chin upward in a glean of pride. "Tomorrow evening, I intend to give a speech upon these very steps. I will be presenting to the constituents of this kingdom a summary of changes that have been made and of the changes that are to still to come. Write me this speech, Quinn, and present it to me, in full, tomorrow at eight in the morning. If it is acceptable, I will read it to the masses that night, and you shall have yourself a role in my royal court. On the other hand, if your words prove to be uninspiring, we shall find you a... more appropriate role."

Luke returned with a folded paper that he handed to Quinn.

"This list shall provide you with all the facts you will need to include in this speech."

Quinn took the paper in his dry and cracking fingers, lowering his head in fealty. "Thank you, Mister Presider. You shan't regret this."

"I hope not, Quinn, and so should you."

With that, the man spun about and marched himself back up the steps; back into the spaces hidden within the courthouse.

With shaking steps, Quinn turned to proceed down the length of the avenue. He would meet Willie, Beatrice—and hopefully Maxine—that evening to share his acquired proximity to the presider. He, of course, had no intention of writing the speech, which in-effect accelerated their timetable for action dramatically. But a planned, intimate meeting with the Presider... that's something they could work with.

But little thought could be given to the matter just yet as his hunger and thirst made critical thinking all but impossible. His eyes darted from one edge of the road to the next, seeking anything that might give respite to his biological lacking.

The long sullen line extending from the open doors of the nutrient-distribution post continued its centipede crawl from its doors. If he were to ask the saints, or enter the long line in order to receive his ordained rations, he would easily find relief for his hunger and thirst. But something in either prospect so repulsed him that he instead chose to seek sustenance on his own rather than accept their offered assistance. It was a pastime he was long familiar with, after all.

But as Quinn tested each of the spots that had previously offered easy procurement of food or water, the wells behind the storefronts, the chicken coops once filled with eggs, he found all to be either empty, uprooted, or filled with dirt.

As such, Quinn finally began to comprehend the absolute control that the town's new leadership had gained over its resources. Not that it was a town, anymore. It was something else entirely. Something monstrous and full of fear.

Out of a burgeoning curiosity, he produced from his pocket the paper that Luke had given him. On it were the items that were to be included in the following day's speech. He wasn't forced to read far to be further doused in horror.

On the coming sabbath, there was to be closed-door interrogations to evaluate the town's knowledge of scription. For those that were found to be lacking, decimation—in the Roman style—was to be practiced, soon thereafter. That's to say, that one in every ten would be clubbed to death by their brethren.

"To instill discipline," read the parchment.

Madness. Through and through. He'd have thought such a concept to be impossible, but at seeing what had already come to pass so easily by the hands of the believers, of his neighbors and friends, he held no steady faith that it would not indeed come to pass.

At suddenly finding it difficult to think, Quinn relented, found a steel bucket from behind what was once Xavior's smithy, and took his place in the bread line. Coincidentally, he found that both Willie and Beatrice stood immediately before him in waiting. Not that either turned around to say hello. They would see each other that night to discuss means of never again being forced to endure such a circumstance.

Thirty-Six

Shae nearly followed Vale off the back of Benevolence, the sheriff being his primary means of remaining on the quarter horse in the first place. But just before sliding equally to the dirt, Shae narrowly grasped the horn, pulled himself into the saddle, and jerked sharply upon the reins to implore the beast to stop.

Benevolence skid to a halt but continued to pace about, neighing unhappily. It was clearly terrified of the bear. Shae looked back to see two lumps lying upon the earth. The further, the colossal carcass of a bear. Vale lay closer.

Neither moved in the gentle breeze that worried the grass about them.

Shae kicked into the horse's sides to bring him closer to Vale's motionless body, but the horse wouldn't have it. It nervously paraded side to side whinnying, vehemently refusing to step any closer to the bear that lay a few dozen feet beyond Vale. Shae was ready to dismount and run to him, but realized that the horse would likely be eager to bolt, should he relinquish its reins.

"Vale!!!" he shouted, hoping that the man would simply sit up and make the situation a simple one. But there was no such luck. Vale remained motionless upon the ground, his face in the dirt.

Shae decided to dismount and try his hand at pulling the horse but found the beast to be shockingly strong. With each tug of the reins, Benevolence resisted with an equally stubborn anchor. And with each doomed pull, Shae grew further overwhelmed with a sense of impotence.

Here he was, in the middle of nowhere at the bequest of devils, without food, chased by bears, and now likely without his guide. He clenched the reins in his fists and screamed at the earth until his vision grew dots, forcing him to drop to a knee and take deep breaths in the hopes of retaining a steady grip on his consciousness.

But as he knelt, grasping for air and damning the horse whose reins he resentfully gripped, he looked up, beneath the horse's barrel, to see a further development to arrest his breath. On the grass but thirty feet away stood six Indians beside a pair of speckled packhorses. Amongst them were two adult males tightly grasping their rifles, a boy of maybe ten or eleven, a pair of woman standing cautiously behind the horses, and an elderly female standing stoically between the men.

The men didn't appear imminently ready to aim their rifles, although they equally made no effort to conceal the control they demanded of their weapons.

The males, including the young boy, wore what appeared to be elk-hide leggings beneath wool shirts of tan and embroidered turquoise ribbons. The women wore crimson cloth dresses that danced with the shells of their necklaces and the braids of their hair. The elder woman wore what appeared to be ceremonial garb of some kind, including a turquoise shawl about her shoulders and a cascading necklace of alternating color. A trio of feathers protruded from the band that arrested her forehead.

All amongst them bore faces of sorrow.

Shae was frozen at the sight. As such, he lacked the gumption to make the first move. They simply watched him as if he were an exhibit to be casually lamented. But after what felt to Shae to be a dreadfully long time, the elder turned her head to speak to one of the rifle-armed men flanking her. The man then relayed the message to the boy, prompting him and the child to step forward, toward Shae.

Shae gently stood and, still holding the reins, circumnavigated the still frightened horse to put himself between the approaching Indians and the animal. As he did, Benevolence neighed with disdain. Shae paid it no mind. He instead kept his eye trained upon those approaching, particularly on the trigger finger of the man carrying the rifle. He paid his own pistol no mind. If the approaching Indians wanted him dead, so it would be.

Shae was generally ambivalent toward the natives. He'd met enough of them throughout the years to understand that they were simply people. As such, they came as good as they came and as bad as they do. And just like any other collection of human beings, the American Indian was one that was capable of immense kindness, generosity, and love when given the opportunity to practice such tenants. But also, just like any other collection of humanity, when put into the vice of grim circumstance, they also have the capacity to practice reciprocity of affronts committed, both real and conjured.

But the man and the boy approached him casually without neither fear nor malice in their faces; only sadness. Shae relaxed at the sight, but also at his sudden recognition of the clothing worn by the group—likely that of the Eastern Shoshone tribe, a culture with which he'd encountered on more than one occasion over the years. In one such meeting—traders passing through Bastion, some years back—he was taught how to greet them in their way. He only remembered it because of the peculiarity in its pronunciation, specifically how its verbal components sounded so similar to that of his organs of sight.

"Ai Ai," he said, cautiously raising his free hand.

The adult man nodded slightly in acknowledgement, but said nothing. The boy, however, proceeded to speak in such flawless English that it brought a sadness to Shae's ear.

"Grandmother will see to your man, so long as you make words with the great puha before the wind takes him. My cousin, Tobia Tuwani," he gestured to the man beside him, "will keep your horse amongst us as you do."

Shae was both puzzled and apprehensive. He knew well enough that the horse was his sole lifeline, and without it... well.

"Puha?" he asked, wishing to dismiss his puzzlement before addressing his anxiety.

"The bear. He was a speaker. And now, he speaks no more. Grandmother says that you must make words with it as it goes. And in exchange, she will see to your friend. She will see if she can help him."

Shae soon realized that he had little choice in the matter. Vale had killed an animal of significance to them, it appeared. If he declined the gesture and refused to trust their offered assistance, the best-case scenario was that they would leave him alone to struggle with the horse while Vale remained face-down in the dirt. He didn't want to discover what the worst-case scenario might be.

Slowly, he extended the reins to Tobia while looking into his eyes with intensity. He wanted the man to know that he understood what he handed him. The man returned only a flat glance. It was obvious that he held no sympathy for Shae and only acted on the direction of his elder.

Shae jogged off toward Vale. He gently rolled him onto his back and saw that, although his eyes remained closed, he was breathing; something he wasn't all too confident in finding.

Shae looked up to see the elder female approaching, whispering softly to herself. He recalled what the boy had said. That he was to "make words with the bear." He didn't know exactly what they wanted him to do with the dead bear, but figured that it would be easy enough for him to stand near its carcass if the woman could do anything for Vale.

He saw that Tobia still stood holding the reins of Benevolence. Both looked into the distance of the rolling hills.

Shae left Vale to the approaching woman as he ambled unsteadily toward the bear. It too lay with its face in the dirt.

The creature was of astounding size, and the word "boulder" came to mind when he drew near it. Its coat was a thick matted rug of swirling strands of fur. He'd seen rugs similar in the homes of Hess's, but what truly captured his attention were the size of the monster's claws; behemoth razorblades that would have happily seen his chest opened had he given them the chance. He considered the back of the skull and torso expecting to see an exit wound but found none. Whether Vale's bullet had found its brain or its heart, the lead remained somewhere deep inside the hulking carcass of the creature.

Again he wondered... what did she want him to do with the bear? He looked back to the woman. She knelt beside Vale with her hand resting lightly on his chest, her chin lowered in meditation. Was that what she asked of him? To meditate beside the bear? He'd been forced to endure worse over the past days. Why not? He lowered himself to a seated position beside the beast and rested his arms upon the pleated knees of his checkered pants.

In his stillness, he was reminded of the emptiness of his stomach. It churned in protest over his brain's authority over its circumstance. It seemed to proclaim, in no uncertain terms, that he had proven himself unworthy of providing for its wants and would eat him alive until it was satiated.

He shifted his sight from the unremarkable rolling plains and back toward the valley and its stream. Near the water, the two baby cubs were seen stalking a deer that had since wandered into the enclave.

"I'm sorry," he said at last to the beast. "Such is just the way of the world."

He wished to be sitting beside Ginny in the bar, Henry drunkenly hammering the keys behind them. He wondered what Quinn was up to. He pictured the Irishman locking himself within the confines of the bar with a sign on the door reading *Closed for the Summer*. The thought raised a chuckle in him while a strong breeze rose to tussle his hair, the grass, and the fur of the dead bear beside him.

He looked back to see both the elder Indian and young interpreter approaching from the direction of Vale, still lying upon the earth. They stopped only a few feet before Shae when the woman proceeded to speak at length in a language that he could not understand. Despondence filled her tone.

"She says that your friend won't die this day, but the spirits call to him," said the boy.

The woman spoke again as another wind scattered her long, braided hair. The boy looked up at the woman in slight shock at what she said, before hesitantly repeating it back to Shae.

"She says... that we will take him with us. We will do what we can. But *you* must leave. That *you* must come to know the silence that you have given the bear."

"What? I just did. Didn't you see me?"

"Silence comes when one is alone," said the woman in awkward English, surprising Shae.

Why not just gut him then and there, he thought, wisely keeping it to himself. And yet, still, he hadn't much in the way of choices. She awaited his answer mournfully.

"I'm hungry," he said at last.

The boy relayed the words to the woman who then considered the statement for several moments before finally speaking at length, although gently, in return.

"She says that we will give you a pouch of pemmican," translated the boy. "It will last you two days. If you travel east for such time, you will encounter a great cloud of dust traveling south, a cattle train led by many white men. You are white too, so they will feed you."

The thought of traveling upon the landscape so unforgiving—and apparently filled with bears—filled Shae with dread. But, again, choice had abandoned him. At least Vale would be looked after. As stern as the natives appeared, he knew that they would do whatever they could for the sheriff if they could realistically do anything at all.

Shae awkwardly stood and bowed to the woman.

"Tell her that I am thankful, and that I will do my best to know the bear's silence."

Neither the boy nor the woman replied.

True to their word, Shae was given a large pouch of dried tallow, of which he immediately indulged in greedy mouthfuls to the disgust of the Indians. By their furrowed and worried brows, Shae sensed that they had never seen such gluttony. He didn't care. All that mattered in that moment were the thick handfuls of the paste that he scooped into his mouth to satiate the twisting of his stomach

When he was finally content, Shae packed what remained of the pemmican into the saddlebags of Benevolence. He looked back toward Vale, who the males were begrudgingly, albeit carefully, hoisting onto the back of one of their pack horses.

The boy that had translated for him earlier approached, apparently having noticed the worry in his gaze.

"He'll be okay. One way or another, he'll be as he's meant to be."

"Where will I find him? If I need to?"

"We're returning from pilgrimage, back to what your people call the Shoshone Indian Reservation. If your man doesn't return on his own, that's where he'll be."

Shae hoped that he wouldn't be obliged to ever do so, but deep down, he suspected that on some brighter day, out of a tug of conscience, that he very well might be forced to.

Before he knew it, and without a word further, the Shoshone departed and traveled west over the presiding hillside. They went in the direction of a home that had been assigned to them. They soon escaped his view.

"Goodbye, Sheriff," Shae said aloud. "I'd say it's been fun...but I won't."

Thirty-Seven

The flames of the fireplace crackled, leading Thadeus to liken the sound to a clamoring chorus of whispers.

The interior of the Courthouse's study had grown decidedly more refined over the past week, as the items that had been confiscated and deemed worthy filled the presider's chamber of contemplation. He looked up, high above the fireplace, to admire the imposing trophy of a grizzly's head jutting out from the plaster of the wall. Its mouth was wide, mid roar; its teeth glistening in the reflection of the flames beneath it.

Thadeus thought it a splendid sight.

The armchair on which he sat, plush with its refined leather, hugged his arms snuggly. It aided him in the tiresome nature of his deliberations. It was no easy feat being the presider, after all, with so many important decisions coming to him and him alone. He hadn't even a cabinet to confide or confer with.

It seemed that he could only rely on Luke, as of late. Mathius had all but abandoned him since the day of his appointment, promptly retreating to the haughty church in the hills thereafter. Thadeus couldn't help but assume Mathius to be envious of his ordainment.

And yet, on what grounds could the outsider reasonably rely upon in protest? Thadeus knew that he alone was the natural choice for the position, and it wasn't like he had influenced Luke in any way to name him Presider. It was the decision of God himself, speaking through his nephew, not blood promoting blood. No. Nepotism played no part in the ordeal and he resented even the implication of such by Mathius's abandonment of him.

Be gone then! Be gone to your steeple! It means little amongst the pews of the kingdom. God may have given you petty gifts to disperse, but the second of your promised three gave only breath to the voice that claimed ME King...Presider... was there truly a difference?

Thadeus came to recognize, then, that he had been talking aloud. It mattered not. No one could hear him in his private study.

He shifted his gaze from his vantage of the fire to appreciate the helm resting atop its pedestal across the room. Its metallic face glittered like the teeth of the bear above him. How he suddenly desired to feel its confines embracing his scalp. He nearly went to stand, to close the space that separated he and it, to don it and remind himself that its dimensions still encapsulated his skull with instinct. But as he contemplated the action, a shift in its glittering reflection startled him, furrowing his brow. It almost appeared as if something had shifted in the charcoal darkness behind him.

Thadeus wrapped his fingers about the fire poker's handle rising vertically beside him. He pulled it from its cast iron holster with a metallic shimmer.

"Trespassers plenty to inherit the abyss," he said, carefully annunciating each syllable.

Thadeus stood and turned to face that which had shifted the shadows of his helmet's reflection. The room before him appeared empty beyond the finery that decorated the space. His globe in one corner. The gramophone in another. A mounted telescope and a taxidermized fox standing atop an oriental rug in the room's center, all before the backdrop of a perimeter of bookshelves.

Everything in the room, including the books that lined the walls, were coated in the warm glow of the fireplace's tickling flames. But as the presider further scanned the room, nothing appeared amiss, that is, until he came to recognize an uncanny shadow occupying the room's far corner.

"Thy hearth betrays thee."

At Thaddeus's words, the shadow abandoned its stillness, stepping into the orange hue emitted by the fireplace.

It was Jebediah Lovely, a tearful quiver upon his face.

"What has gotten into you, child?" asked the presider. "I might have killed you."

Jebediah stuttered tearfully before eventually responding. "I didn't... I didn't want the others to know of your audience with me, Presider. You have fewer allies than you know."

Thadeus lifted the poker, aiming its heavy end toward the boy. "I don't take well to being snuck up upon, child. Speak quickly in your defense, lest I call the guard to lend both you and others example."

"I come bearing news of treachery. Debasers of your kingdom. I thought that you would prefer to know it over not."

A twinge of interest mingled with the presider's existing ire. Of course he would like to know of such a thing. He had already been suspecting more than a few of betrayal. It would serve him and his forthcoming decisions well to have external accounts of specific usurpers... usurping.

He lowered the poker, retaining a tight grip upon its handle.

"Proceed then, but do not dally nor tell a lie! God sees all things."

"Indeed, he does," replied Jebediah, stepping leisurely into the center of the room, his head cocked to the side as he approached the fox. The taxidermied animal stood with a sly demeanor all its own. "I know it to be true... I know other things too."

Jebediah drug his hand down the back of the fox's spine, raising his gaze to meet the presider's.

"Mathius makes for the crown."

Thadeus's left brow raised. He had become assured of the fact in himself. But to hear another say it so bluntly, so out in the open... The boy's words were as vindicating as they were intrinsically alarming.

"From what I've gathered from eavesdropping on conversations as slyly as I'd entered this very room, Mathius was unended by Luke's proclamation of your title. He had come to assume such a position to be his, and his alone... He intends to assemble an army of fanatics to make it happen."

Thadeus felt the corner of his lip tremble upon a coalescing rage. He had, at first, assumed the man to be a Charleton. He then, thought him to be the light. But now, he knew Mathius to be a snake, slithering in the tall grass.

"Why do you bring this knowledge before me?" he muttered.

Jebediah looked away, regaining a bashfully tearful appearance. "He murdered my parents."

Thadeus had nearly forgotten the context of the boy's recent history. What a terrible business that was. "Why didn't you say something sooner, Jebediah? Why have you allowed this deceiver to climb to such heights? Why hadn't you bemoaned him on his initial, daylight jaunt into town?! Why didn't you..."

He found himself again clutching the grip of the poker with blistering tightness, his breath heavy with wrath. He wished only to see blood and incur it. The boy brought news of usurpers in his holy lands but only after practicing a deceit all his own. He gripped the poker tighter, fully intending to raise it with malicious intent but caught himself when the orphan pitifully began to sob into his hands.

"I don't know!" he cried. "I was so.... I was just so afraid."

The boy continued his weeping, suddenly diffusing the presiders acute need for retribution. Not that it was fully abandoned. No. He stored it away in the atriums of his heart. In consolation, he took comfort in knowing that it would soon fall upon the man plotting in the hills.

"Be gone from me."

Jebediah turned to leave, still sobbing.

"And Jebediah," called Thadeus before the former could pull open the door and exit the room, "Find Luke... I wish to speak with him."

The boy rapidly departed.

Shortly after, the saint that had been assigned to guard the study's entrance, a stocky and boring man by the name of Nathaniel Gilway peaked into the room with fearful eyes.

"Sir! Where did he come from?! I've been standing right here, just beyond the door all night long!"

"It's quite alright, Nathaniel," spoke Thadeus in a calming tone. "Everything is fine. But I'm glad you're here. Come. Could you help me with something?"

"Of course!"

Nathaniel stepped into the room with eager fealty.

"It's this damn plank of wood, the one at the base of the globe there. Could you take a look at it, for me?"

The man promptly obliged and leaned down to investigate whatever it was that was wrong with the hardwood.

Thadeus raised the poker high above his head and fell it upon the man's skull.

A splash of arterial splatter painted the presider's face with the impact.

Nathaniel fell to the floor, emphatically convulsing, until a second impact of the poker brought stillness, forever, to his limbs.

Thadeus cast the weapon to the floor in a bassy clutter, breathing heavily over the body. The blood upon his face dripped into his mouth, and with its taste, he pondered what specific fate he wished to befall Mathius.

But as much as he wished to continue ruminating on the thought, an all-encompassing tingling suddenly enveloped him, distracting this thoughts. It felt like a thick cloud of mist had suddenly overtaken him. Then, without context, a single word came to the forefront of his mind.

Stop.

“Uncle,” spoke Luke from the threshold of the room, snapping Thadeus back to his senses. “You called for me.”

“Ah, yes... I did,” muttered Thadeus, at last wiping the blood from his face. Luke didn’t bat an eye at the terrible sight lying at the presider’s feet.

“It appears that there is foulness in the holy water. We must throw it into the graveyard’s well, for even the plants don’t deserve its rot.”

Luke nodded in understanding.

“Come and find me when it’s done.”

Thirty-Eight

For two days, Shae endured the silence of the plains with only Benevolence and his thoughts to keep him company. A looming concern persisted in his mind as to the exact location of the cattle drive, if there even was one.

For the duration of both days, cloud-cover evaded the horizon, baking Shae insistently under the Sun's heavy gaze. He might have been more inclined to curse the fact if not for his long, curly hair shading his ears, neck, and scalp from the relentlessness of the sun. Plus, the number of streams that he and Benevolence crossed provided more than enough opportunities for both he and the horse to dunk their heads.

Still, the days were mercilessly long while the nights proved haunting in their peering emptiness. He'd sit by each night's fire thinking on what the old woman had said, that he was to "endure the silence" that he and Vale had incurred upon the bear. There, surrounded in the engulfing shadows of the plains, he'd often consider the possibility that the phrase was nothing more than a polite euphemism for stranding him to die upon that endless sea.

During the long, hot days, he was thankful for the emptiness that surrounded him. It aided in the dulling of his mind, allowing him to dissolve into a hypnosis of travel that was closer to sleep than the medium of his dreams. Dreams that were, more often than not, filled with fouler things.

He missed the company of the sheriff, a sentiment that surprised him. But more than anything, he missed Ginny.

Over the course of the week that had passed, his response to the loss of the gunsmith had evolved from that of quiet despondence, to a murderous rage, and finally, to a sour bitterness that writhed upon the lining of his heart. Just like all grief, he knew, it would take time for it to embrace its final form: a silent wraith; ever present, but with less effect upon his emotions; forever fading, but never gone.

And then, on occasion, he'd think of Bastion and everything that was happening back there. He could only imagine what had transpired since he'd departed in such a huff. He'd always assumed that Bastion would remain nothing more than a dull town full of high talkers and slow walkers, but nothing more.

How he wished his cynical boredom had been proven right.

But since hearing what Vale had to say regarding his encounter upon the cart, and the awful memory of Jebediah's voice conjuring a wyrm of bloodlust within him, he had never been more convinced of anything in his life. Something terrible was happening back in Bastion, and the memory of Ginny's contorted corpse was evidence enough to enforce it. Regardless of its nature, he would return to Bastion to dissolve it of its cancer. He would do whatever it took to unclasp its tendrils from his home.

For Ginny, if nothing else.

The hours remained long and resoundingly empty as he and Benevolence tread forward over a landscape that, at times, seemed more similar to the moon than a landscape friendly to man. The wind was a constant commodity, eventually dissolving into a white noise of unending familiarity. Even the stinging upon his knuckles, ever protesting from their unending exposure to the sun, liquified into a blanket of passivity.

Everything became a slow crescendo of hillsides. Everything was as it was and would ever be. Where the things that he considered important truly as significant as he held them to be? Or were his loves, ambitions, worries, and even virtues only passing winds to trouble the grasses of his days? He hadn't an answer, and—instead of pursuing one—embraced a liquification of his attention. With each passing hour, he retreated into a nothingness of thought that more intuitively accompanied the nature of the plains.

In the dreams of his third night's rest, when sleep came to greet him like an old friend, he dreamt that he was in space, floating amongst the stars; lost and searching hopelessly for an earth that was nowhere to be found.

It felt somehow familiar. Nostalgia vague.

He awoke before dawn with a start, dew coating the exterior of his clothes. He was happier than he thought possible to be lying upon the endless yellow of the prairie.

He resumed his trek, not waiting for the sun to rise. A redemptive fog—drenched in the light-blue of the moon—lingered about his and the horse's slow amble forward. But before very long, the passage of time becoming a fickle thing, the slow-encroaching sunrise banished both the fog and the moon from his company. And when the sun itself rose high enough to kiss the burnt red of his cheeks, he began to earnestly believe—and increasingly accept—that his voyage upon the plains might be one as ill-fated as a transient mist in the light of the moon; one soon, too, to be banished by the unending sight of the Sun.

It was only when Shae accepted the soon-to-come silence of his death did he ascend a small knoll to find a fantastic cloud of dust inching south along the horizon—its mass painted gold by the ascending Sun.

At first, he couldn't comprehend what he was looking at. Did death manifest itself in such a way? But when he noticed the cloud being produced by a thousand cattle—and some two dozen men on horseback—he finally came to recognize what he saw.

A cattle drive.

And in that moment, while he processed his deliverance from the isolation that had become him, Shae silently bid adieu to his resignation. He would know it again, somewhere down the line. Best not to part with it on bad terms.

He let it go gently to dissolve in the sunlight.

Thirty-Nine

"Wouldn't you agree, Marshal?"

Colt had forgotten the men standing before him and only returned his presence to their company with the question.

"I'm sorry, gentleman. I... I must have drifted off. What was the question?"

Marshal Colt McLane didn't hear what the men had said due to what had caught his eye between the pomade heads of the cattle barons standing before him, each intent on drowning him in pretentious conversation. Through the smoke of their cigars, his sight had been resting upon a floating glass case hugging the wall behind them. It displayed a rusted set of manacles. Beneath it, in gold plated lettering, read the words "Early Southern Restraints."

"I was simply defending my position," said one of the barons adorned by a thick walrus mustache, "that the Romans were better off before Caesar crossed the Rubicon.

That he was a tyrant, intending only on seeing his ego reach heights that not even..."

"Oh, c'mon now Steve!" spoke another, his teeth balancing the end of a protruding cigar. "Would we even be talking about Rome right now if it hadn't transcended into an empire?"

"The United States is a Republic. Should we disband the constitution in favor of an empire? Of a kingdom? I'm sure Roosevelt wouldn't mind wearing the crown!"

"Apples and bacon, Steve! Apples and bacon. What do you think, Marshal? Was the Roman experiment better off under a republic, or as a *mighty* empire?"

Colt was impressed by the lengths to which the men appeared willing to go in order to impress him. They'd done their homework, or, more likely, one of their underlings had. There was no way in holy hell that this group of nepotistic wealth would be discussing such topics if he wasn't their prized guest for the evening. More likely whores, he assumed, by the looks of them.

Of course, he'd read all there was to read on the former topic. Cicero's speeches. *The Twelve Caesars*. Plutarch's famous retellings were his favorite with their vivid verbose color—a rarity for the time. And indeed, he had his opinions on the question presented to him. But among his ambitions for how he saw the remainder of the evening unfolding, discussing ancient Rome with the group before him mingled amongst his least desirable. Furthermore, he didn't want to encourage their bootlicking.

"It's complicated," he murmured.

"Of course it is," the walrus-mustache baron replied brightly, "So are sweetbreads. But the complexities of both are what make them so enjoyable. Indulge us, Marshal, what are your thoughts?"

Colt sighed, poorly disguising his exhaustion. It wasn't only the question that burdened him. In all honesty, he was physically spent. The train ride to Cheyenne from Memphis had been a long one, and he hadn't even had the pleasure of settling into his room before being swept off to the dinner that he now found himself at. Not that being wooed by the local money was all that surprising. It was almost customary for the congealing powers—of small towns especially—to promptly flatter any new U.S. Marshals to arrive in town. He knew their end, and rather than fight it, used such opportunities as a means of getting eyes on them. In all likelihood, he'd be discussing greed related crimes with them down the road.

But as for tonight, he just wished that he had been given a chance to settle in for a soak before indulging their courtship.

He looked about the men and saw that they were unlikely to relent with their pompous questions of Rome and its empire without, in the very least, a reply disguised as genuine.

"Your question is flawed, I'm afraid."

"How so?"

"By false dichotomy. The republic was better at some things, the empire others. They each served their purpose. And frankly, it's dangerous, if not outright lazy to label different governmental systems in such broad strokes. I find that such... stereotypes... can lead one down the path of misinformation." He wanted to look at the glass case behind them as he said it, but decided against it. Best to keep his sheep's clothing on for now. Regardless, he wondered if any of them had entertained a graduated African American before.

"Bold claims, Sir Marshal!" exclaimed the baron most intent on pressing the topic upon him. "Would you be willing to provide an example? I still struggle to see how the meager republic was more capable than the ferocity of the empire at its peak."

Colt pulled in a deep and tedious breath as if readying a cannon, when—to his relief—a tightly dressed servant in French buns entered the room, bowing before the men.

"Gentlemen. Dinner is served."

***

Colt emerged from the Cheyenne Club with a stomach lined with prime rib, a pocket filled with cigarettes—reportedly hand-rolled in New York City—and a mental list of likely suspects for when *he* would be asking the questions.

He was glad to be free of the place. As opulent as it was with its polished mahogany and attentive staff, the mansion's overall aura did little but convey a stench of perceived superiority. The fact was made all the more plain as he strolled languidly from its steps and through the modest city beyond. The smell of manure and burning coal dovetailed in the warm summer evening, and with it, he couldn't help but think of his home in Appalachia.

How long had it been since he'd been home?

The night was in its waning hours, and although the streets of the city were empty, distant and muted cacophonies of saloons in the unseen corners of that town played a backdrop to his slow walk back to the hotel. This town must really put 'em back, he thought, listening to the sounds of far-off jubilees.

Colt pulled his Stetson low over his eyes and retrieved a New York cigarette from his pocket. With a swift crack of a match, he gave it a light. The smell of sulfur turned to that of burning tobacco, and with it, his memory drifted to Memphis, his last place of appointment.

Colt had never been a smoker before Memphis, but the long hours of standing on street corners pretending to read newspapers outside the residence of Bobby Black—formerly known as Johnny Two Toes—had driven him to the habit to help pass the time. No one in the agency had volunteered for the dig, as protecting those in the witness protection agency was far from a glamourous assignment. But he drew the straw, or at least, that's what he'd been told.

But Colt was no fool. He knew how those decisions were made. And despite the benevolent words of those atop the marshal service, he understood the realities and bigotry of the country in which he lived.

From somewhere not far off, the slow grinding of steel upon steel announced a slowly braking train approaching the station. He wondered what one might think of its ominous, high pitched hysterics without the context of knowing what a train was; what it did, and how it worked.

Part of him wondered if the railway city of Cheyenne was a racket similar to his placement in Memphis. After all, the last marshal assigned to the state was shot dead in the street—not far from where he walked now, in fact. But even if it was, he was just happy to be far and away from Tennessee.

He turned a final corner and approached the Plains Hotel, its vertical corner-sign engulfed in the warm glow of electric globe lamps. But before he could reach its lobby, he passed the tall glass windows of a shuttered tailor, noticing a verbose sign plastered upon its glass. With it, the distant parties suddenly made sense. It's bold headline proclaimed in bright-red font: *The Second Annual Cheyenne Frontier Days!!!* Beneath it, a cowboy was drawn hanging onto the reins of a bucking horse. Below that—in smaller text still—read the words: *Come one, come all for two whole days of Saddle Bronc Riding, Steer Roping, Wild Horse Racing, Frontier Pageantry, and More! August 12th and 13th Only.*

Colt was walking through the final hours of the 11th. No wonder the town was drowning their wells. He knew enough about cowboys to know that if you gave 'em a holiday, they'd make the most of it. That was for sure.

With no distractions further, Colt ascended the stairs of the Plains Hotel. He found his floor, the third, and collapsed upon the room's sharply made bed with his clothes still on.

He didn't stir again until the late of morning when the sound of gunshots outside his window startled him awake.

Colt stumbled near the window, drawing his revolver. He leaned against the plaster flanking the window and used the barrel of the weapon to pull back the sheer white drapes from the glass. Through the opening that it created, Colt looked out to see that a large crowd of onlookers watched as a mock-shootout took place in the street down below. In his fatigued stupor, he had all but forgotten the revelries that he'd seen advertised the night before.

White smoke erupted from the aimed pistols of the gunfighters as two more shots rang out—clearly blanks. One of the duelers reached for and grasped his chest as his weapon tumbled to the floor.

When Colt descended to the street himself, throngs of cowboys and tourists alike walked about in bustling crowds. Barkers called to all from the entrances of pop-up shops flanking the road while scattered clouds dappled the otherwise blue sky making for a serene background to the Union Pacific Depot. The impressive sand-stone of the train station was the first to greet him when he arrived in Cheyenne, the day before.

As he stood and admired the building's reaching belfry, he noticed something in the corner of his eye. High atop an alleyway dissecting a meat market and The Normandie Hotel, a series of cables carried the carcasses of pig and cattle, high upon the breeze. The high-pitched whirring of a train's whistle suddenly made itself known and a curling plume of smoke projected itself above its crawling departure from the station. Colt thought the bustling crowds, lively sounds, and dovetailing smells to each be fine ambassadors to a town celebrating the vivaciousness of its soul.

Colt made his way through the busy streets in search of the sheriff's office. It was high time that he made himself known there, as Cheyenne apparently harbored enemies beyond that of cattle barons. That much was made clear by the still-drying pool of his predecessor's blood. None were charged in the murder, and it was Colt's lingering suspicion that the sheriff wasn't all that eager to help.

The whole thing just reeked of dirty money, and he—at the very least—wanted the sheriff to know that he was onto them.

He'd written the building's address on the back of a business card that he'd acquired from his favorite barber back in Memphis. He pulled it from his pant pocket and examined its face, its finely etched paper and lifted lettering objectively superfluous for that of a barber. On its front it read: *Jackson Wise: Barber; Comedian; Trumpet Extraordinaire.*

He flipped it to its backside to reveal the address that he'd scribbled onto it only two days prior: *300 Carey*

Street. In parentheses, he'd written, *Northwest of rail station*.

Such was the only guidance that he was given by the delegating captain. Again, he could only assume that the United States Marshal service had more intelligence regarding the exact location of Cheyenne's Sheriff's Office, and that the lack of transparency was yet another slight handed to one of the only African American's willing to take up the mantle of the U.S. Marshal service.

Colt walked in a direction he was fairly confident to be northwest. It was difficult to tell with the midday sun being so directly overhead. But sure enough, he soon approached Carey Street, turned right, and came upon a square brick building with a black sign atop its doors reading *Sheriff's Office.*

Multiple horses were hitched outside the building while a pair of deputies leaned against its brick, smoking cigarettes. One of the men noticed Colt approaching and raised the brim of his hat with his thumb.

"Whatchu lookin for, blackie?" he asked with a forked tongue.

Colt reached into the interior pocket of the duster to retrieve his badge, taking care to keep the gold star pressed tightly to his palm so that only its leather backing could be seen when he extended it outward in offering.

"Howdy sir. I was hoping you might help me out by taking a look at this."

The deputy scoffed as he stepped toward Colt, clearly annoyed at being forced to recess his leisure.

"You people are always needin somethin. Goooood grief. What do we got here?"

The deputy lifted the badge from Colt's open palm, flipping it about to find the gold star of the U.S. Marshal Service gleaning back at him. His jaw dropped as his eyes lifted to meet Colt's grin.

"Marshal. I... I'm awful sorry about all..."

The knuckles of Colt's right fist cracked the deputy's nose.

"Ahhhh!!" screamed the man, raising his hands to cover the blood quickly pouring from his nostrils. "Motha fuckin Nigg..."

Colt's left fist cracked the deputy's jaw, crumpling him to the dirt. The deputy that the man had been chatting with made to pull his pistol from his side when he froze at seeing Colt's right hand already holding his own, aiming it squarely at his face.

"Now, don't do nothin silly, boy. You're man'll be alright. Just needs to learn some manners, that's all." Colt holstered his gun to walk past the deputy still standing stupidly beside the building's entrance.

"Splash some water on him."

The lobby that received Colt was a meager room filled with wooden benches, a metal door leading into the building's interior, and an imposing countertop. The counter held aloft several heavy, vertical bars that rose to meet the ceiling, intermittently obstructing the view of a blonde clerk sitting lazily behind the counter, filing her nails with a long black file.

The woman hardly looked up when Colt approached. He dropped his badge heavily upon its wood in the hopes of reducing any further bigotry.

"U.S. Marshal Colt McLane. I'm here to see the sheriff."

The woman continued her attention upon her nails. "Sheriff's in a meeting right now, darlin," she spoke in a thick southern drawl. "You can take a seat if you'd like."

Colt turned about to examine the crudeness of the benches hugging the lobby's walls.

"Nope," he replied, shifting back to the receptionist.

"You can stand then, I s'pose"

"Or you can let me in now so I don't have to tell the sheriff that his receptionist hindered the duties of a federal officer. Now, today's already been a long week, darlin, and I'm awful sorry for being rude, but I'd appreciate it if you'd let me through that door right there so I can do my job."

The woman sat in silence for several more seconds before eventually rising with a sigh to open the metal door leading further into the building.

There was no difficulty in finding the office where the sheriff was having his meeting, for as Colt strode through the wood paneled hallways, the sounds of an impassioned argument happening within a particular room made his destination obvious. From the few emphatic words that bled through the door, it sounded like someone was imploring the sheriff for help while the latter refused.

Colt twisted the door's handle and stepped inside, sharply halting the argument as each of the three men within looked up to see who had interrupted their dispute.

Narrow slits of windows, like those of a basement, lined the upper boundary of the wall, flooding the room in muted daylight. A man clearly identifiable as the sheriff stood behind a desk, his hands pressed firmly atop its wood. In the corner behind him stood a burly bearded fellow with his arms crossed tightly across his chest. Finally, a man coated in a thick layer of dirt stood nearest Colt. His hair was long, curly, and brown, its strands congealed into a filthy matte. He wore checkered, pleated pants beneath a long-sleeved dusty t-shirt of fine fabric.

"And who the hell are you!?" shouted the sheriff, his nostrils flaring.

Colt flashed a smile.

"Name's Colt McLane... U.S. Marshal."

Forty

His uncle was beyond saving, that much was clear.

Luke saw it to be obvious even before Thadeus had thrust the sharp of the poker into Nathaniel's skull. But when he witnessed the act, Luke knew that he had to at least *try* to get through to the great Hess of Hess's.

For the sake of those around him, if nothing else.

He had known Thadeus all his life and had generally looked up to the man. So to see him descend to such depths, to such barbarism, conjured in Luke a sorrow to mix with his otherwise drifting dejection.

Ever since he'd so helplessly watched his own body rise to life without him, he felt unable to comprehend much of anything. The sight and slow recognition of his circumstances hollowed him so thoroughly that he thereafter only meandered through the streets for the days that then followed. At times, his body—whatever that was—felt as if its components were relatively normal and precisely in place, complete with transient bouts of itchiness, warmth, and even pain. But just when he would come to appreciate the warmth of the sunlight or the kiss of the breeze upon his transparent limbs, the sensations would abruptly become replaced by vacuous feelings of nothingness, or worse, amorphous floating pressures upon his phantom limbs.

In his aimless meanderings, he found that a select few appeared capable of perceiving him—to a certain degree, at least. Most others, meanwhile, remained completely unaware of his presence. Quinn was among the most capable, it appeared, while his mother too responded to his company at times. When he would walk solemnly beside her as she attended to the various tasks assigned to the "Mother of Bread", she would occasionally pause and turn in his direction to furrow her brow with searching eyes.

How he wished he could grasp her fingers and tell her that all would be okay. How he wished that he could believe the words himself.

How terrible it was to watch Bastion, his one and only home, descend so surely toward the abyss. If nothing else, he took solace in knowing that he did what he could to push Quinn and the others in an admirable direction, although he admittedly doubted that a minor rebellion of schoolteachers, store clerks, stable masters, and drunkards could do much in the face of such villainy.

He felt a similar pessimism as he watched his uncle lower the fire poker upon the head of Nathaniel. And yet, Luke felt obligated, in some vague revolt against his circumstance, to make an attempt at swaying his uncle's further actions, even if he knew such a pursuit to likely be folly.

He stepped into Thadeus's space, just as he had done with the others, and screamed as loudly as he could. But as he stepped back, his uncle appeared largely oblivious to his emphatic objections. Only a glassy, flat stare looked off into a wayward corner.

"Uncle..."

Luke turned to see what was once his body standing attentively in the doorway.

"You called for me."

It was the first time that he'd run into his old body since he'd been ejected from it so unceremoniously days before.

"It appears that there is foulness in the holy water," said his uncle. "We must throw it into the graveyard's well, for even the plants don't deserve its rot."

His former eyes turned with the rest of his body and left the room. For whatever reason, maybe only a morbid curiosity, Luke felt inclined to follow. What did Thadeus mean by such a command?

But before he crossed the room to follow his former body out the door, he turned to see his uncle looking down upon the body that he had so ruthlessly dispatched. Luke paused, searching for even a glimmer of humanity in his uncle's eyes, but instead witnessed only the same grey dullness that he'd perceived in that which used to be his.

"Goodbye uncle."

Luke expected to never see Thadeus Hess again, at least not how he knew him to be.

Luke stepped out into the night in pursuit of his former body. The legs that carried him forward did so without feeling. He looked out upon the avenue and caught a glimpse of his flesh ascending the path into the hills. Numbly, he followed his autonomous former self all the way to the church where it pulled open its cherry doors and stepped inside. Luke, instead, chose to traverse the building's exterior walls, an action that he'd commonly taken throughout his grim wanderings. It was one of the few advantages of being ethereal, after all.

Inside, a dozen votive candles flickered along the banisters and ledges illuminating in soft-orange the interior of the space and its occupants.

Luke looked on as his former body turned into a row of pews to sit beside Mathius. There, the two sat in quiet observation of the murmuring sermon being given by Reverend Gilroy upon the rise.

The reverend stood feebly behind the wooden pulpit, his hands pressed firmly upon its platform. Bloody, empty sockets peered out from where his eyes had once resided while two vertical columns of dried blood descended below them. His mouth muttered an unceasing jumble of words at a restrictively quiet volume, each syllable simultaneously bleeding into the next, the spaces between the words abandoned. Luke focused on the reverend's speech in the hopes of deciphering its intention but found the words either too tightly compressed to be unraveled or of a different language altogether. Possibly both.

Meanwhile, in the second to last row of the opposite side of the aisle sat Jebediah Lovely in an equally still and observant manner. At the sight, the curiosity that Luke had given Jebediah's presence in his uncle's study was promoted to that of bewilderment.

How did Jebediah Lovely fit into all this?

Luke's former body leaned its head gently toward Mathius to utter something into his ear. Whatever it was, it prompted Mathius to stand and make his way up the corridor and outside.

Luke followed. The reverend's mumbling words were making him uneasy.

Mathius circled around the building and into the graveyard behind the church, its epitaphs nestled under the looming watch of the surrounding cliff faces. Overhead, tall cottonwoods and aspens swayed in the breeze of the late evening.

Luke followed close behind as Mathius walked directly toward the well rising from the overgrown clearing in the graveyard's center.

Luke thought the well nearly beckoning in the heaving moonlight, as if promising sure transport to the land exclusively inhabited by those lying in the graves nearby.

Luke expected Mathius to stop when he reached the well's wall. To maybe lean over and gaze into its depths or perform some esoteric ritual near it. But when Mathius met the ledge of the well, he didn't stop at all. Instead, he unceremoniously bent over, and slid into its swallowing darkness headfirst. A splash in the deep soon followed.

Had he lungs, Luke might have gasped.

But before he could make an attempt at processing what he had just witnessed, the entirety of his being—whatever that was—suddenly began to tingle with an electricity set apart from his other newfound sensations. This one was distinct, unusual, and hitting all at once. It was as if a thousand cactus needles suddenly pressed upon his skin without breaking its barrier; only making themselves unambiguously known with a sharp threat to go deeper, if they so wished.

Luke rotated slowly about to find Jebediah Lovely standing a short distance behind him in the moonlight.

The boy's head cocked far to one side.

Forty-One

"I don't give a hog's bottom who you are and even less who you think you are. Where I come from, which ain't too far from here, barging inta meetins unannounced is jus' bad manners," proclaimed the sheriff.

"Well God forbid I hurt yer goddamn delicate feelings, Sheriff," mocked Colt, an insultingly weepy demeanor on his face. "Where might I find ya a tissue?" He looked about the room searching for a lavendered handkerchief to provide the man.

"You're the marshal!?" spat the dirt-coated man. An air of optimism shone upon his face as he extended an open palm toward Colt. "My name is Shae Mackenzie. I've been looking for you."

"Well ain't this fuckin cute," snarled the sheriff still standing imposingly behind the desk. "Does this mean that you will leave me be, Mr. Mackenzie?"

"Gladly," spoke Shae, still shaking Colt's hand. "Marshal, I would appreciate a word with you in friendly company, that's to say, away from here."

Colt scrupulously examined the man in an attempt at discerning if he were eccentric or not. He was certainly a fascinating looking character, his mustache drooping over the edges of his mouth pitifully. His eyes suggested a recent, exhaustive journey, as did the stench that virulently radiated from him. But more than anything, he displayed all the features of a man desperate, a far cry from the chaotic proclivities of one seeking only an audience for ravings.

Colt shifted his attention back to the sheriff. "I wanted to introduce myself to you, Sheriff. I'm Marshal Brett Scott's replacement. Shame what happened to him on your watch, and all. But given that my primary duty is to the citizens of this state, I reckon I'll give Mr... Mackenzie, was it?"

Shae nodded in affirmation.

"...Mr. Mackenzie his requested audience, seeing that you won't. Now if you need me, I'll be staying at the Plains. Oh, and a bit of advice, Sheriff, teach yer men some God damned manners, would ya?"

Colt backed out of the room before giving the sheriff or his lacky a chance to retort, quickly retracing his steps out of the building. When he stepped back onto the patio, he retrieved another New York cigarette from his pocket, lighting it with a match that he drug across the wooden beam beside him. It lit with a crack.

The deputies that had antagonized his initial approach were nowhere to be seen, although Mr. Mackenzie met him at his side as he shook out the match.

"Have you heard of a town called Bastion, Mashal?"

He hadn't.

"Figured not. Anyway, I've come an awful long way to tell you about it," spoke the man picking dirt from his eyes. "But being that you were nowhere to be found when I arrived in Cheyenne two days ago, I was left to sing my piece to that goddamn mute back inside. My God, I've never met a thicker imbecile in my life."

"You must not travel much," said Colt, stepping from the building in a direction that just then seemed to suit him. He was eager to lay eyes on more of the town and figured there was nothing wrong with doing so in such a manner. He'd end up where he'd ent up, he figured.

"No, sir. I don't. Regardless, I'm hoping you're going to be more receptive to what I have to say than he was. I've no reason to pull your leg all the way up to Bastion without a good reason, after all. Hell, I wish I wasn't here in the first place. I wish I was back home, sitting on my bar stools drinking whiskey. But it ain't, and I need you to listen to what I have to tell you."

They turned down a dusty road flanked by cowhands eyeing them suspiciously. Likely never seen a colored lawman before, thought Colt.

"Now, that thick bastard was convinced that I was full of it. Maybe he just didn't want to do nothin about it. Too lazy, more likely. But I'm tell you now, Marshal, I wouldn't be here if a strong wind hadn't pushed me all this way."

Colt halted his march before a wide, open field. A dozen bales of hay rested intermittently across its yawning acres.

"You look like you just got off a cattle push, son. I can understand his hesitation, at least."

"I'm more of a saloon man. I'd still be there now if it weren't for..."

"I'll be honest with ya, you talk more than I prefer. Let's just hear what you have to say before the coyotes join in with ya."

And so, Shae did just that. As the pair resumed their stroll through the dusty streets coated in the warm aromas of burnt coal and livestock, Shae shared the story of how Mathius had ridden into town on an otherwise unassuming Sunday to upend the normalcy of his life. He told of the mayor's speech and it's not-so vague allusions to secession. He retold, with halting difficulty, the arrival of

Vale with Ginny's corpse in tow. And finally, he shared the whispers of Jebediah and the resulting visions of red that had taken him.

"Now, this all might sound odd to you Marshal. Hell, it does to me too. But if my instincts serve me, and they usually do, something awful is happening up in Bastion. At the very least, blood has been spilled there, the blood of an innocent woman and the town's young deputy..."

"At the hand of this Sheriff Kingsbury, by the sound of it."

"Vale didn't do it." snapped Shae. "As much as I'd love to accept an answer so simple, he didn't do it. I saw it in his eyes. And believe you me, Marshal, you serve enough drinks and you learn to know an awful lot from someone's eyes. I'm telling you here and now, he was being influenced by the very same that had driven me from Bastion in his pursuit. And if nobody does nothing about it..."

"I'm not a priest, son," replied Colt.

"But you are the marshal, which leads me to the worst-case scenario. The one that should concern you the most, Mr. Representative of the United Goddamn States of America..."

"Watch your mouth, son."

"...I shared with you the mayor's speech, where he spoke of 'independence from men distant and unworthy to dictate their lives' and other horse shit. He means to separate the town from the authority of this country, Marshal, and it's your GODDAMN job to investigate potential cases of insurrection. Is it not?!"

Shae concluded his defense in a holler, prompting Colt to stop his saunter to face the man in earnest. He was beginning to wish that the man was in fact only a mad man wishing to ramble to a willing ear. He had only just arrived in the city. Was he to leave it so soon?

"It is," he muttered, in surrender. "But let's say, for the sake of argument, that you and I travel all the way up to your little town and find that things are just fine, that in fact you've wasted weeks of my time. What then?"

"If such is the case, Marshal, my happiness at such a sight would oblige me to lend my services to you, as your deputy, for as long as you wish."

Colt amused himself envisioning the lanky, dirt encased man as his deputy.

"But I follow your question with one of my own," continued Shae, "what shall *you* do, if we indeed travel all the way up to Bastion and find ourselves face to face with the devil? What then?"

"I s'pose I'd shoot him."

Shae laughed, somewhat relieving the marshal. "You lawman are all the same, aren't you? Never seen a bug you can't squash. You remind me of Vale."

"That sheriff you mentioned? Hopefully after the red had passed him."

Shae spat at the dirt.

"I'm afraid that's yet to be seen, Marshal, but I sure do hope so."

Forty-Two

"I must say, Luke, you are a pleasant surprise."

Jebediah took a step to his left, and then another, both in the opposite direction from which his head leaned. He walked a wide circle around Luke, stepping carefully amongst the epitaphs and marble of the old graveyard. It was older than the church itself, many of the town's first residents buried within it.

A slowly intensifying breeze rustled the leaves of the foliage surrounding them.

"Some say," he continued in his boyish tongue, "that when a soul refuses to depart this world, to accept that they have been heralded elsewhere, it is because they have business that has been left unattended. And I must admit, I overlooked your zeal. I overlooked your gumption. I took you as a pawn when you were a rook. And yet, all is the same, as it ever was, only more... colorful." He flashed a toothy grin. "In fact, I owe you a great deal of thanks. My fun here would have been but a grey wind had you not come along."

Luke spun about—as if on a top—tracking Jebediah's encirclement of him. It drew tighter and closer with each revolution.

Jebediah continued. "But I see it now. You were instrumental all along. You were the piece that carried the work from triviality into that of triumph! You are the brush I didn't even know I held, bristles dancing with the elegance of the gazelle! You astound me, young one, and I owe you a debt."

"Mathius fell into the well." said Luke, fear dovetailing with his perplexity. "Why would he do that?"

"Oh, him?" laughed the boy, "Mathius was only doing what the presider had instructed him to do. I think he called it, 'tossing the holy water down the well."

Luke thought back to what Thadeus had said to his former body, following his hacking of Nathaniel.

"Your uncle certainly has a way with words, doesn't he? But as an equally entertaining sideshow, I'm quite curious to see how such a fate will look on him, given the terms of their contract and all. But regardless," Jebediah gestured to the well, "that old zealot was only a tool... another paintbrush, you could say. Just like you.

"I don't understand."

The boy briefly halted his circumnavigation to roll his eyes. "Oh c'mon Lucius, as your mother used to call you. Sure you do! Mathius was just a way to get those churchgoers all riled up; just a shadow that I beckoned to Bastion to help with the matter. You see, all you have to do is give the crowd a bell, raise a deputy from the dead..." he winked, "drape it in the wrappings of a prophet and BAM! They get all... crazy... It's quite fun to watch, if I'm being honest."

Jebediah resumed his circular march.

"Mathius. Jebediah. The blacksmith. Your uncle. All brushes of unique texture. The bartender's sure a fun one. He should be arriving any day now, delivering me a *fine* prize."

The distance between them was half what it was initially, only mere yards now separating Luke from the still circling Jebediah.

"Can you not see it? This is art in its most pure and splendid form, the muse giving herself to us in the nude. I'm afraid, after all these eons, that it's the only thing left that brings me any joy..." He gestured to the air overhead. "Can you smell it?"

Luke inhaled deeply. It was a clean smell. Wet and earthy. The unmistakable scent of an approaching storm to conjure in Luke a thousand half-memories.

"It's going to rain tomorrow. A storm whose wind shall be the canvas to receive your enlightened paint. And yet, look at you. You don't even know it. What a dance! What a ballet! What shall you have, young champion? What shall be your worthy prize? What does your heart desire?"

"Are you the devil?" asked Luke, suddenly.

Jebediah stopped in his tracks. He raised his stare from the dirt to meet Luke's gaze. A wind troubled the leaves overhead while two minuscule dots of white light, like those of a star's distant shimmer, shone brightly from the depths of Jebediah's eyes.

"Is that you're wish? Is such an answer your lonesome desire?"

"No," replied Luke quickly. "I don't think I'd like it much to consort with a fallen angel."

The rustling of the cottonwoods went mute. As did the chirping of the crickets and all other contributors to the white noise of the enclave.

"Bold words for fodder."

"Maybe," said Luke, suddenly brave. "But I would rather drift forever as a wraith, unseen and alone, than parley with you."

"Funny. Jebediah said something similar after inviting me here, into his home; into your town. This bushel of brushes. You see, Luke, I could relieve you from your limbo. Give breath to lungs anew. I could give your mother riches she wouldn't believe. Hell, I could make you the single Hess worthy of your ancestor's helm."

The boy's final statement caught Luke's attention. He was still a Hess, after all. But the first sentence continued to supersede the last in the triage of his mind.

"What happened to Lovely?"

"I thought we don't consort with fallen angels?"

"He was a friend of mine and you masquerade in his skin. The least you could do is share with me what became of him."

"The least I could do..." the boy began, stopping himself short. The skin of Luke's former peer then smiled, raising its palms upward in capitulation. "Oh, what the hell. It's a fine story, after all.

Without warning, Jebediah raised his palm to Luke's face, using his fingers to lower the former deputy's fearful and translucent eyelids to occlusion.

All was again darkness for Luke, and for a fleeting moment, he recalled with dreadful acuity the blankness that followed the bullet that found him.

But then, at first grainy and off-color, his sight returned. He was standing in the carefully manicured front yard of the Lovely home in the bright light of a sunny day. A diverse and happy pair of garden beds lay beside the brick walkway leading to the house's front door. Luke heard the sound of a latch becoming undone and turned to see Simon, the mailman, stepping through the gate carrying a burlap wrapped package strewn tightly with string.

But before he could rest the package against the doorstep, the door cracked open and a pair of eager eyes, Jebediah's—still distinctively full of joy—met Simon's approach.

"It actually came!" he called. "It actually came!!"

Simon laughed and ruffled the boy's hair as he gave him the parcel.

"Whatcha order, Jebbie? New toy er sump'n?"

"Uhh, yea!" he replied. "Actually, it's a gift for my parents. For their anniversary! So don't tell them about it, okay?"

Simon smiled, tipping his hat. "Whadya's doin for the fourth tomorrow, Jebby?

"Ummm, I dunno," said Jebediah in innocent impatience. "But I gotta go. Bye, Simon!"

Jebediah closed the door behind him with a slam. As Simon returned to his cart, Luke approached the Lovely home to traverse its walls and look inside.

He followed the boy to his room where Jebediah sharply shut the door to hurriedly—albeit carefully—unwrap the package. It was a book. A large, elegantly printed book coated in emerald trim dancing along its borders. Its title, *Tome of Instruction*, was printed upon the leather of its cover in raised crimson lettering.

Jebediah cracked the volume's spine and flipped to a random page, landing on what appeared to be something akin to a thickly detailed instruction manual. At the top of the page that he'd landed on, the words "Summoning Further Entities" pronounced itself in bold.

"Cooooooool," said Jebediah.

The sound of the home's front door opening led Jebediah to slam the book shut and scan the room for a place to hide the tome.

"Jebbie!" called his mother. "Are ya home, Lovely?"

Something drew Luke's attention out the boy's window. He looked out and saw a porchlight lighting the face of the Lovely home in the dead of night; the very home in which he still stood in seemingly perfect daylight.

At Luke's feet, Jebediah darted about. He stashed the book under his mattress, collected himself, and stepped into the living room to greet his mother.

Luke walked outside, through the wall, and into the nighttime garden that separated the day home from its nocturnal iteration. The same brick walkway that had led him to the door many times in his memory, complete with blooming flanks of roses, daffodils, cosmos, and junipers.

He looked back to see Susan and Jebediah pleasantly conversing in the home's still sun-drenched living room. But when he shifted his gaze toward the home at night, each of the window's drapes were pulled shut while a flickering orange light danced dimly behind the cloth obscuring Jebediah's bedroom window.

Luke stepped toward the night-time home and traversed the same walls that had led him to Luke's bedroom in daylight. Within, he found the desk's chair propped against the doorknob while the boy sat cross legged on the floor, carefully reading from the open tome. On the floor surrounding him lay the book, a knife, a small clump of hair, and the flickering flame of a candle. Jebediah was quietly muttering words that Luke couldn't understand. But when he leaned in close to hear them more clearly, the boy abruptly stopped his utterances, grasped the bundle of hair, and placed it over the flames of the candle. When the hair was fully inhaled by the flames, filling the room with a sickly scent, Jebediah grasped the knife and drug its sharpness across his open palm. The boy grimaced in pain as he then held his hand over the candle's fire, allowing his dripping blood to fall upon its dance.

"What're you doing, Jeb?" muttered Luke, no sound coming from his lips.

The first drop of blood that landed upon the flame turned its color from orange to a radiant ebony marbled with veins of white. Upon the second drop, the candle was extinguished and all was dark in the room.

In the resulting silhouette of shadows, Luke saw Jebediah's arm remain outstretched although no further movement was seen from the boy for several silent seconds. Still facing away, the boy's head then cocked itself lazily to the side as a rasping breath emitted from somewhere inexact in the room.

Jebediah lowered his previously outstretched hand and grasped the knife from the floor, dragging its serrated end upon the wooden planks as he did. He stood, turned, and walked slowly across the room to the door. With his free hand Jebediah removed the propped-up chair that had held it shut. He went to step through the doorway, to enter the darkness of the slumbering home, but before doing so turned to gaze directly at Luke.

"Do you want to see the rest? Do you want to see what I did to them? Do you want to see how they begged for life while choking on their blood?"

"No... I've seen enough."

"You haven't seen anything. Just wait... Just wait until you see what you've painted."

Luke suddenly found himself standing—as much as his ethereal self could "stand"—in the long parallel rows of the orchard in the bright light of day.

He felt a strong yearning for his mother and went off to find her.

Forty-Three

Just before Sunday's dawn, Shae Mackenzie and Marshal Colt McLane departed Cheyenne, heading north.

Colt acquisitioned a fine Missouri Fox Trotter for Shae to ride, as the saloon keeper's steed had apparently gone lame on its arrival into Cheyenne.

"He wasn't meant for what we put him through," lamented Shae, recounting the sad tale. "I think... when he finally saw the finish line, something in him knew that he'd done his job. That he could finally rest. That poor horse."

They hit the trail before dawn and were soon beyond the northern borders of the city.

Shae wasn't all too eager to be back on the trail but was nonetheless quick to appreciate the advantage of riding a horse actually bred and tacked with such a journey in mind. Not to mention, his clothing was much better suited this time around.

"I won't be seen riding alongside a man so decorated by disgrace," Colt had said the day before they left. "Here's twenty dollars. Go and buy yourself something that won't embarrass me."

Shae was understandably shocked by the gesture and did what he could to refuse but was curtly denied by the marshal.

"This isn't a gesture of philanthropy, Mackenzie. You're appearance is repulsive. Go and get yourself right for the love of God."

And so he did. Shae found a clothier along the main artery of the town where he purchased himself a decent pair of denim trousers, two thick flannel shirts, a pair of good riding boots, a checkered bandana, and a gambler hat wide enough to engulf the entirety of his thick, curly hair. After that, he spent his final few dollars on a room at the Plains.

"Well if you ain't ready for the ball," laughed Colt when they met in the street the following morning. "Let's go."

As the smell of smoke and fertilizer dissipated behind them, Shae recognized that it wouldn't be long for the dirt, sunburns, and tenderness of his thighs to return. But just as he caught himself slipping into an aching somberness at the prospect of another long ride, Colt, riding ahead of him, emitted a crisp whistling melody that took Shae by surprise. It was a sound that wasn't altogether novel in itself, nor was the song obscure—*After the Ball* by Charles Harris. What was pleasantly jarring was how naturally the melody complimented the endlessness of the brightening sky beside them.

It was like a small splash of water accompanying cold whiskey in the glass. The sound knew the sunrise well, he thought. And before very long at all, his morosity dissipated and the remainder of their travels that day were pleasant and plain.

***

"You must meet all sorts of ignorance, being a black lawman and all," said Shae in the soft glow of the fire.

Colt nodded with a gruff laugh.

"You wouldn't believe the hate that walks free in this world."

"I mean, from how I understand it, you're out here representing the interests of a country that was forced to have a long and bloody war just to decide if it would allow people like yourself, good people, an opportunity to live free lives, to be treated with humanity. How do you reconcile that? If I were you, I'd want nothing to do with this damned place."

Colt looked silently to his hands, their knuckles suddenly grasping one another.

"Sorry... Not my place."

"No," responded Colt quickly, "I was just thinking about my mamma... I asked her the same questions when I was little. You know what she said to me? She said, 'There'll always be dragons in this world, son, and that's why God sends us knights... to slay em.'"

The days that followed were long, dry, and largely unremarkable. Colt proved to be a steady and pleasant companion on the trail, as both his frequent whistling and penchant for intelligent dialectics agreed with Shae; a welcome contrast to that of the self-assuredness of Vale Kingsbury. Regardless, the days dragged on with an aching dullness that reiterated Shae's longing for his home with each passing hour.

On the twelfth day they approached the spanning granite of Butcher's Pass. Considering everything that stood north of its obscuring rise, the sight of it took on a decidedly more ominous appearance than it did the last time he'd seen it.

They traversed the rock in the lateness of the afternoon. It was, in all practicality, the final major landmark between the dull tranquility of their travels and whatever it was that waited for them in Bastion.

Through the winding crag of the rock, they rode with Colt in front and Shae behind. As they did, it struck Shae just how quiet it became inside the crevasse when no wind was blowing—a rare occasion. It was a different quiet than the muteness of the plains where the sound of one's voice drifts away forever into nothing. This was an absorbing quiet; one that soaked up all sounds in craggy permanence. Somewhere within its rock existed his confrontation with Vale. He hoped the man was okay, wherever the Shoshone had taken him.

Hell, knowing the stubbornness of the man, Shae half expected him to be in Bastion already when they got there, having beaten them there by a week.

As dusk approached, the duo entered the final leg of their journey. A few hours of wordless travel ensued, concluding when Colt led them atop a high knoll, insisting that they make camp in the now complete darkness of the evening.

"We're no more than fifteen miles from town," said Shae. "Can't we just push through?"

"We arrive in the morning. Rested, with clear heads and vigilant eyes."

And that was that.

They hobbled the horses, removed their socks, and finished their arrangements for bed.

Shae lay on his bedroll, staring at the wide, star speckled sky while Colt sat nearby in the flickering light of the lantern. The marshal intermittently cussed while attending to the straps of his tack when, suddenly, soft footsteps approached the camp from somewhere in the unseen darkness surrounding them.

Shae arrested his breath to listen, simultaneously turning to see Colt already standing—pistol in hand—aiming in the direction of the now halted footsteps.

"This is the voice of U.S. Marshal Colt McLane," he uttered, his voice disappearing into the darkness. "We know you're there. Now come into the light with your hands raised high. I want to see you plain."

Twelve-year-old Jebediah Lovely emerged into the flickering light of Colt's lantern. His open palms raised slightly, no higher than his shoulders.

Forty-Four

Jebediah lowered his hands slowly.

"I didn't say you could do that. Put your hands back up and tell me your business, quick like!" shouted Colt.

"I'm unarmed, sir," said Jebediah in his boyish tongue. "I only want to tell you a story."

"Colt," shuddered Shae. "It's not a kid."

Colt looked over at him, perplexed.

"Sure looks like a kid."

"It ain't."

"Again, I only wish to tell you a story."

"Well, we don't wanna hear it!" retorted the marshal, whipping his gaze back toward Jebediah. "Now what's your business?! I'm losing my patience here, son"

"Storytelling," mocked the boy. "You see, I'm a traveling historian and, given where you've chosen to make camp," he gestured to the knoll on which they stood, "I figured you might like to hear a story relevant to the specific earth on which you now stand."

A cool wind troubled Jebediah's hair while Colt's revolver remained trained upon his chest.

"That's Jebediah," said Shae, with a quiver. "Or his body, at least. That's who I told you about... In the bedroom above the bar."

"*That's* our friend?" asked Colt, amused. "*This* is the beast incarnate?"

Shae nodded.

"You're sure?"

"Yes."

Crack!

Smoke snuck out, away, and up from the barrel of colt's gun.

Jebediah looked down at his chest, then back at Colt without so much as a flinch in his bored demeanor.

"Well... That was rude."

Colt lowered his pistol, acknowledging his weapon to be a moot vessel of effect upon the situation at hand. His eyes dropped to the dirt in contemplation.

"Like I said," said Jebediah, casually probing his chest wound with a finger, "I only want to tell you a story."

A silence stood in the open air, and, apparently taking the extended hush as approval, Jebediah began to speak.

"Thirty-four thousand years ago, thirty-four thousand, three hundred, and sixty-three, to be exact, the earth below the hill on which you now stand, this very hill, became revered by a civilization whose existence has since been swept away by the ice, wind, sun, and blood of the years that followed. God, or as they pronounced her then, Vaa, showed her face in the bark of a tree that once rose from the since covered earth below us. The bark spoke in an audible creaking of its wood, and the people that were present found, to their surprise, that they could understand what it said. It spoke of joy and righteousness, in disrespective order. They relayed her words to those in places distant, saying that Vaa had insisted upon building a caliphate on the location to protect the tree at all costs, for it was holy, and those that shared in its presence and defended its knots, roots, and limbs would be blessed to live forever. And so, they did. They built walls of stone surrounding the blessed arboreal and manned its sentries with means of violence. A man rose among them, declared himself to be chosen, and led the devout in its organized defense. They called themselves the People of the Tree, and they drew blood from any that threatened it. They went so far as to proactively cut down the lives of those with any reason to see their holy tree burn. And so, they went on campaign and levelled vast collections of humanity surrounding them. But one day, they spilt the blood of those that wouldn't see such an act unavenged. The wounded peoples rose up and summoned an alliance of all those that were also affected by the People of the Tree, and together, they moved in tremendous numbers against the caliphate. The risen army descended upon the earth with such force that the ground shook and the defenders trembled; for they knew that they were fated to die for the ambitions of their wooden god. The army broke through the walls and cut down the tree with a thousand and one cuts of their axes. And when the tree met the extent of its entropy, and its defenders were none left to suffer, they piled upon the chopped wood their bones, and upon their bones they piled the stones taken from the walls surrounding. It took a month to lift the final boulder upon the heap, but when it was, the men rejoiced, departed, and lived in peace until their next reason to fear and die in community..."

From somewhere far off, a pack of coyote's howled.

"None alive know this story, except for you now... I just thought that you should know it, being that you stand upon the stones, bones, and limbs of righteous conviction"

A wind rose to flutter the lantern's flame.

"You didn't come here to tell us a story. What do you want?" asked Colt, suspicious.

"A word with you, Marshal... in private."

"Don't," interrupted Shae, suddenly witnessing the danger unfolding before him.

"You're old enough to make your own decisions, aren't you Marshal?"

"He's a snake, Colt. A liar. You know it as much as I do."

"He suggests that you cup your hands over your ears, like a child while the parents speak."

"I don't think I'd enjoy, nor benefit, from speaking with you," said Colt to Shae's minor relief. "I'm not so sure we'd have much in common."

"Enjoyment is rarely synonymous with success. You know this. Don't pretend to be dull just for the sake of the dullard's presence amongst us."

"The fuck?!" exclaimed Shae. "Careful who you call dull, snake."

"Oh?" asked Jeb with amusement. "Were you not he so easily persuaded to murder a lawman for motives so tame? You hardly knew her, Shae."

"Liar."

"Yes, but not here. Not this time. Think about it. I'm guessing that you only came to appreciate your love for poor Ginny after you heard the ringing of that bell. While you cut citrus and spilled blood upon the drinker's ledge, maybe?"

It wasn't true. It couldn't be. He had piles of recollections of him and Ginny having long, silent companies together and… was that truly all? Were his affections—still persistent and strong as ever—only manifestations… specters imbedded in his heart for the sole purpose of driving him to bloodshed?

"But it's okay. You can keep your affections of the woman. In fact, I'm not so sure that you could reverse it, even if you wanted to," laughed Jebediah. "Think of it as a gift. One that was taken, ultimately, without payment."

"Why didn't you just kill him? If you wanted the sheriff dead, why didn't you just do it yourself?"

"Because it's not about killing. It never was. It's about the dance, Shae. If you'd like, I could come whisper in your ear once again and teach you how to move through this existence with pleasure."

"Goddamn you," spat Shae.

"She already did."

Jebediah shifted his gaze back to Colt in the flickering light.

"Like I said, Marshal, I simply want a word."

"Then speak."

"Colt!" exclaimed Shae.

"Quiet!!" the marshal shouted in sudden defiance. "We haven't exactly leverage here… I'm not so sure we have another play." He looked genuinely afraid, thought Shae. It was an appearance he'd yet to witness in the man, a sight that saddened him. The marshal had been a totem, up till then. Now, he was only human, as he must have been all along.

"Wise words, Marshal. I shan't bite, and you shall return to your lantern light and easy company very soon. Come, my words will be short, I assure you."

With that, Jebediah turned and walked back into the darkness from whence he'd come.

"Colt," Shae begged once more. "No."

But Colt only frowned and looked passively at the gun in his hand, examining its impotence. He dropped the weapon to the floor as he stepped forward to enter the encircling shadow lying beyond the light of the lantern.

As much as he hated to, Shae was forced to acknowledge the fact that he may be forced to kill Colt if things went south. Who knew what whispers were being spun into the man's ear?

He scrambled to where Colt's pistol lie in the dirt. He hurriedly grasped it and pushed out the rotating cylinder to find five bullets nestled inside. He clicked it back into place.

"What're you doing?" Colt asked from the edge of the light.

A cold impulse crossed him. He could raise the weapon right then and finish it before it began. He could cut the snake's designs short with the single pull of a trigger. The wyrm's words would become dust with the marshal's blood upon the dirt. He squeezed the grip and contemplated the seduction of raising its sights upon the man. Don't give it a chance to speak. Do it, spoke a voice behind his ear.

The sound of the gun falling to the ground startled Shae as Colt calmy—albeit quickly—approached the pistol to replace it in his holster.

Shae lowered himself to his knees.

"I'm sorry, Marshal. I don't know what...I don't know what came over me."

Colt lowered himself beside his tack to stare emptily at the barkeeper. He no longer looked afraid. Only tired.

"He's gone... You wanna know what he told me?"

Shae stared flatly ahead.

"He said that he was leaving this place...said us Americans know how to dance just fine without him."

Forty-Five

Beneath the spiked ceiling of its belfry, Bastion's church bell rang seven times in the early morning air. At the sound, Willie Boyle walked into the tree line that decorated the southern edge of the livery.

On his back and in his clenched fists he carried three sloshing containers provided by Maxine the night before. She had indeed been met with luck—if not outright providence—on her excursion to Gillette.

From what she relayed to her fellow saboteurs on her return, she hadn't even made it to the nearby town, but rather encountered a traveling snake-oil salesman rolling along the plains atop a monstruous mule-led cart.

"I heard it before I saw it," she recalled. "It was all jingling and jangling like a right choir of glass. And when I came upon him, I saw that he sat atop a makeshift throne of dressers and drawers all strung together with rope. He was clearly mad, the man, and spoke at me for nearly fifteen minutes before I could even introduce myself. But when something got caught in his throat, it might have been a fly, I batted my eyes and flattered his ego. That's all a man ever wants, after all. Anyway, once I got him giggling, I asked if he 'had anything that might, say, burn down a forest'. He laughed mightily at the question, but promptly dug through his chest of drawers and gave me these." She laughed as she gestured to the collection of jugs and five-gallon tin cans at her feet, each painted with skulls and crossbones.

"Well, I'll be," sighed Willie at the sight.

The memory was only a few hours old, and yet, it felt as if it had been days.

Once in the shielding of the tree line, Willie came upon Beatrice, just as they had arranged. A can was tied to her back as well, and they each carried jugs in their hands.

They shared a nod, but that was all. The coming minutes were to be the most consequential—and dangerous—of their carefully orchestrated dance.

"Here's the plan," Beatrice had whispered to her fellow saboteurs, only an hour before. "Willie, you and I will run the kerosene from the livery to the orchard at seven o'clock sharp."

"What if we get caught?" asked Willie nervously. "That's a long scamper."

"Let's not get caught."

Willie looked away into the pre-dawn darkness, clearly taken by anxiety.

"Meanwhile, Quinn, you've got your meeting with Thadeus at eight. Take this." She handed the Irishman a pistol. "It's got a single bullet in it. Don't waste it."

Quinn examined the weapon curiously. "Where'd you hide this?"

She smiled. "Don't worry about it. Now if Willie and I succeed on our side of things... *When* we succeed, everyone in town should be plenty distracted by the time of your meeting. With any luck, your meeting with the presider should be a private one."

Willie leaned out from the trees and scanned the field. Only a desolate landscape of dew laden grass looked back at him. A lingering layer of smoke, likely from the previous night's chimney fires, hung lightly upon the field. Only one thing surprised him. A bulging anvil of dark, threatening clouds coalescing on the western horizon. Storms of such a sight rarely descended into the Buckshaw Valley in the mornings; they belonged to the afternoons. It was a curious thing, and certainly not ideal considering their plans, but there was no time for hesitation.

He returned his sight to Beatrice and gave her a nod. It was time.

Side by side, they bolted into the field while a distant roll of thunder rumbled in the distance. The containers they carried swished and swashed in waves of frustrated momentum, making for a challenging sprint. To make matters worse, Willie found that the field through which they ran was covered in gopher holes. The last thing they could afford was a broken ankle.

"Careful," he muttered between racing breaths. Beatrice didn't respond and only sprinted ahead of him in an impressive display of coordination. He enjoyed watching her go. But just as he was becoming enraptured in the sight of her remarkable jaunt, he felt his own ankle slip into a hole and nearly roll over on itself. It was a miraculous thing that he didn't trip, and from that point on, he kept his gaze low and focused.

Soon enough, they reached the end of the field, skidding to a stop in the cover of the thinly spaced apple trees. Willie heaved in desperate breath.

"Us stablemen aren't meant for sprinting, ya know?" he gasped.

"I think that's just you Willie," she smiled, "c'mon."

Willie followed Beatrice into the heart of the orchard, toward its innermost branches; towards trees they intended to douse with so much kerosene that the resulting blaze would frustrate even the most efficient of bucket brigades.

"Do you think it'll work?" he asked, jogging behind her. He knew it was a silly question, one that she couldn't rightfully answer. And yet, he felt compelled to ask it. Maybe he just wanted to hear her voice to quell the racing of his heart.

Beatrice stopped her trek with a heavy breath all her own, gazing down at the mulched and shaded ground beneath her. The shadows of the tightly columned trees were strewn long and sharp from the freshly risen sun.

"Have faith, Willie."

She grasped his chin lightly and tilted it upwards to face hers. "The lord is with you... You'll see."

It was as good of a response as he could have asked for.

"I'm glad you're with me, Bee."

She smiled a quintessentially Beatrice smile, in her bashful and knowing way. She leaned in and quickly kissed him on the lips. It wasn't the first time that such a thing had happened but it was the first time in many years. In another life, maybe he would have had as much courage in love as he did in rebellion... In another life, he might have said and done what he knew inside himself to be true. *In another life,* he thought in a bittersweet moment.

"You'll see," she smiled.

They resumed their trek toward the heart of the orchard and within minutes they arrived.

Without ceremony, Beatrice undid the lid of her first jug and began to pour its contents liberally upon the trunks and low hanging limbs of the closest unfortunate tree. Willie followed suit, bending over to undo the screwcap of his own container when something in his peripheral vision froze him in place. Something... someone... stood between the rising tree-trunks only a dozen feet away. It was Luke Hess, a sawed-off shotgun dangling from his hanging hand.

"Whatcha doin?"

Neither Willie nor Beatrice said a word. There was little to say that wasn't already understood by all that were present. Luke raised the barrel of the shotgun, bringing it parallel with the floor. He aimed it at Beatrice, prompting Willie to step between them.

"I never said it, Bee. But I love you."

Willie closed his eyes and steeled himself to stand, soon, before his God.

"Luke!" called a voice at first unfamiliar. Willie's eyes shot open to see Penelope, Luke's mother, striding toward them through the trees.

"Luke!" she shouted again, "Wait!"

Luke begrudgingly obliged, still staring at the trespassers with both his own eyes and the long of the barrel.

Penelope slowed to a stop beside her son and leaned in close to share a quiet word, her hand resting tenderly on his shoulder. She was long winded in whatever she said, but all that Willie managed to make out were the words, "allow me."

Luke hesitated at first, but ultimately lowered the weapon, smiling at the dirt.

"It's your orchard, Mother." He turned his gaze upward to meet hers. "And indeed, it is yours to defend."

He handed her the shotgun.

Penelope stared intensely at the wood infused metal in her hands. It was a finely crafted weapon, blue steel erupting from the cherry-stained pine of its stock. She clearly knew how to use it, too, evidenced by the sharp pumping of the weapon's forend along its magazine tube, injecting a shell into the receiver. She stepped toward Willie with anger in her eyes. And not just any old anger. A pure, white-hot rage. The rage of a mother.

As fast as the wind, Penelope spun herself around, raised the shotgun's barrel to Luke, and pulled the trigger.

The boy's body, or at least every part of it beyond the portions of his forehead that were obliterated by angry, hot beads, collapsed to the mulch in a heap.

Penelope walked to the body to stand over it.

"You're not my son," she said, softly shaking.

But to the horror of all present, with half his face missing, the boy abruptly began to laugh in a bloody garble; a vile, damp sound. Penelope re-aimed the weapon and again pulled the trigger, this time splashing both herself and the grass in gore.

She looked to the saboteurs.

“Burn it down.”

The two obliged without hesitation.

Within a matter of minutes, they poured all four jugs—and both of their five-gallon cans—upon eight tightly clumped trees. While they worked, Penelope lifted what remained of her son’s body upon her shoulders and hoisted it into the cradling limbs of one of the most thoroughly soaked trees. The act resulted in a river of the body’s blood flowing over her, coating her face, arms, and a good majority of her denim. When she was satisfied that Luke’s body was secure in the soon to be burning tree, she bent over to pick up the shotgun and walked off in the direction from whence she’d come.

A vivacious roll of thunder accompanied her departure.

Soon, the sound of a shotgun’s crack pronounced itself from somewhere in the direction that Penelope had gone. Then another. Then, finally, a chorus of smaller arms—likely pistols—erupted in response. Nothing further was heard, not that the saboteurs were eager to stick around and find out if more black powdered verbiage was to be spoken.

Beatrice lit a match and tossed it upon the tree cradling Luke Hess. It released a tall plume of smoke that mixed eagerly with the swirling clouds overhead.

Forty-Six

"Fire! Fire at the orchard!" called a saint sprinting onto the avenue. "All that are able must come at once! Go! Jump on the bucket line!"

Quinn stood upon the road flat footed, facing the courthouse. He carried in his hands an envelope, a red wax-stamp rendering it sealed.

"You!" shouted a hastily passing saint, the red lasso about his neck jostling as he ran. "Get to the orchard! Now!"

A sharp crack of thunder erupted overhead, pulling each of their attentions briefly to the sky. But when Quinn returned himself to the saint and his crimson necklace, he only extended his hands forward, brandishing the envelope.

"I have an audience with the presider at eight o'clock sharp. I don't intend to be late, sir."

"I don't give a damn about yer audience, mick!"

"Well then I'll be telling both him *and* the deputy that you're the one that delayed his cabinet meeting!" It was a rehearsed fury, but the slur that had been slung at him was providential in raising genuine anger.

"Goddamn you then!" replied the man, mercifully ambling off.

It seemed as if most of the town—half with crimson halos dangling about their necks—ran toward the black smoke rising in the south.

They'd done it, he thought. Those brave, silly, bastards had really done it.

As he waited for the final saints to depart the avenue, he looked up to acknowledge the vast, imposing clouds descending into the valley from the mountain range in the west. It was a wide front, clearly infused with bad intentions. A peculiar green peered out from the dark bulbous contours of its approach. Had he not been engrossed in what he assumed to be the cumulative moments of his life, Quinn might have spent the coming minutes seeking shelter. But now was not the time for shelter. Quite the opposite, in fact.

"Just don't 'cha drench that fire too soon, now," he whispered at the sky. "Give me ten minutes, then ye can do whatchu will." He laughed, suddenly chipper. He was glad to be there, approaching whatever end. It'd been quite the road, hadn't it?

Quinn lowered his sights to the steps of the courthouse, marched forward, and ascended its rise. When he reached the top, he found the building's doors—doors that he never once dreamt of entering—without guard. It appeared that everyone capable had indeed run off in the direction of the orchard.

Maybe, just maybe, hope still remained.

Quinn pulled open the heavy doors and stepped into the circular foyer within. A glimmering chandelier of glass hung above him, illuminating its walls and muraled floor. Mozart played from somewhere unseen.

Isolated nails hung upon the walls, apparently only recently absolved of holding their paintings aloft. Only one painting remained on the rounded walls of the chamber, a massive lithograph of a painting that Quinn had never seen before. And yet, despite that fact, he sensed—in a curious way—somehow acquainted with the scene of the painting. He stepped toward it, completely forgetting his purpose in the room.

It was déjà vu; nostalgic and terrible.

The lithograph depicted a widely cast scene of murder; the sacking of a city by an army of the dead. Skeletons slayed bodies by the hundreds with spears, swords, and scythes. Dogs ate at bodies lying face down in the mud while kings, peasants, knights, and clergymen equally bled into their hands and pleaded with the sky. A cart filled with skulls trampled a carpet of bodies while led by a horse stricken by famine; its bones bulging from its hinges. In the far distance, parades of skeletons marched across further hills while billows of smoke erupted from their plunder. A tall mound of corpses—that of men, women, children, and horses—were piled in a heap in the foreground. A nobleman stood beside it, shakily grasping the hilt of his still sheathed sword.

"It's really something, isn't it?"

Quinn flung himself around to find the presider standing in the shadows of a flanking hallway. Thadeus wore a white, flowing garment decorated with golden stitching along its borders. The entirety of his neck and face—eyes and mouth not excluded—were covered in cloth bandages. Evidence of moisture bled through the wrappings.

Atop his head rested the golden helm.

"Pieter Bruegel the Elder painted it in the Netherlands in the sixteenth-century. God only knows what inspired him to paint such a scene."

"Yes," replied Quinn with a hollowness that surprised him. The sight of the man so decorated conjured in him a shiver that he wasn't expecting.

"Oh this?" asked Thadeus, gesturing to his face. "It's nothing, really. A peculiar condition of the skin, it seems." His head cocked slowly to the side while, overhead, the blunt banging of heavy rain—if not outright hail—made itself known upon the ceiling. A whistling wind tested the walls.

"Would you like to see?" he asked curtly.

Quinn didn't answer. He didn't, but for whatever reason could summon neither words nor actions to prevent the man from reaching into his shirt's slacked neckline to begin unraveling the bandage. To Quinn's horror, each upward rotation of the wrapping's undoing exposed an unceasing echelon of sopping, waxy, and bloated skin; rotten and mottled. Quinn's nostrils soon filled with the mingling perfumes of putrid gas and rot.

It wasn't until the wrappings were fully undone, exposing two cavernously empty eye-sockets of pale sodden skin, did Quinn recall what he was doing in such a place, with such a man. With a start, he reached behind him to grasp the six-shooter wedged between his waistband and the small of his back, aiming it squarely at the chest of the sloughing man before him.

At the sight of the gun, Thadeus emitted a gentle, almost timid chuckle that grew patiently into a full-throated howl. It mingled fittingly with the wind that beckoned, louder and louder, outside.

"You can't kill me!" he cackled. "I'm chosen by God! I'm his perfect wish. For generations upon generations, the Hess line has existed for the sole purpose of bringing me, His chosen presider, into being. And here I am, in all of the glory of He that is undying. Look!" he reached to his mandible, grasped a hunk of sopping skin and pulled it clean from his cheek in a squish. "See?" he bellowed in hilarity. "Beyond you and yours, son. So why don't you do yourself a favor, old man, turn that gun on your own face, and relieve yourself of an otherwise bloody and painful future." He took a step toward Quinn, his foot squishing upon the tiled floor. "Have you ever heard of peeling? By red hot tongs? It came to me in a dream recently, but apparently it was once quite popular. You see..." *Squish.* Quinn stepped back in impulsive, babbling fear. "For the worst of the worst, back when justice was made clear to all, they'd string 'em up real high so everyone could see..." *Squish.* "Then, they'd pull out tongs that'd been resting in beds of coal..." *Squish.* "...and they'd use 'em to peel at the skin of sinners, like jerky, piece by piece..." *Squish.* "And if the poor sinner would grow unconscious from the pain..." *Squish.* "...they'd splash a pail of water on em, for the crowd was due an hour in full..." *Squish.* "...and that's what I'm going to do to you, paddy. I'm going to give the good people of God's kingdom, of New Jerusalem, an hour of *you*!"

Quinn went to take a step further backward, maybe even run, but when he went to do so, he felt his heel hit upon a wall immediately behind him. He leaned against it and felt the frame of the lithograph pressing against him.

Without conscious intention, Quinn sensed the recoil of the gun in his hand and the sound of its action. But the presider—already missing a chunk of his check—only cackled while a stream of putrid water spew from the fresh cavity in his belly.

But his raucous laughter suddenly became outdone by a tremendous sound, a colossal roar pushing against the building's walls. It sounded as if a locomotive was barreling down the length of College Avenue, hurtling straight for them. Before either man could move themselves from their positions in the foyer, the roof was torn from its feeble walls while a fiery hellscape of fire, wind, and debris exploded overhead, pulling Quinn, Thadeus, and much of the room itself into the scorching flames of a swirling banshee wind.

Forty-Seven

Before dawn, Colt and Shae set out on the final leg of their journey. As they ambled north and away from their campsite, Shae turned back to admire the tall mound of earth on which they had rested the night before.

"Do you think the story was true? About the People of the Tree and all that?"

"I'm more curious if what he said about leaving was true."

Shae spit at the ground. "I sure hope so. I hope I never hear that boy's voice again. Not that I blame Jebediah, the real Jebediah, that is. He was a good kid, from what I've been told."

"What if he really did leave?" asked Colt. "What should we expect to find in Bastion if its villain has departed?"

Shae pondered the question for a long while.

"I haven't an earthly idea, Marshal, but it's my great hope that I have made you ride all this way for nothing."

Colt descended into silence before emitting a romantic whistle some minutes on. It was a melancholy tune, Red River Valley, and as Shae had come to expect from his companion's whistled melodies it nestled itself intuitively against the dull soft blue of their pre-dawn ride.

He wasn't sure if it was the melody, or the hue of the air, but something in the moment made him think of Ginny. Fabricated or not, he was terribly hers.

The final miles to Bastion were decidedly more hilly than the slow-rolling plains of which they had grown accustomed. At seeing the landscape change in such a way, a giddiness overcame Shae. He was nearly home.

But when they overcame a tall overlook that allowed the men to look clearly upon the Buckshaw Valley—with Bastion at its center—two things became readily apparent, each drawing distinct and valid concerns. The most imposing of the two was a massive wall of black and dark clouds spilling into the valley from the east. Shae hadn't seen such an aerial showing in years. It approached the town in a long, horizontal line like a phalanx of moisture marching ever onward with spears of lightning at the ready. His most enduring memory of a similarly angry sky resulted in hail the size of baseballs that killed a dozen cattle and bust more than a few holes in the roof of the saloon.

All that to say, the approaching storm was not a welcome sight for those riding upon the hills without cover.

But what compounded his worry was the second visual novelty before them: a thick and rapidly accelerating column of black smoke billowing from the apple orchard, just south of town. By the looks of it, it was an angry fire smack-dab in the orchard's center, inching outward by the second.

"Not good," he said aloud. Once again, Colt didn't respond.

They dug their spurs into the flanks of the horses and raced down the hillside toward the town. But before they could get much closer, the swiftness of the storm overtook them, releasing a deluge of hail, lightning, and wind.

"We can't stay out in the open like this!" yelled Colt. "Follow me!"

Shae trailed closely behind the marshal as he led their horses into a ravine where a modest grove of cottonwoods huddled.

"What about the lightning!?" shouted Shae.

Colt waited to respond until his frightened mare was settled beneath the cover of the trees. "Frankly, I'm more worried about me or Sally getting concussed! When the hail stops, we'll find somewhere better!"

Colt was wise to seek cover when he did, for seemingly just as they came to rest under the protection of the sprawling branches, the hail doubled in size. It was a feat in itself to keep the horses beneath their legs as they endured the storm, the animals flinging their heads violently to and fro, neighing and hoofing at the mud.

But as quick as the sky had ripped itself open to unleash such a cluster of ice upon them, the hail, at last, stopped. Colt nodded to Shae in a nonverbal suggestion that they depart the lightning rods above them as the lightning remained persistent, constant, and deafening.

They pulled their reluctant steeds away from the ravine and continued a hurried trek toward Bastion. The sooner they got to cover, the better. But as they summited a narrow ridgeline with a clear view of the town, both men were compelled to yank at their reins as they were confronted by a sight both terrible and astonishing.

Reaching from the underbelly of the sea-green clouds was a twisting vortex of debris, earth, and everything in-between. It contorted itself in a capricious dance that moved north—directly for the increasingly emboldened blaze.

Shae's eyes bulged in horror as he watched the two extremes of nature and their quickly approaching convergence.

"Maybe it'll put it out!" he shouted.

Colt nearly smiled. "I don't think a blaze like that has much in common with a candle's flame, Shae."

Shae returned his attention to the twister as the sound of its hurtling, twisting wind came to roost in his conscious comprehension. It was the sound of air being twisted as if it were metal. If hell had a sound, it was surely similar.

The twister reached the edge of the enraptured blaze. There, the twin columns—one a tight swirl of dust and debris, the other a rising plume of hot carbon—met, coalesced, and consumed each other in an instant. What took their place was a massive vortex of smoke that, within the blink of an eye, ignited into flame, resulting in a twisting inferno ripping through the orchard on a steady dance north toward the heart of Bastion.

"What do we do!?" exclaimed Shae in saturated terror. "It's going to destroy the town!!"

"What do you mean? We wait for that monster to move on. That's all we *can* do."

Shae shook with adrenaline still enraptured in the subconscious belief that he should be doing something, anything. But Colt was right. There was nothing to be done but watch the disaster unfold before them. He wanted to turn away, but that too seemed a woeful impossibility.

Rooftops joined the curling rise of the flaming tornado, as did bricks, lumber, and mortar; a trail of disheveled civilization left scattered in its jagged path. And as the monstrosity met the center of town, specifically the courthouse, Shae watched in incredulity as the gilded bookend of the avenue was torn to shreds by the twisting and howling conflagration.

The twister continued north, but by the time it met the hills, the flames of its body dissipated at last, returning its composition to that of simple debris, dust, and swirling wind.

Meanwhile, back at the orchard, the blaze burned on with fresh vigor. Shae thought the sight akin to watching two prized bulls meeting in a field, tussling in a furious dust-up, and, having agreed that they were equals, moving on in the search of lesser beasts to devour.

The tornado crept up the hills and, just before it met the walls of the church, lost its gumption to fade into nothing but a whisp of wind; the final act of a play introduced by the batting of a butterfly's wings.

When it was apparent that the heaviest of the storm was behind them, Shae and Colt resumed their approach to the town with eyes ever trained upon the sky. But in the minutes it took them to close the final stretch of land between themselves and Bastion, no rogue clouds appeared and all signs pointed to the sky resuming a mild nature, as if nothing had happened at all.

A gentle precipitation more comparable to a morning mist than a tornado's rain continued to fall upon them, although blue skies could already be seen approaching from the crest of the western horizon.

All was quiet—save for the stubborn billowing of the still raging blaze—when the hooves of their tired horses tread upon College Avenue and into Bastion proper. Shae briefly acknowledged the saloon still standing to his right, although his attention remained primarily upon the tall mound of destruction rising where the courthouse once stood at the end of the avenue.

Miscellaneous debris, from the shingles of homes to the bricks of chimneys, littered the ground, and with each meter tread their paths became increasingly filled with obstacles upon the ground.

No onlookers were present to gawk at their arrival, a departure from Shae's imaginings of the moment, visions that had been filled with either combative crowds decrying their approach or groveling masses appealing to their mercy.

What he hadn't expected was such destruction nor the billowing silence.

Colt encouraged his mare into the rubble where the courthouse once stood. Shae made to follow, but when he heard a cough, and then another coming from behind a fallen door lying against a pile of debris, Shae jumped hurriedly from his saddle, no longer worried where his horse might venture. He approached the door to peel back its weight.

Underneath, he found a bloodied and bruised Quinn O'Callaghan. The Irishman smiled and coughed once more.

"Well, well, well..." he said in a raspy voice. "If the master barkeeper himself hasn't returned."

Forty-Eight

The fire that turned the orchard to soot ran out of trees to burn.

When it was at last extinguished, the rudderless crowds observing its feeding dejectedly returned to the heart of the town to examine the destruction that awaited them. But instead of empty smolders and tear-soaked apathy, the crowds were met by an energized Colt McLane steadily pulling back the layers of fallen timber and stone amassed where the courthouse once stood.

"Quit your gawking and help!" he hollered at the stunned onlookers. "There could be people under here!"

The crowd immediately obliged the order and went about searching for bodies in the rubble. The marshal guided the effort, directing the ever-arriving masses toward areas of destruction that still required searching. He flashed his badge, shouted instructions, and quickly delegated persons to positions of authority. The mob immediately gravitated to his decisiveness. It was as if they'd forgotten how to operate without authoritative guidance; their muscles of initiative atrophied to nothing.

The marshal, in his charismatic way, easily filled the void.

From what Shae could gather from those that would speak on the matter, Penelope, the matriarch of the Hess family, had abruptly gone mad that morning. Apparently, she emerged from the orchard with a sawed-off shotgun, shooting at anyone that crossed her path. That had been right around when the fire had started, and many suspected that the fire itself was likely her doing. As such, many were forced to acknowledge the likelihood of the headless, charred body found in the orchard's smoldering ashes to be that of her son's.

How peculiar, thought Shae. How sad and peculiar.

But as the efforts to unearth any of those potentially buried in the felled buildings continued, the circumstances that had brought him back to Bastion with such foreboding returned to his mind, especially when Quinn provided a brief recap of what the town had been through while he was away.

"Where's our dear leader, then? Where's Hess gone off to?" asked Shae of his old, Irish friend. But after a moment's silence, Shae turned to notice a troubled gaze residing on Quinns face. It was something he'd never seen on the man.

"I only wish to know, so that I may turn about, and go the other way," he said, at last.

Not a further moment passed before the crowd, one by one, stood where they did to gaze silently to the pathway that led into the hills. Shae, too, turned to see what had so enraptured their attention. There, draped in midnight-black robes strode Mathius Patmos onto the littered dirt of the Avenue.

"Brothers and sisters!" he bellowed, raising his hands to the sky. "The lord has bequeathed thee with a vengeance to match thy pride! For this, we should be grateful."

A heated murmur rose about the crowd. Shae thought it a similar sound to the rumblings that had responded to Thadeus's initial pitch of secession, right before Kingsbury had so distracted them by death.

"Do not grumble, my friends. For I shall willingly leave you to your despondence. I have been called elsewhere, to enlighten sheep anew in shores distant. But fear not, for I have not forgotten the third of three blessings that I have promised thee. It awaits your gaze in the hills, atop thy steeple."

A gunshot rang out. A river of blood suddenly gushed from Mathius's forehead coating his face and chest in a current of crimson.

Shae looked over, in shock, to see Colt standing upon the mountain of debris, a line of smoke rising from the portal of his still aimed pistol.

The sound of the dark-red liquid descending steadily, like a waterfall, from Mathius's forehead and onto the dirt was the only sound left to be heard. It was a sickly sound. A terrible sound. But what was worse than its pronouncement was the fact that Mathius remained standing tall, his eyes open, staring straight ahead. Suddenly, his retinas shot upward—without any shift in his facial muscles—to stare at he that had shot him. And as the blood began to amass into a wide pond of gore, a river of blood still flowing eagerly from his forehead, he took a step forward, splashing the bloody puddle with the soles of his feet.

He wavered slightly as he spoke.

"Bless you... Marshal."

He took a second step forward, but with this foot's fall, the entirety of his body fell through the scarlet puddle as if it were the mantle of the ocean itself.

And he was gone.

***

When the crowd collected themselves from what they had just witnessed, a large collection of them—Shae included—scurried up the hillside to see the aforementioned third blessing.

In all that went, apprehension lingered naturally with their curiosity.

But at reaching the plateau that held the church, nausea became the predominant sentiment of the crowd. For on the dirt before them kneeled Reverend Gilroy and Xavior Jenkins, each eye-less and incoherently mumbling. In their outstretched arms, they reached for that which was skewered upon the sharp, pinnacled spire atop the church's belfry: the impaled, bloated, and sloughing body of Thadeus Hess.

It vibrated as the bell began to ring.

Forty-Nine

Shae and Quinn sat together on the floor behind the saloon's obscuring bar to avoid the ongoing efforts being had outside. They drank from tall glasses of whiskey.

Although many of the crowd took to producing sweat to process the horrors that they'd witnessed that day, the bartender and his favorite customer took a different approach, one preferred by men of leisure such as themselves.

As Quinn had expected, the bar had been emptied of its liquors. But the one unopened bottle of Old Forester that Shae had stored in the back of the piano's upright casing, for such an occasion, remained.

"Why'd it go this way, Quinn?" asked Shae of the Irishman. "How'd it go so bad, so fast?"

Quinn's eyes were closed in a quiet appreciation of the bourbon upon his lips. Shae thought he'd never seen such serenity upon the face of a man.

"I think," Quinn uttered at last, "that everyone secretly wants to be there, at the end of the world... to know that they won't miss a thing when they're gone. To be amongst the last to see the sunrise, and the last to see it fall. We all just want to be there... to know how it ends. So, when the end professes itself to the willing, they nurse it like a babe and sharpen its barbs. And when it comes of age and suckles from their neck the blood of their virtues, they say, 'the ends will forgive us'. And when it slices the necks of their kin, they profess, 'patience, the time is nigh'. And finally, when it salts the fields and brokers their undoing, they close their eyes, certain that their end will be all's."

Shae could think of nothing to say and only stared at the rafters above them. A thought appeared at the forefront of his mind. Something unexpected.

"There isn't anything left for me here, Quinn... I thought maybe there was while I was away, but now that I'm here, and I see these walls, I'm thinking maybe it's time I go somewhere new... I've never seen the ocean, you know, and I think, maybe, I'd like to go and do that. Maybe I'll go off and find San Francisco."

He took a sip from the glass and admired the burning of his throat. It agreed with him.

"But I've traveled alone before, Quinn. I've endured that silence, and to be honest, I don't think I'd like to again... Would you come with me?"

Quinn smirked doubtfully at the thought of him embarking on another long adventure across another unforgiving wilderness. The last time he'd traveled such distances, he was a substantially younger man and his bones were growing heavier by the day. And yet, he couldn't help but agree that such an adventure sounded exciting. He knew that the town would, from then on, be nothing but an injured thing and he had little desire to spend his waning years as a maggot fettered to an open wound.

"You find me a carriage and enough whiskey to get me there and you have yerself a deal, master barkeeper. Just don't go expecting much from me in the way of manual labor."

***

In the coming days, Shae sold the saloon to the highest bidder, which just so happened to be Dr. Stevenson.

"I suppose I'll use that backroom there for my evaluations and leave the front room just the same."

"You're going to see patients... out of a bar?" asked Shae, incredulously.

"My good man, can't you see an opportunity for novel innovation when it calls? Why, half of my patients are drunkards anyway. It'll save them a trip, and for that I dare say they'll be thankful."

Shae thought the concept rife for disaster but cared not. He was just happy to have found a buyer so soon. He was growing eager to head west before the weather turned cold.

With his newfound financial liquidity, he purchased a pair of horses and a carriage from Willie at the livery. Quinn had told Shae of his shared insurgency with the stable master, but Shae knew better than to mention it.

"Where'd ya get off to?" asked Willie at the conclusion of their transaction. "I didn't see ya round here when things went south. Wish I was as smart as you."

Shae grinned, looking downward.

"Just got lucky, I guess."

"Did you see the sheriff? He never did come back, after he got run off. I suppose if I were him I wouldn't have come back either. Not after what he'd done to poor Ginny."

Again, Shae was wiser than to invite conversation on either topic. He was content to let things lie as they were and leave both Vale and Ginny in the past; to simply tread west into the exfoliating waves of the ocean. He'd come to embrace the idea. Just get to the water.

"No," was all he said.

Just after dawn on the morning of their approaching departure, Colt approached the carriage that Shae and Quinn eagerly loaded with supplies. They did so on the dirt path that lay just east of the old sheriff's office, a building that Colt had come to inhabit as his own.

"Word is that you're headed for San Francisco. Anything I could say to keep you around these parts? We could use good men such as yourselves while we get this place back on its feet."

Shae laughed. Quinn groaned.

"If I were to stay here much longer, Marshal, I'm afraid you'd soon come to realize that I'm not quite as good as you think I am." He winked and both men chuckled. "What about you? When are you are leaving this place? Won't you be needed back in Cheyenne?"

"My obligation is to the people of this territory, when and where it's needed. And after all that's happened to this town, I struggle to imagine my services being more valuable anywhere else. Besides, I suspect that the presence of the federal government might be beneficial ... you know... considering the whole succession thing and all."

Shae smiled in understanding, extending his hand in closure.

"It was a pleasure to have met you, Marshal."

Colt met Shae's hand with his own.

"Take care of yourself, Shae. I don't suspect I'll see you again."

"No," agreed Shae. "I doubt you will."

Colt departed and walked back toward College, the town already bustling with the sounds of sawing and hammering.

But as Shae watched him go, a curious tingling, like a heavy mist encompassing the entirety of his body, suddenly overcame him. It was as if the entirety of his being had suddenly grown tendrils that were being brushed by a passing hand. It wasn't a painful thing, only... odd. Then, strangely enough, a single word emphatically came to the forefront of his mind, demanding his attention.

Jebediah.

Shae could find no reason for conjuring the boy's name while watching Colt walk back toward the town. But after pondering it for only a moment longer, he decided to let it go. He was tired of thinking of the boy and whatever it was that had possessed him.

"Let's go already!" called Quinn from the back of the cart.

Shae climbed upon the seat, grasped its reins, and encouraged the horses forward to leave Bastion behind forever.

Fifty

The sky was dappled with a gentle smattering of clouds passing idly overhead.

"I won't miss the wind here," said Quinn, lounging behind Shae. "It never quits. Saturday, it blows. Sunday, it blows. Monday, it blows. But I don't have to tell you that, do I, Shae."

Shae grinned, thinking it might have been the only time he'd ever heard the man use his rightful name. He could sense a joyful energy in Quinn's voice, although he was beginning to suspect that he might soon regret inviting the talkative Irishman—already drunk—on the extensive journey.

At least he'd be asleep by noon, he figured.

"What's the weather like, in San Francisco? From what I understand, it's right on the coast. Ya suppose it's anything like Ireland?"

"I've been told it's exactly like Ireland," shouted Shae. "With misty mornings, and high grass fields that go on and on, as far as you can see them."

A long silence followed, and after some time, Shae looked back to see Quinn pleasantly gazing upwards at the clouds.

Come midday, the speckling of the clouds dissolved, replaced only by a pristine blue that covered them like a sheet. They followed a southwestern route that circumnavigated the Bighorn Mountains, a path of steeply rolling hills that overcame ridgeline after ridgeline in an inconveniently perpendicular manner. But despite the nature of its turbulence, Shae, wearing the very same denims and leathers that he'd been gifted by Colt in Cheyenne, was glad to be back on the trail. What a feeling, he thought. To be so unencumbered by the walls of one's comfort. It wasn't always that way, of course. But in this moment, with such an optimistic sky beckoning him forward, with so many miles of opportunity still ahead, he found no reason not to smile and appreciate the landscape as it met him.

He proceeded, then, to whistle a song that he knew well but couldn't recall the name.

As they rode toward it, the late day's sun began to dip and approach the western horizon. On it, Shae noticed a tight clumping of tipi's. An unbothered, vertical line of smoke rose from the triangle shelters.

He and Quinn must have entered the reservation, he realized only then.

He decided it best to approach the camp. Shadows were growing long in the approaching dusk and if they were to camp nearby, it would be smart to introduce themselves before doing so.

He called back to Quinn to ask his opinion on the matter but found the Irishman soundly asleep.

Shae encouraged the wagon in the direction of the encampment, and as they drew near, two adult males and a boy walked out to greet them.

Well serendipity, thought Shae. If it wasn't the very same group that he had met after the incident with the bear. What were the odds of that?

"Ai Ai," he shouted to the trio "We're passing through and intend to camp nearby."

Quinn snored boorishly behind him.

"That is fine," spoke the boy. "But before you do, you must walk with me into camp. You will be glad for it."

Vale. Could he be alive, after all?

"You must leave this here," said the boy, gesturing toward the carriage. "The elders are not eager to receive your wagon. But you, and you alone, may enter on foot."

Shae looked back towards Quinn. The man slept soundly in the depths of his snoring.

Shae dismounted to walk to the nearby camp, the boy translator marching beside him. They strode upon the long shadows of the tipis as Shae admired the dust that had been cast golden in the approaching twilight.

"Did you come to know the silence?" asked the boy.

Shae hesitated, contemplating an honest answer to the question. Sincerity was due, if nothing else.

"From time to time," he replied at last.

As they entered the encampment, a dozen tipis surrounded a central, communal space where a small fire burned. A handful of women huddled near a tanning rack, shielding just as many children against their hips.

Beside them sat Vale Kingsbury on a wide, felled log, his arm draped around Ginny Samson.

Startled, the ragged gunsmith looked up to meet Shae's suddenly tearful gaze.

"Have *you* seen my boy?"

About the Author

Nathaniel Shrake is a Marine Corps Veteran and Arizona State Alumnus. When not writing, Nathaniel enjoys watching horror movies, shooting pool, and traveling the American west. He is a contributing writer for Veterans Life Magazine and currently resides in Cheyenne, Wyoming.

ShrakeWrites.com

@Nathaniel_Shrake

Also by Nathaniel Shrake

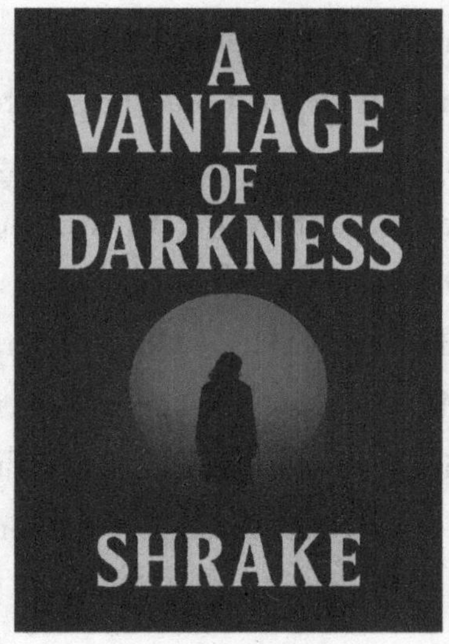

In the 1890's, a homesteading family stakes their claim to a plot of land in the forest outside of Flagstaff, their hubris disregarding warnings of the soil being sour. Before long, that which watches between the trees makes itself known to the family's young daughter, Mae Barrett, bestowing upon her a curse of undeath, a curse that isn't understood until years later, when death would have otherwise taken her. But before she can understand the depths of her circumstance, Mae attends university where her aptitude toward the arcane is fostered by an enigmatic teacher of magic that sees promise in the girl. Soon, Mae develops practical skills in the occult, skills that risk inflating the hubris of her genetics. But immortality isn't the blessing one might assume it to be. When Mae comes to fully understand its implications, she goes to dark lengths to grasp at any straws that might undo that which makes her unable to die. Unfortunately, such pursuits collect collateral damage and innocent lives. Lives like Sam Yellowstone's—a modern Marine Corps Veteran only trying to find himself after achieving his freedom from the military. In grasping for quiet, he finds himself taking a job as the caretaker of an estate located in the forest outside of Flagstaff.

With lush prose, haunting atmosphere, and a deep existential undercurrent, *A Vantage of Darkness* is a cosmic horror tale that blends the psychological, supernatural, and philosophical into a singular, unforgettable experience.

A Vantage of Darkness is **available now** on Amazon.

www.ingramcontent.com/pod-product-compliance
Lightning Source LLC
La Vergne TN
LVHW031334150826
845673LV00012B/2885

* 9 7 9 8 9 9 8 9 9 7 0 3 7 *